Elizabeth Mundy's grandmother was a Hungarian immigrant to America who raised five children on a chicken farm in Indiana. An English Literature graduate from Edinburgh University, Elizabeth is a marketing director for an investment firm and lives in London with her untidy husband and two young children. *A Messy Affair* is the third novel in the Lena Szarka mystery series.

Also by Elizabeth Mundy

In Strangers' Houses
A Clean Canvas

A MESSY AFFAIR

A Lena Szarka Mystery

ELIZABETH MUNDY

CONSTABLE

CONSTABLE

First published in Great Britain in 2020 by Constable

Copyright © Elizabeth Mundy, 2020

1 3 5 7 9 10 8 6 4 2

The moral right of the author has been asserted.

*All characters and events in this publication, other than those clearly
in the public domain, are fictitious and any resemblance to real persons,
living or dead, is purely coincidental.*

A CIP catalogue record for this book
is available from the British Library.

ISBN: 978-1-47212-639-9

Typeset in Bembo by Photoprint, Torquay
Printed and bound in Great Britain by Clays Ltd. Elcograf S.p.A.

Papers used by Constable are from well-managed forests and other
responsible sources.

MIX
Paper from
responsible sources
FSC
www.fsc.org   FSC® C104740

Constable
An imprint of
Little, Brown Book Group
Carmelite House
50 Victoria Embankment
London EC4Y 0DZ

An Hachette UK Company
www.hachette.co.uk

www.littlebrown.co.uk

For Violet

CHAPTER 1

He's not yours. He's mine. Do not touch him again. If you do you'll both regret it.

Lena Szarka held the paper by its edges, trying not to get her fingerprints on it. 'You have no idea who sent this note to you?' she asked again, looking at her cousin Sarika. She could feel dread settling in her stomach like her mother's heavy *haluska* dumplings.

'No idea,' replied Sarika. She pouted as she brushed blusher along her cheekbones and squinted into her grubby mirror. 'But I'm not worried. Terry's had a note too. He gets threats all the time, mostly on Twitter. It's no big deal.'

'You must take this note to the police,' said Lena, trying to ignore the make-up streaks on her cousin's mirror. She'd rented a flat for them to share, but was finding the state in which Sarika kept her room hard to bear. 'You could be in danger. We must go there now, instead of on this double date.' Although it was just the two of them, she spoke in English, lapsing now and then into Hungarian. Lena was determined to keep practising until she'd achieved the fluency that still eluded her. Frustratingly, Sarika's English was already much better than her own.

'Terry said crazy fans are just the price you pay for starring in *N1 Angels*,' said Sarika, her voice tinged with pride. 'Being in the public eye like he is, you are bound to attract attention.'

'You are not in the public eye. You work for me.'

'Maybe next series,' said Sarika, her voice wistful. 'Imagine, a cleaner from Hungary in an Islington reality TV show.'

'This person knows where you live,' said Lena, still looking at the note. 'And there was no stamp, no address?'

'Not even an envelope,' said Sarika.

'That means that whoever wrote this must have been here,' said Lena. 'Right up to our door. Sarika, this is serious.'

'Drop it,' snapped Sarika, finally looking up from the mirror. 'If I make a fuss, Terry will think I can't hack the limelight. You don't understand.'

'You are right, I do not understand,' said Lena, extracting her mug of coffee from Sarika's dressing table, which was strewn with brightly coloured pots of powders and myriad brushes. 'But if I got a note like this, I would do something. London is not the village. Terrible things can happen here.' She thought of Timea. Her best friend, murdered in Islington just over a year ago.

'Like us being late for the date,' said Sarika. She looked Lena up and down and frowned. 'You need to get changed.'

'I think perhaps the date is not such a good idea,' said Lena. 'Maybe I will stay home.'

'You can't pine for PC Cartwright for ever,' said Sarika.

'I do not pine!' exclaimed Lena. 'I have been working hard all day and I am tired.'

'Look how well I've got over Dragg,' continued Sarika, ignoring her. 'When I was sitting in the flat with you every night sobbing my eyes out, it seemed hopeless.'

Lena nodded. Sarika had gone through all Lena's tissues in the weeks after Dragg stopped returning her calls. Lena had never doled out as many hugs in her life.

'But I got online and met someone better,' said Sarika, applying another layer of mascara. 'If Cartwright calls you need to be out. That is how you catch a man. Make him jealous.' She turned to Lena. 'You should have let me put your profile on Bienvenue. com. That's how I met my darling Terry.'

'I do not want to date online.'

'That's why I've fixed you up. This date will do you good. You can't stay in on a Thursday night.'

'I do want to meet your boyfriend,' admitted Lena. 'You've been dating since December and now it's nearly February. I think it's time.' She pulled herself up. Much as she was reluctant to take advice from her cousin Sarika, ten years her junior and barely in her twenties, she had to admit the girl had a more active love life than she did. And she wanted to see what Terry was like. Sarika seemed smitten already. Lena felt like she had a responsibility to her family to check that he was good for her cousin. 'I will come.'

'You won't regret it,' said Sarika. 'Your date is hot.' She grinned at Lena.

Lena looked down at the note again. She was still holding it by the edges. 'But tomorrow we will take this to the police,' she said.

Sarika leaned forwards and snatched the note from Lena's hands.

'Do not touch it,' said Lena, trying to grab it back. 'It might have fingerprints.'

'Fingerprints are no use,' said Sarika. 'Because I am not going to the police.' She tore the paper into long shreds, like chicken destined for a *paprikash*. 'See, it does not matter,' she said, going into the kitchen to dispose of the note. 'Now, I will paint my nails,' she said, disappearing into the bathroom. 'Don't wear those baggy old jeans again. And put some heels on.'

Lena listened as the bathroom door shut, then she went into the kitchen and over to the bin. Emptying the bin was one of the few tasks in the house she'd delegated to Sarika and the girl always waited until it was overflowing and stinky before she'd finally lug it out, leaving a trail of tissues and biscuit wrappers behind her. Lena extracted the shreds of paper. She pieced the note back together and read the words again. Jealousy oozed from the page like bleach from a bottle. And jealousy, she knew from experience, was the most dangerous emotion there was. It was why Timea had been murdered.

She used Sellotape to stick the pieces back together. Since it wasn't going to the police in any case, she ran her own fingers along the paper. She could feel the indents from the force of the pen. Whoever had written it had been pressing down so hard the paper had almost ripped. She looked at the page itself: plain, white A4, like in the offices in the City she used to clean when she first came to London more than three years ago, before she got regular clients and started her own business, Lena's Cleaners. There'd probably be paper like this in every office in the world. She raised it to her nose and sniffed. There was a faint hint of perfume, but not one she recognised.

Lena put the note down again, feeling ridiculous. She knew smelling toast was meant to be a sign of a stroke, but was sniffing paper an early sign of madness? She hoped that Sarika was right and there was nothing to worry about. But Lena found she couldn't shake the anxiety rising up in her. She got up. Perhaps a chocolate-chip biscuit would help calm her down. Then she'd get ready for the ordeal of the evening, stretching ahead of her like the long muddy bank of the Danube.

Lena shifted uncomfortably on her bar stool and tried to smile at the man sitting in front of her. She took a sip of her slightly flat gin and tonic and strained to hear what he was saying over the din of the bar music. The song lyrics were interfering with his story and even with her best concentration she couldn't follow what he was on about. She wasn't sure if the problem lay with the three overpriced pints the man had consumed since they'd arrived an hour ago, or if it was her own faulty English. It was at times like this that Lena wished she was back home in Hungary, where she didn't have the linguistic and cultural barriers that faced her here. Not that there was much choice of eligible men back in her village. Unless she fancied a life raising pigs on the Lisdtok boys' family farm.

The man was laughing at his own story. Lena strained a smile in response. He would, she supposed, be considered attractive. A tight-fitting T-shirt wrapped an impressively muscular physique. He'd clearly spent a lot of time in the gym. Surely he had better things to do, thought Lena. PC Cartwright was muscular too, but in a less ostentatious way, she decided. She couldn't imagine him wasting his time on a treadmill or lifting weights. His muscles were from saving people on the streets. Catching criminals. Doling out justice.

Lena told herself off. She wasn't meant to be thinking about Cartwright. The man in front of her was probably perfectly nice. The fact that he wasn't PC Cartwright was hardly his fault. She let her mind drift back to her policeman for a moment, mentally enjoying the memory of his sandy hair and eyes the colour of Lake Balaton. His breath, always faintly smelling of bergamot. Only recently, while picking used tea bags out of the sink at her client Penelope's house had she realised where the scent must come from: the Earl Grey tea he always drank so enthusiastically.

But he wasn't here, she reminded herself. Each time they had arranged to meet up, he'd cancelled at the last minute. Maybe Sarika was right, she thought. She needed to be less available. Perhaps next it would be her who would cancel. A cleaning emergency, she decided. He wasn't the only one with an important job.

Thinking of absent people, where on earth had Sarika got to? She'd barely had a chance to be dazzled by the brilliance of Terry's blue eyes and the depth of his dimples when the two of them had disappeared for a cigarette. Those eyes would get all bloodshot if he continued to smoke, thought Lena. And the dimples would wrinkle. But even she had to admit, he was an extremely handsome man. He had the same way about him as her childhood sweetheart Istvan: a presence that made you feel as if you were sitting in the sunshine. It was no surprise that both men had ended up on television.

Lena cast a surreptitious glance at her watch. Sarika and Terry had been smoking for half an hour now. That was a long cigarette. Lena started to wonder what else they might be up to.

She looked again at the man opposite to distract herself. She decided to glean what information she could from him about Terry. Despite his handsome looks, Lena had yet to be convinced Terry was good news for her rather gullible young cousin. Istvan certainly hadn't been good news for Lena. She waited for Raz to stop talking so she could change the subject, but he was in full flow and didn't even seem to pause for breath. To hell with politeness, thought Lena, and began to speak over him.

'How did you meet Terry?' she asked, leaning forwards so she'd have the best chance of hearing, and understanding, the response.

He smiled at her and she noticed his gaze drop. Lena adjusted her top to conceal her modest cleavage. 'We worked together,' he replied. 'Of course.'

'What do you do?'

'You're joking, right?'

Lena looked at him. 'I did not joke?' she said, baffled. She thought she had the measure of English humour now, but perhaps she was wrong.

'Really?' he replied. 'I wondered why you hadn't asked for a selfie with me. You haven't seen the show?'

'I do not watch much television,' Lena replied politely.

'That's rare,' Raz replied. 'You must have heard of it though. *N1 Angels*. The Islington reality show? Season two only ended a couple of months ago.'

'Sarika told me Terry was on it.'

'He was the star,' said Raz. 'But don't you recognise me at all? You're sure? I'm big on Instagram too.' He grinned at her. 'How about now?' he asked, pulling his T-shirt sleeve to his shoulder and rippling his muscles in what Lena guessed must be his trademark pose.

'No,' said Lena, feeling vaguely sorry for the man. 'What is the show about?'

'Us,' he said, with another smile. 'Well, Terry and the others mainly. I'm only in a few of the episodes. Get my top off, though. Got me 120,000 Instagram followers, just like that,' he said, clicking his fingers. 'Raz98gunsout. Look me up.'

Lena nodded, having no intention of doing so.

'Sarika told Terry you run your own events business?' said Raz. 'That sounds cool.'

Lena paused for a moment, wondering whether to set him straight. Sarika liked saying she worked in events, and Lena supposed it was true, in a way. The girl did help out with the odd job that the cleaning agency got catering small events and dinner parties; cleaning before and after, of course. But it was very much a sideline to her main role as Lena's assistant cleaner.

'Among other things,' said Lena, thinking Sarika owed her one. She clearly didn't want her new TV-star boyfriend to know what she really did. Lena saw no reason to be ashamed of the noble art of cleaning, but she knew her image-conscious cousin thought otherwise.

The smell of smoke and a giggle announced Sarika's return. She'd wrapped herself around Terry's athletic frame, making it awkward for the two of them to progress through the bar, even though it was near empty. They knocked bar stools as they went. Sarika accidentally nudged the pint of a man in a suit, spilling it on to his shirt. He turned to her, his stance filled with aggression. Terry pushed her behind him and squared up to the man, towering above him. From the droop of the other man's shoulders, it seemed he backed down quickly.

Sarika skipped on past to Lena. She grinned at her. 'Terry is so brave,' she said, in English. 'And isn't this better than sitting at home on your own?' she added, breaking into Hungarian.

'No,' replied Lena, in English. 'Not at all.'

Raz thumped Terry on the back. 'This lovely lady has never seen the show,' he said. 'Can you believe it?'

Terry turned to Lena and gave her a brilliant smile. His dimples made it seem like his whole face was delighted to see her. Despite never having heard of him, Lena felt a little star-struck.

'We're hoping for a third series,' he told her. He put his arm around Sarika and Lena could almost hear her cousin purring.

'Good luck,' said Lena, wondering how Terry's teeth could possibly be so white and perfect. Perhaps she should switch toothpastes. 'It is set near here?'

'Lots of it is set in this bar,' Sarika told Lena, jumping in. 'That is why we are here.'

There had to be a reason, thought Lena, looking at the sticky surfaces and dirty floor.

'Me and my uncle own the place,' said Terry, running his fingers through his shiny brown hair. 'N1 Demons. I've renamed it, after the show. Get it? It's been here for donkeys' – in my dad's day it was just the Dog and Devil, a cruddy old man's pub. I wish he was still alive to see it now. I've even put in a fire pit.' He smiled again. 'I hope my dad would have been proud,' he added.

Lena looked around again. The fire pit Terry mentioned was really a small gas fire in something that resembled a concrete bowl. It looked nice, thought Lena, but it seemed a dangerous ornament to put in a bar.

'My new boyfriend is a TV star and successful businessman,' said Sarika, gazing adoringly at Terry.

Terry leaned in and gave Sarika an affectionate kiss. Lena felt the *Tojáskrém* egg sandwich she'd had for lunch travelling back up her gullet. 'I am lucky,' he said, pulling his face away but leaving his hand still squeezing Sarika's. 'And I've finally found a nice honest girl to share it with.' He grinned at her and winked. 'A nice honest Hungarian girl who is drop-dead gorgeous.'

Sarika wriggled in her chair with pleasure at the compliment.

'Terry is the gorgeous one,' she said. 'Lena, do you want to see his new tattoo?' She began to tug Terry's shirt up, revealing a rippling six-pack.

'No,' said Lena, in alarm. She sucked the remainder of her drink up through her straw. It was mainly melted ice.

'I'll get you another,' said Terry, smiling magnanimously. 'Drinks are on the house when you're with me. Uncle Barry,' he said, gesturing to the scrawny man behind the bar. 'Another round please for these gorgeous ladies. And turn up the music. Let's make this a party.' Barry fetched the drinks and slammed them down on the table.

'There you go, little prince,' he said with a sneer.

'He's a miserable old sod,' said Terry, with a laugh. 'Hey Uncle, tell them about your luck with women!'

Barry responded by giving him the finger. Terry continued, his voice loud above the din of music. 'He was seeing this woman, Anastasia, off the internet. Russian. Hot as. Thought she loved him, silly old guy. Then she came round one night and emptied the till and our safe. Wiped him out. Daft bugger had told her the combination. Not my idea of pillow talk, but there we go.'

'That's awful,' said Sarika. 'Poor Uncle Barry.'

'It's the only way the old sod could get some action!' laughed Terry. 'I reckon he got a good deal.'

Lena watched Barry fidgeting behind the bar. He was rearranging shot glasses in a straight line on the shelf. His hands shook as he did so. 'Your uncle is not married?' she asked.

9

'He was,' said Terry, his laugh evaporating. 'His wife died fifteen years ago. Cancer.'

'I do not think we should judge people for being lonely,' she said.

Terry's smile faded for a moment. 'You are right,' he agreed. 'It's not easy, being alone.' His blue eyes looked mournful for a moment. But then he smiled again, bouncing back like a ball. 'But hey,' he added. 'I'm not the bad guy here. I had to bail the place out after that. You're not going to get an insurance pay-out when you've been that daft.'

'You are very generous,' said Sarika, gazing into his eyes.

Terry rewarded the compliment with another kiss. Then he pulled away. 'Hey Bazza, I asked you to turn up the music,' said Terry. Barry obliged and the music further swamped the bar. Lena could see Barry muttering something under his breath.

He needn't have bothered. She could understand nothing of the conversation now with the drumbeat reverberating around her ears. She didn't think she was missing much.

CHAPTER 2

The next evening Lena found herself enjoying work much more than she had her date. She hovered at the edge of the kitchen watching her chef Lucia work her magic. This new business venture was working a treat. Here they were, in a client's kitchen on a Friday night, preparing an elaborate meal for a dinner party. Lena had cleaned the house before the guests arrived, Lucia was cooking a delicious meal, Lena and Sarika would serve it and clean up afterwards, leaving the house spotless. Already a number of Lena's cleaning clients had taken her up on the offer and it was proving to be a gold mine. Lucia had even hired an assistant cook, Irina, to help her on such occasions. The only problem was that Sarika was late again, leaving Lena to clean alone.

'You are quiet tonight, Lena,' said Lucia. She was chopping an onion so quickly Lena could barely see her fingers.

'I am tired,' said Lena. 'I was on a date last night.'

'Really?' said Lucia, sounding a little more surprised than Lena would have liked.

'Yes,' said Lena.

Even Irina looked interested for once. She glanced up from the carrot that she was struggling to peel. The girl had proven herself a terrible cook, but she was the little sister of Lucia's terrifying flatmate Kat, so Lucia insisted they give her a chance. Lena's own patience was already wearing thin.

'Cartwright finally called you?' asked Lucia.

'No,' replied Lena. She saw Lucia's look of sympathy and couldn't stand it. 'Cartwright is not the only man for me,' she lied.

'Who was it then?' asked Irina. 'Any action?'

'It was a double date,' said Lena, choosing to ignore the second part of the question. 'With Sarika, her boyfriend and a friend of his.'

Irina laughed. 'I was partying with many men last night,' she said. 'Out till five a.m. The men, they love to watch me dance.' She wriggled a little for the women's benefit. 'Tongues hanging out,' she added, 'like dogs.' Lena had to admit, although Irina was tiny, she had a voluptuous figure and knew how to move it.

'I do not know how you still have the energy to cook,' said Lucia. Both she and Lena watched the girl. She'd barely managed to peel a single carrot, wielding the peeler awkwardly with her long red nails. The colour of dried blood, Lena decided, and shuddered.

Lucia glanced at the clock on the kitchen wall. '*Dio mio!*' she exclaimed. 'The time is flying. Irina, fry those quails' eggs for the *primi*.' Irina stood by the stove, looking blank and clutching her carrot. 'Just like you would fry a normal egg,' explained Lucia, looking at the girl. 'Except they are smaller so need less time.'

'In water?' questioned Irina. Lena looked at her. The girl was pretty, she'd give her that. But even Lena knew how to fry an egg.

'Never mind,' said Lucia. 'I'll do it. Can you just finish off the *pan di spagna*? The batter is all there.' She stuck a spoon into the mixture and sampled it. 'I think you need to add two more teaspoons of sugar and some lemon zest, it is not flavourful enough. Then pour it into the baking dish and pop it into the oven. Thirty minutes and do not open the door or it will deflate.' She turned to the stove and poured some olive oil into a frying pan before breaking the tiny quails' eggs in, one by one. 'Lena,' she said, without taking her eyes from the pan. Lena's usually

12

placid chef was starting to sound as frazzled as bacon. 'Pass me those mini ciabattas.'

Lena obeyed.

'I've already spread them with tapenade, I just need to add the eggs,' Lucia said, doing it deftly as she spoke. 'And a sprinkle of salt, where's the salt?' Irina passed it to her. 'No that's sugar,' she said. 'The salt is in the other bag.'

'Oh,' said Irina, looking a little uncomfortable.

'Try one,' said Lucia. Lena didn't need to be asked twice. She took it in a single bite. The quail's egg oozed hotly over her tongue, the fat offset by the saltiness of the tapenade. 'Delicious,' she said.

'The cake won't be ready yet,' said Lucia, watching Irina opening the oven.

'Um,' said Irina. 'I think I might have . . .'

'What now?' asked Lucia. She pushed past the girl, grabbed an oven mitt and took the dish out. With the Teflon hand of a cook, she dipped a finger into the still soft batter and tasted it again. 'You put salt in here, didn't you?' she said, emptying the container in the bin. 'And what did we say about the difference between a teaspoon and a tablespoon?'

'I hate working here,' declared Irina. 'It is stupid.'

'It is not the work that is stupid,' said Lena, feeling defensive of her new business.

'Not everyone is cut out to be a chef,' said Lucia, patiently. 'Lena here, for example. But she is a good cleaner.' She turned to Lena. 'I don't suppose you need any extra help cleaning?'

'No,' said Lena and Irina, simultaneously. 'I do better at cooking,' said Irina, with a quick smile. 'But not for long,' she continued. 'I have other work too. Pretty girls do not need to slave in a kitchen for ever.'

Lena and Lucia both stared daggers at her. 'I have no openings anyway,' said Lena.

'I need my break now,' said Irina, looking at her phone. 'My boss is calling me.'

'I am your boss,' said Lucia.

'My other boss,' replied Irina. 'She is not a woman you keep waiting.' She fled the kitchen.

'Is she the best you could get?' asked Lena.

'I cannot fire her, she's my flatmate's sister. And she is just over from Russia and only seventeen. Give her a chance. Although, she hates cooking so much I don't think I'm doing anyone a favour.'

'Like Sarika,' sympathised Lena. 'She does not like to clean. These young people,' she added, despite the fact she was only a little past thirty. 'They do not want to do proper work.'

'She'll learn,' said Lucia. 'Luckily I have some of my famous Nutella gelato in the freezer. That will be fine for dessert on its own. Things could be worse.'

'At least Irina is here,' said Lena. 'Sarika has not even showed up yet.'

'Finally,' said Lena, when Sarika appeared. 'I had to clean the house without you.'

'What's she doing here?' hissed Sarika, glaring at Irina.

'We told you Lucia needed an assistant chef,' said Lena.

'She hates me.'

'You did steal her sister's boyfriend.'

Sarika snorted in response.

'Anyway,' said Lena, herding Sarika to the kitchen. 'Why are you late?'

'Since I cannot see Terry tonight because you are making me work,' she said, shooting a dirty glance at Lena, 'I tried to meet him earlier.'

'You can have a night apart,' said Lena. 'It will not kill you.'

'Two nights. He has to work tomorrow,' she said. 'He is doing a paid appearance at a birthday party,' she added loudly. 'We will miss each other so much.'

'Women will be all over him at the party if that TV show is anything to go by,' contributed Irina. 'If he's even telling the truth about where he will be. Perhaps he has another date?' Sarika scowled at her, picking a cold bottle of white wine from the fridge to serve to the guests.

'I think it is sweet,' said Lucia, as she chopped a tomato ferociously. 'I bet he was pleased to see you.'

'He did not pick up the phone,' said Sarika. 'He must not have heard it. So I tried N1 Demons but he wasn't there. And I cannot go to his house because of Marsela.'

'Marsela?' asked Lena.

'His real girlfriend,' said Irina.

'His fake girlfriend,' corrected Sarika. 'On the show.'

'She is very pretty,' Irina added, looking at Sarika. 'And Terry loves her. Perhaps you shouldn't try to steal him from her. But I forget, that is your thing.'

'Shut up,' replied Sarika. 'You do not know anything about it.'

'It is real,' said Irina. 'Kat knows Marsela. Their relationship is not for show.'

'Your stupid sister is just bitter because Dragg chose me over her,' said Sarika, stabbing the top of the wine bottle with a corkscrew.

'And that worked out well?' asked Irina, her voice seeping with fake innocence. 'I heard that he fled the country to get away from you.' Lena put her hand on Sarika's shoulder, but the girl shrugged it off.

'I do not care about Dragg any more,' said Sarika. 'And Marsela and Terry are just pretending for the cameras. Terry loves me.'

Irina laughed. Sarika ignored her. 'It is called a "showmance",' Sarika told them. 'It just means that we can't stay at his, because of his contract. So we go to hotels and this damn bottle will not open.'

'He has a girlfriend?' said Lena, taking her cousin to the hallway. 'You did not tell me this.' She took the bottle from Sarika and twisted the screw top open.

'It is just for the show,' insisted Sarika, going back into the kitchen. They all watched Lucia drizzle her pesto over the plate. Lena smiled at her chef's handiwork: the food was making her mouth water. Lucia was her secret weapon.

The talk of the dinner party was the disappearance of Sebastian Brown, and Josephine Brown's subsequent fury. Lena picked up pieces of the conversation as she put a plate in front of each guest.

'She waited a week to call the police, you know.'

'I heard his passport was missing.'

'I bet he ran off with some girl from Bienvenue.com.'

'That website is a disgrace. I've heard half the men in Islington use it now.'

'Poor Josie.'

'Poor Seb. If he does come back, Josie will have his guts for garters.'

Sarika was lingering to pick up gossip. Lena tried to get her back to the kitchen, but the girl promptly grabbed a bottle of wine and returned to the dining room to slowly refill not yet empty glasses. Lena, finding herself bereft of a task, made her way back to the kitchen to see how she could assist Lucia.

Lucia was peacefully stirring a risotto that was emitting a pleasant odour of buttery, fresh asparagus. 'Let me help,' said Lena.

'No thank you, Lena,' said Lucia. 'You are a great cleaner but a dreadful cook. Last time you touched my wooden spoon, the rice immediately clung on to the bottom of my pan and my porcini risotto was ruined. You are almost as bad a cook as Irina.'

Lena had to agree. Her skills were many, but they did not extend to the culinary world, much to her mother's despair.

Sarika re-entered the room. 'I miss Terry,' she moaned

'Pull yourself together and grate some Parmesan,' said Lena, handing her the lump of pungent cheese. 'Work is the best remedy.'

Two days later, to her surprise, Lena found herself missing Sarika as the day drew to a close. She settled back into her sofa and pulled her blanket around herself. The previous evening had been lovely. It was Saturday night and, with Terry busy, Sarika had been home for once. They had ordered pizza, sprinkled it with Hungarian paprika, cracked open a bottle of Tokaji wine and watched *Kontroll*, one of her favourite Hungarian films, before both having an early night. It was the kind of evening she used to enjoy with Timea when Lena's ex-boyfriend Tomek went to his Polish social club on *kielbasa* night to eat his body weight in sausages.

But now the two nights Sarika and Terry had to be apart were over and Lena found herself alone. She thought about calling Cartwright. Maybe later. Right now, she'd listen to music. She pressed play on the remote control and let the calming sounds of cellos wash over her.

Lena stretched out on the sofa, wondering whether the heated joys of a bath were worth the effort of running the water and having to dry off afterwards. She decided they were not and closed her eyes, feeling the music carry sleep gently towards her.

And then she was awake.

Wide awake.

Lena blinked in confusion. The music was still playing in a gentle diminuendo. She reached for the remote and switched it off. The sound. It happened again. A crash. Definitely not part of the music. Lena got up and ran to the window but she couldn't see anything out of the ordinary. Traffic lumbering by. People hurrying along the pavement.

She took a deep breath. She'd been nervous of loud noises since she'd been shot. She had to relax and accept that it was her mind playing tricks on her.

Lena sat back on the sofa, in silence now. She took some more deep breaths. Maybe she needed a huge dog to protect her? Lena shuddered. She could smell that distinctive dog odour already, see the fur on her sofa, the pee stains on the rug. No need for such a drastic measure. She'd be fine. Slowly she felt herself begin to relax again, allowing her tiredness to make her limbs feel heavy. Perhaps if she shut her eyes for a moment, and thought peaceful, dog- and intruder-free thoughts . . .

'I will kill him.'

Lena's eyes shot open. She saw an irate Sarika standing in front of her. Sarika's hair was perfectly curled and her lips painted a brilliant pink. But her cheeks were flushed and her eyes flashed angrily.

'You are back early,' commented Lena, shifting herself on the sofa to make room for Sarika.

'I need a drink,' she said.

'Coffee?' offered Lena.

'A proper drink,' said Sarika. 'I've had the worst night ever.' The girl sat down with such force Lena felt the ricochets. She heaved herself up and went to the kitchen, pulling a bottle of red wine and two glasses from the cupboard. She filled both up and returned.

Sarika snatched the glass from Lena and took a deep swig. Lena watched as a drip ran from the stem of the glass and gathered at the base, threatening to leap to the sofa and memorialise itself forever as a burgundy spot. 'That *fasz*,' said Sarika. 'I hate him.'

'What did Terry do?' asked Lena, feeling concern for her cousin mingle with concern for her sofa. She went to the kitchen to grab a piece of kitchen roll. She returned and tried to wipe at Sarika's glass, but the girl was back to swigging and held the glass out of

18

Lena's reach. She didn't try to grab it, fearful of knocking the whole thing from Sarika's hand. Instead she bided her time and tried to listen to what her cousin had to say.

'It is Dragg all over again,' declared Sarika. 'Terry didn't show up for our date and now he won't answer my calls.' She turned her face to Lena. Her lip was trembling, her cheeks remained flushed and her eyes were beginning to glisten with tears. 'Why do all men ghost me?' she said. 'Disappear like they never existed? Dragg went all the way back to Greece to get away from me. He didn't even tell me he was going. Now Terry stands me up. Am I so ugly?'

Lena embraced her cousin, doing her best to ignore the dangerously tipped wine glass. 'You are beautiful,' she said. 'But more important, you are . . .' Lena wanted to tell her she was a clever, independent woman, but she found her lips wouldn't contort to that lie. 'Lots of fun,' she finished.

'I *am* lots of fun,' said Sarika, downing the rest of her wine and slamming the glass on the coffee table. 'They are missing out. Your policeman is missing out too. You are . . .' Sarika looked at Lena. Lena listened as the girl struggled to tell Lena she was fun too and couldn't manage a lie either. 'Forceful,' she said finally.

Lena laughed.

'Lots of men like that,' Sarika reassured her. Lena reached for the bottle of wine and refilled Sarika's glass. 'Terry is a *malac*,' Lena said.

'A stinky fat *malac*,' agreed Sarika. She took another swig. 'I didn't think he was like that,' she said, staring into the wine glass as though it held the answers. 'He said he loved how real I was, how I'd never lie to him. He seemed to like me so much.'

'That is what they always seem,' said Lena, taking a good gulp of her own wine. 'So that you fall for them. Then once they have you hooked, they reveal their true colours.' She thought of PC

19

Cartwright. He'd seemed so keen, then suddenly had no time for Lena with his important cases. Never-ending important cases.

'Unless . . .' said Sarika. 'Because he is not answering his phone. Something could have happened to him. Perhaps I will try to call him again.'

'Put the phone away,' said Lena. 'Nothing has happened to him. He is just a man.'

'Something terrible has happened,' continued Sarika. 'That is it. I should call the hospitals. The police too.'

'I do not think you should bother the police,' said Lena.

'But I have a bad feeling,' said Sarika. 'I can feel it here.' She gestured dramatically to her heart and a splash of wine flew from her glass on to her dress. 'What about that note? Something could have happened to him.'

'I am sure Terry is fine,' said Lena. She exchanged the glass in Sarika's hand for a wet dishcloth for her to dab out the spot.

'But he could be my soulmate!' said Sarika, grabbing back the glass. 'I cannot let my soulmate slip through my fingers. Perhaps there has been a misunderstanding. Maybe I got the wrong night . . .'

'I do not think . . .' began Lena.

'And besides, I will not be twenty-one for ever,' said Sarika. 'And I want to be married at twenty-five. I couldn't bear to be thirty and not have a husband and two children. What a failure I would feel.'

Lena took another swig of wine.

'I didn't mean that badly,' said Sarika, quickly. 'Some people, like you, are happy on their own.'

Lena got up. 'I am going to bed,' she said.

'It's only nine o'clock,' objected Sarika.

'I am happy in my bedroom,' replied Lena. 'On my own.'

CHAPTER 3

Lena bent down to collect a dog bowl, licked clean. Some people were gluttons for punishment, she thought to herself. Her client Penelope, already struggling with the demands of two toddlers and a hectic job in PR, had done what Lena could only believe was the worst possible thing imaginable. She'd bought herself a puppy.

And not just any puppy.

A St Bernard. A giant puppy that would grow to be an enormous slobbering source of mess, fur, bad smells and general disasters.

Back in her village, people only kept pets if they had a purpose. If they could herd sheep or catch mice. But in Islington, with their flats and patio gardens, people seemed to want to get the largest, most expensive, most impractical dog they could physically fit through their Georgian front doors.

Lena shrugged to herself and resumed her task, popping the bowl into the dishwasher and turning her attention to the dried Plasticine clinging to the granite worktops. She could hear Sarika frolicking in the small garden with the two children and the puppy. She smiled: it had been a nightmare trying to clean this house on her own and manage the menagerie of children and animals. It was such a relief to have Sarika to help.

'I miss Terry,' sighed her cousin, coming back into the house from the garden. The puppy followed her and sniffed hopefully around the area his bowl had been. 'I hardly slept last night, without him there. I will call him again.'

'Remember what you said to me about Cartwright,' said Lena. 'You want to be unavailable.' She reached for a clean bowl and shook some unappetising brown dog biscuits into it. 'Maybe you could go on a date with someone else. Like you are always telling me to.' The dog jumped at her and she held the bowl above her head, attempting to stare him down. 'That would make him jealous.'

'I couldn't!' said Sarika. 'Lena, I'm worried that something has happened to Terry. It isn't like him not to call.'

'You have not known him for long,' said Lena. 'A couple of months only. You do not know if this is like him or not.' The puppy licked her leg, leaving a smelly damp patch on her jeans. 'Bad dog,' she scolded. He licked her again and gazed up, an adoring look in his eyes.

'When you know you know,' said Sarika. 'I love him.'

Lena put the bowl down and slid it across the kitchen floor. The puppy scrambled after it, leaving a trail of muddy footprints the size of a bear cub's in its wake. It was hardly worth cleaning a house with a dog, thought Lena. Or children, for that matter, she thought, looking out at the toddlers who appeared to be crafting cakes from mud in the freezing cold garden.

'Did you not think you knew with Dragg too?'

'That was different,' replied Sarika. 'Dragg was a boy. Terry is a man.'

Lena rolled her eyes and began to run the hot tap in the sink. 'Just be careful.'

'We had a special date planned for tomorrow,' said Sarika. 'To the bar first for a free bottle of champagne, then somewhere fancy in town.' She leaned forwards and turned off the hot tap.

Lena turned to look at her. 'I think he was going to tell me he loves me.'

'Do not get too excited too soon.' She thought of her own slow-burning romance with Cartwright. So slow it had all but fizzled entirely. Maybe she wasn't the person to give advice. 'I am sorry,' she said, looking at Sarika's crestfallen face. 'Maybe he was. But I do not think you should get your hopes up. And I had a bad feeling about him. He was unkind to his uncle.'

'They are like that together,' said Sarika. 'Bants, Terry calls it.' Sarika scooped up the larger of the two muddy toddlers who had wandered inside. 'Mrs Sarika Tibbs,' she said. 'It has a ring to it. Perhaps I'll be in the next series of his show. Instead of that awful Marsela he has to pretend is still his girlfriend.'

'Are you sure she is not?' asked Lena, carefully.

'He only lives with her because it's in his contract.'

'But he does live with her. I would not want my boyfriend living with another woman that everyone thinks is his girlfriend. That does not seem good to me.'

'It's no big deal,' said Sarika, sitting the child down by the sink and reaching for a paper towel to wipe his face. 'They're not right for each other. You'd know if you watched the show.'

'Maybe I should,' said Lena. 'But if he has a girlfriend, and he stops calling, don't you think . . . ?' Her voice trailed off as she watched Sarika's face. Lena had meant what she said from the best place. This man had clearly lost interest and the best thing for Sarika to do was move on. But from the tears welling in her cousin's eyes she clearly wasn't ready for that. 'I am sorry,' began Lena, but it was too late.

'If that's what you think I can't be around you,' declared Sarika. 'My Terry is missing and all you can be is spiteful. No wonder Cartwright doesn't like you any more.' Lena started back, feeling as if she'd been hit. Sarika lifted the child back down. Evidently sensing anger, he escaped to the garden, his little brother and the giant puppy trailing after him. 'You are bitter and mean and don't want me to be happy,' Sarika said. 'I'm going.'

Lena watched her leave. She worried about her young cousin. Quick to trust and quick to love, like Timea had been. But Lena had been too harsh, she knew she had.

Lena poked her head into the garden. The dog was lying on its back and both children were rubbing its belly. They looked happy, enjoying each other's company. Lena came back inside to an empty kitchen and proceeded to finish loading the dishwasher. Perhaps having more creatures in your life wasn't such a bad idea after all.

Lena was exhausted as she sat on the bus on the way home. Sarika storming out meant she'd had to clean all day by herself, not to mention looking after Penelope's menagerie of children and dogs. Typically, Penelope had arrived back late, so Lena had to finish at the last house of the day when the owners were home' already. From the dirty looks they'd given her as they grabbed a wine bottle from the kitchen she'd been scrubbing, she was clearly in the way. They left a trail of dirty footprints behind them and it had been dark for a couple of hours by the time Lena was finished.

Her phone rang as she approached her stop. Lena rummaged in her bag to answer it, at the same time ringing the bell on the bus and heaving herself up from her seat. This had better be an apology from Sarika for leaving her with all the work, she thought, not even glancing at the screen to confirm.

'I hope you do not think that I will pay you a full day,' she said as she stepped off the bus. *Szar*, she thought. She'd meant to say sorry.

'What?' said the voice at the other end of the phone. It was a man.

24

'Who is this?' asked Lena, glancing both ways as she walked along the deserted pavement, remembering the warning signs she'd seen in the police station about using your mobile on the street at night. Not that hers was worth much, but she still didn't fancy the inconvenience of having it snatched. She saw someone disappear into an alley under her gaze. She carried on walking but glanced back to the alley regularly.

'Raz,' said the man.

'Who?'

'You know. We double-dated with Sarika and Terry. Thursday night. You remember, babe. Off the telly. Raz98gunsout.'

'Oh,' said Lena. Was this what Sarika would call a drunk dial? 'I did not give you my number,' she added.

'Terry did,' he said. 'Before he . . .' His voice stopped abruptly.

'Before he what?' encouraged Lena.

'I have some bad news,' he said, his voice slow. 'Will you tell Sarika?'

'If you tell me,' said Lena. Was Terry breaking up with Sarika via his friend to her friend over the phone? Surely even a social-media dump was more intimate than that. 'But I do not think this is the right way to do it.'

'What?' said Raz. 'I'm sorry, I haven't done this before.'

'Good,' replied Lena. 'Now come on.' She searched for the English expression. 'Spit it up.'

'What?' repeated Raz.

'Tell me the bad news,' said Lena. She froze for a second, thinking she could hear someone behind her. She turned around. No one was there. 'I think I can guess,' she said, wishing she hadn't become so jumpy.

'It is about Terry,' said Raz. 'I just found out. I had a call from Mars.'

'Mars?'

'Marsela. His co-star. She's practically Mrs Tibbs.'

'So it was real?' said Lena, feeling a little vindicated.

'What's real?' said Raz. 'Who knows? It doesn't matter now anyway. Listen, I don't think it's been in the papers yet, but just in case it's online . . .

'Online?' said Lena. Had that *fasz* dumped Sarika on Twitter? 'Just tell me. I want to hear what he has to say. Sarika will ask.'

'What? He doesn't have anything to say. There was no time.'

Lena paused to watch a fox dash across the road. It stopped outside a derelict front garden and stared at her accusingly.

'Has he gone somewhere?' said Lena. 'Run away?' Even to her, this sounded a bit extreme. He could just have ended the relationship.

'Sort of,' said Raz. 'He's dead.'

CHAPTER 4

Lena didn't often indulge in spirits, but she was pleased that, like all good Hungarians, she kept a bottle of Unicum in the cupboard for evenings like this. She poured herself a glass and took a sip of the thick, bitter liquor, then sat on the sofa and waited for Sarika to arrive home.

She didn't know any more details about what had happened to Terry, but she felt a nagging worry. That note. Sarika told her Terry had received one too. And now he was dead.

She took another swig of Unicum and tried to calm herself, looking at her watch all the same. Sarika was late. But she was often late. Maybe she'd gone out with Lucia. Lena grabbed her phone and dialled Sarika. No reply. She was probably still angry.

She was being ridiculous, Lena told herself. Terry could have died of natural causes for all she knew. Now was not the time to worry. Sarika was not Timea. But perhaps Lucia would answer, thought Lena, dialling her. She did not.

She mustn't worry. Not about Sarika. Not yet.

Instead, Lena tried to work out the best way to tell her cousin about Terry. She thought back to when she'd found out that her best friend Timea was dead. The police had told her. She had barely absorbed anything else they'd said that day; she'd been too preoccupied by her own grief.

This was different. Lena grew up with Timea; they'd been

friends for over twenty years. Sarika had known this man for a couple of months.

But it was still death.

Still grief.

Lena closed her eyes and allowed her own sadness to wash over her again. Timea gone, Timea's son Laszlo growing up without a mother. Even though the person responsible was now in prison, it still didn't feel like justice. Nothing ever could.

Lena awoke to the appetising aroma of bacon sizzling. She'd fallen asleep on the sofa again. She blinked and looked to the open-plan kitchen. Sarika was busy cracking eggs over a frying pan. Lena pulled herself to her feet, relief flooding through her like water down a drainpipe.

'Awake finally, are you?' said Sarika. 'I'll pour you a coffee.' Sarika handed Lena a cup, which she took and drank from greedily. 'I've decided to forgive you,' Sarika continued. 'And I'm sorry for what I said about PC Cartwright. It's none of my business. I'm making you breakfast so you'll forgive me. You will, won't you?'

'Yes,' said Lena. 'And I am sorry too.' She wondered whether she should tell Sarika about Terry before or after breakfast. It seemed callous to eat eggs and bacon, knowing what she did. But it was pretty rare for Sarika to go to this much effort and she didn't want to spoil it. Was bad news better on a full stomach? She took another sip of coffee and decided it couldn't wait. But Sarika had already plated up the bacon and eggs and was struggling to smear hard butter from the fridge over the toast.

'There you go,' she said, setting the plate in front of Lena.

'Thank you,' said Lena. 'But there is something I must tell you.'

'There is something I must tell you too,' said Sarika. 'You can probably tell I'm in a better mood than I was yesterday.'

'About that,' said Lena, unable to resist putting a forkful of bacon into her mouth.

'I am going to see Terry later,' said Sarika. Lena nearly choked on her bacon.

'What?'

'His phone must be broken, so I'm going to go to his house. Marsela or no Marsela. He'll want to see me. I know he will.'

'I don't think he'll be able to . . .' started Lena, carefully.

'Listen, you might not think much of him, but he's a good guy. And he cares about me.'

Lena put her fork down. 'Maybe he did care about you,' she said.

'Did? What do you mean?'

'Sarika, I had a phone call last night. From Raz. Sarika, I'm sorry, but Terry is dead.'

Lena rinsed the frying pan under the tap. She'd sat with Sarika for hours, stroking the girl's hair and comforting her as much she could. Eventually Sarika had gone to her own room to call her mother. The phone call had ended, the sobs had subsided, and now Lena could hear the reassuring sounds of Sarika's gentle snoring.

Lena gathered the plates from the table. She rescued a piece of crispy bacon, popped it into her mouth and regretfully scraped the remains of the cold eggs into the bin. Chewing the bacon, she wished she knew more about what had happened. She couldn't get over the uneasy feeling that it had something to do with the notes. The notes that both Terry and Sarika had received.

She was being ridiculous, she told herself, as she opened the dishwasher to load the plates. Terry could have died of anything.

A dodgy heart.

A mistimed step in front of a lorry.

A bad oyster.

29

Nonetheless, Lena found herself back in her room, looking at the note. The Sellotape holding it together gave it cheerful shiny strips, but it couldn't conceal the malice behind it. Lena ran her fingers over the lettering again. Felt the anger in the indents made by the pen. She needed to find out what had happened to Terry. And if it was as she feared, this note needed to go to the police.

Lena wished she'd insisted on meeting somewhere different, but she'd gone along with Raz's suggestion of N1 Demons, the bar of Terry's that they'd met in before. At least it was always empty. They settled in a booth that was much more comfortable than the stools on which they'd been perched on Thursday night. It was still ridiculously noisy, though, as if the music wasn't aware that it was 2 p.m. on a chilly February afternoon. As they waited for Raz to arrive, Sarika sat next to her, crying again, this time into a soggy paper napkin. Lena pushed the napkin dispenser towards her and Sarika shakily took another one.

'Last time we were here,' said Sarika with a sob, 'Terry was alive.'

'I know,' said Lena.

'He was happy, wasn't he? With me?'

'It seemed so,' said Lena.

'What happened?'

'That is what we are here to find out,' said Lena. Her Google search had been fruitless: searching Terry's name still yielded nothing but gossip about him and Marsela and a few YouTube clips from the show. News of his death was not yet public.

Lena would feel a lot better when she knew that Terry's demise was not the result of a murderous, note-writing psychopath. But she wouldn't find out anything the way this music was thumping through her skull. She shifted along the bench and stood up, asking the scrawny man she recognised as Terry's uncle to turn the music down. Even through her tear-sodden napkin, Sarika looked embarrassed. To Lena's surprise the man beamed at her.

'I hate this music,' he said. 'It's not what people want when they come for a drink. They want to be able to chat to their friends. That's what they want.' He turned it off completely. 'Ahh,' he said, savouring the moment. 'For the first time in years I can hear myself think.'

Lena looked at him. He did not seem a man heartbroken at the death of a beloved nephew.

Raz entered the bar. He was wearing a tight-fitting black jacket with drainpipe trousers and no socks. His ankles must be freezing, thought Lena as she greeted him. She thought of his little ankle hairs standing on end and felt a small flood of affection for him. 'I am sorry for your loss,' she said.

'I've never known anyone that's died before,' he said. 'It's weird.'

Sarika got up and embraced Raz, sinking her face into his shiny jacket. 'It is so awful,' she said. 'I miss him so much already.'

For once Lena saw Raz's usual cockiness leave his face. He looked uncomfortable. She extracted Sarika and led them both to the bar. There was a damp patch on Raz's shoulder from the girl's tears. Or leaky nose.

'I'm sorry, I don't have long,' said Raz. 'I'm just on my lunch break.'

'I thought you were an actor,' said Lena. 'You are filming today?'

'I'm doing a few shifts at Boots,' Raz replied, looking uncomfortable. 'Just to tide me over till *N1 Angels* starts again.'

'I can't believe you can work at a time like this,' said Sarika. 'I don't know when I'll be able to face life again.'

Lena looked at her. She'd factored in giving the girl today and tomorrow off, but any more than that was going to be a struggle. Already she was paying over-the-odds fees to another agency so that they could both be here now without letting a client down. Lena was planning to cover the rest of Sarika's jobs

31

ELIZABETH MUNDY

herself, but there was a limit to how much she could physically accomplish.

'Uncle Barry,' said Raz, opening his arms to hug the barman. 'I'm so sorry for your loss.'

'I'm not your uncle,' replied Barry, sharply. 'And you're paying for these drinks. No more freebies now Terry's gone.'

They all looked at the man. Raz quietly ordered a cranberry juice, Lena asked for a top-up of coffee and Sarika another vodka and Coke.

'He's not taking it well,' said Raz, as they sat back down.

'We're all grief-stricken,' said Sarika.

'So what do you know?' asked Lena, not wanting to participate in a long, maudlin conversation.

'Not much,' said Raz. 'Marsela hasn't called again. And the story isn't online yet. I'm sure it will be soon, though. Terry's a big noise round here.'

'But what *do* you know?' persisted Lena.

'He died late Saturday night and his body was found on Sunday morning. In a hotel room.'

'Which hotel?' asked Sarika, in a brief pause from sucking up her vodka and Coke through a straw.

'The Goswell,' said Raz.

Sarika emitted another sob. 'That's where we went sometimes,' she said. 'We have special memories there.'

'Who found him?' said Lena. She realised she was getting important information and wished she could write this down. Improvising, she took a napkin from Sarika's dispenser and fished a pen from her bag. She really should carry a notebook.

'The cleaner, I think they said.'

Lena sat back. Discovering a dead body was something she hoped would never feature in her professional career.

'How did he die?' asked Lena.

'I don't know,' said Raz.

'Natural causes?' prompted Lena.

'Marsela didn't say. He did drink a bit. And smoked. But we worked out together. He was in great shape.'

Sarika took the napkin away from her face. 'He had everything to live for.'

'But was the death suspicious?' said Lena, thinking again of the note. 'Was anyone else involved?'

'I don't know,' said Raz. 'Why, do you think someone could have killed him?'

'I do not know,' said Lena. 'But Sarika, now this has happened I think we need to take the note you received to the police.' Lena thought again about Cartwright. He would know the right thing to do.

'What note?' asked Raz. Both women ignored him.

'Lena, do you think the person who wrote the note murdered him?' asked Sarika. 'I could have saved him if I had gone to the police. Couldn't I?'

'We do not know that,' said Lena. 'It is probably not murder.' Cartwright would know the statistics, thought Lena. He'd be able to tell them the chances that the death was a murder or from natural causes, based on Terry's demographics. She looked at Raz, wishing he'd transform into her policeman. 'It is not your fault, Sarika,' she continued, pulling herself back to reality. 'But now you must give the police the note.'

'The police don't know that I had anything to do with Terry,' said Sarika, slowly. 'And I want to keep it that way. You remember what happened before? When that painting went missing, they thought I had taken it.'

'What painting?' asked Raz.

Sarika continued. 'What if they think I'm involved? It's too late to help him anyway. Lena, I can't go through that. Not again.' She grabbed a huge handful of napkins and buried her face in them. 'Not after this.'

'I think you must,' said Lena. She reached for her cousin's hand and gave it a squeeze.

Sarika took her hand away and used it to stab at the lime in her drink with a straw. 'I'm not doing it. No way. I'm not going back to prison.'

'You were in prison?' asked Raz.

'Last time was completely different,' reasoned Lena. 'You ran away at a suspicious time. They thought that meant you had stolen the painting. You will not make that mistake again.'

'The police will think I'm involved,' declared Sarika. 'Just like last time. I don't care what you say. I'm not doing it.'

'Okay,' said Lena. This was an argument she wasn't going to win.

'But you can,' said Sarika suddenly. 'We need to know what happened. Find out from PC Cartwright, but don't mention me. I need to know the truth.'

Lena took a sip of her coffee. It was getting cold. 'I will talk to Cartwright,' she said, feeling a little pleased, despite herself, at having a reason to meet with him. 'I will find out what I can.'

'And do not say anything about me.'

'Okay,' said Lena.

'Promise,' said Sarika.

'Promise,' replied Lena, her voice solemn.

'So anyway,' said Raz. He'd put a comforting hand on Sarika's shoulder while she blew her nose on napkins but his eyes were on Lena. 'You and me.' Lena looked at him in surprise. 'A rematch?'

'What?' said Lena.

'You know, hooking up. Together. Fancy it?'

'Lena, you must,' said Sarika, her eyes red. 'You never know what fate holds.'

'I am busy,' she said. 'I need to find out what has happened to Terry before I can do anything else.'

Raz slurped up the dregs of his cranberry juice through his straw. 'When you're ready,' he said, unperturbed. 'I've got to get back to work now, but let's do it soon. We could come here if you like. Have a big one.'

'We will see,' said Lena.

'I'm going too,' said Sarika suddenly, her attention drawn to her phone. 'Lucia wants to meet before her shift. She's made me her special chocolate truffles.'

Lena watched them leave, then absent-mindedly bent down to pick up one of the tear-stained napkins from where Sarika had dropped it on the floor. Out of habit, she glanced under the booth to see what detritus had gathered there. A few stray wasabi peas glared back at her, and an old Malteser that still looked strangely appealing. There was also a piece of paper. Lena assumed it was a menu card and reached to rescue it.

She was wrong.

It was a note, just like the one Sarika had received. The same office paper, the same handwriting, the same biro. But the words were worse. Much worse.

You've hurt me so much Terry. Now I will hurt you.

Feeling shaky, Lena stood up. She took the paper to the bar. 'You look like you need a brandy,' said Barry. 'What's that you've got?'

'It's a note to Terry,' said Lena. She held it out to him. 'Do you know who it is from?'

Barry took the paper, and without looking at it he scrunched it into a ball and chucked it on to the fire pit.

Lena gasped and reached out to grab it, but it had already gone up in flames.

'Why did you do that?' she asked.

'It's just another piece of fan mail,' he dismissed, turning back to the bar. 'Terry had them sent here – liked to show his mates all the women fawning over him.'

35

'But he is dead . . .' began Lena. 'It could be evidence.'

'Evidence of what?' asked Barry. 'Some bird fancied him? Marsela's been through enough.'

Lena looked to the fire pit again. The paper was gone, but her uneasiness was back. A hundredfold.

Lena waited at the bus stop. Even though it was cold, it felt good to be outside and away from the heat of that evidence-eating fire pit. She sucked in a calming breath of the air, as refreshing as *meggyleves*, the chilled sour-cherry soup she enjoyed in the Hungarian summers. A man at the bus stop across the road was staring at her. Lena looked away, wanting to avoid eye contact. She tried to pull herself together.

She needed to talk to Cartwright. Hopefully he could tell her exactly what had happened to Terry and then she would know whether she needed to worry.

A piercing bleep made her jump. Lena looked around for the culprit before realising it was her own ring tone. She rifled through her handbag and dug it out.

'*Mindenit,*' she exclaimed. Taking another deep breath, Lena answered the phone.

'Cartwright,' she said, trying to sound calm. 'I was thinking about you.' She paused a second, wishing she hadn't said that. She had meant to play it cool.

'I'm sorry to call, out of the blue like this,' said Cartwright, his well-spoken voice sounding breathless. 'I need you.'

'Really?' said Lena, feeling excitement rise in her throat.

'It's Yasemin Avci,' Cartwright continued. Lena felt the excitement turn to dread at the sound of that name. The Turkish gang leader she'd come up against when she was investigating Timea's murder. 'You won't believe this, but she's finally in custody. I need someone to identify her. You're one of the only people who knows exactly what she looks like.'

'Of course,' said Lena, with a shudder. She knew all too well what Yasemin looked like. Yasemin had almost ended Lena's life.

The sense of excitement was palpable in the police station. There were lots of cars parked outside, and a number of senior officers with greying hair and smart uniforms were standing in reception having important-sounding conversations. Lena sat in the waiting room. Despite herself, she ran her fingers through her hair.

Then all of a sudden, he was there. He stepped forwards and shook her hand and she felt the familiar tingling at his touch. 'Thank you for coming,' he said. 'I'm so grateful to you.' He smiled, his hand still holding hers.

'It is busy here,' she replied, trying to sound relaxed as they both pretended they weren't still holding hands. 'It is all for Yasemin? How did you catch her?'

'It's almost unheard of,' said Cartwright, finally letting go of her hand. His excitement had spilled into his voice. 'For an officer of my rank to catch a criminal like Yasemin Avci. In fact, I can't believe how lucky I've been.'

'I am sure it is hard work,' said Lena, politely. 'Not luck.'

'You always know the right thing to say,' said Cartwright. 'Come with me, I'll show you to the room.' He smiled at the officers, several of whom gave him a respectful nod, before leading Lena down one of the corridors. 'I promised myself I'd catch her,' he said. 'After what she almost did to you. And I have finally got her. Yasemin Avci. The drugs dealer, the gang leader, the murderer. Now that she is in custody, I will finally have more time.' He smiled at Lena again. 'I hope that I have not left it too late?'

Lena fought the urge to embrace him then and there. 'We will see,' she said, hoping her voice sounded cooler than she felt. 'I am busy too.'

'Of course,' said Cartwright. 'Thank you so much for coming,' he added, more formally. They were standing outside a locked room.

'I will see her now?' asked Lena. 'In a line-up?' She thought of the movies.

'The Met haven't done a line-up for years,' replied Cartwright. 'We'll use VIPER.' Lena looked blankly at him. 'Sorry, it's a video version of a line-up. It makes a lot of sense,' he added. 'It's traumatic for victims to have to look directly at whoever has hurt them, so this is a way to get the same results without the phys- ical confrontation. We just need to wait for DI Fisher to get here to open the room. I can't be there, of course, as I'm involved in the case, but he's fully trained and will show you a number of videos, one of which is the suspect. It will be up to you to identify if one of them is Yasemin.'

'How did you catch her?' asked Lena.

'In a sting operation,' said Cartwright. 'Of course, it's not really down to me,' he babbled. 'My superior officer, DCI Sutton, was my sponsor, and we've had a massive team on it for a couple of weeks now. You remember what you told me you did, when she captured you? You pretended to have a drugs connection and it tempted her: you said she was incredibly money-hungry. Well, I got a story out that there was a new drug in town: a synthetic opiate. Much cheaper to produce than something you need to grow like marijuana or opium, but the value on the street will be the same. Profits will be tenfold.'

'That is brilliant,' said Lena, feeling like perhaps she should be getting more credit for this than she was.

'She had to arrive with a stash of her own supply to test against the synthetics. Of course, the sample she brought with her isn't substantial, but we've got plenty that we can charge her with now we've got her.'

'Congratulations,' replied Lena. 'She is dangerous. It is good that she will be behind bars.'

'Now we just need the identification to make things official. As you know, she's got multiple aliases but no fingerprints or DNA on file,' said Cartwright. Another officer arrived. 'Perfect timing, DI Fisher,' said Cartwright. 'Let's get this show on the road. Lena, watch all the videos very carefully. Then we'll need you to say which one is Yasemin Avci.'

'Of course,' said Lena. Looking at the excitement on Cartwright's face, she was pleased she'd got another cleaner to cover for her that afternoon. Seeing him happy and proud was most definitely worth it.

'I'll take it from here, Cartwright,' said Fisher, stiffly. He unlocked the room and showed Lena inside. Fisher talked to her at length about what she was about to see, confirmed who she was several times and gave Lena a number of forms, which she completed and signed with a flourish.

Lena sat back and watched the videos, waiting to see Yasemin's small dark eyes glimmering out at her.

Lena didn't recognise the first woman: she was much prettier than she remembered Yasemin, and even on video managed to look seductive. Lena found her mind wandering back to Sarika and Terry. She'd ask Cartwright about Terry as soon as she'd identified Yasemin. She glanced at the second video, but that wasn't Yasemin either. Lena hoped that it was natural causes that had provoked Terry's demise. Although he'd seemed so healthy the other night. Lena didn't recognise the third woman either. It would be much easier if Sarika would let her show the awful note she'd received to the police, thought Lena. Whether or not Terry had been murdered, the note was still a threat. It would be good to figure out who had sent it. Lena felt that Marsela,

Terry's girlfriend (real or otherwise) must be the prime suspect. She would love to investigate that with PC Cartwright. Maybe she could clean for Marsela and discover her secrets. Maybe Cartwright would help her again. It was after they'd discovered who'd murdered Timea that they'd shared their first kiss. It must be time for another one, by now. Lena closed her eyes for a moment, thinking about Cartwright's lips.

'Now it is time to watch them again,' said Fisher.

'I am watching,' said Lena, her eyes snapping open. 'Where is the next video?'

'You have seen them all,' said Fisher. 'I will play them for the second time. Protocol.'

Lena felt a little panic rise up in her, on Cartwright's behalf. 'She was not there,' said Lena. 'That cannot be it.'

'No,' replied Fisher. He pressed play and the first video began again. 'Keep your eyes open this time,' he said. 'That might help.'

'Of course,' said Lena. She was feeling guilty already, although she knew it wasn't her fault. If she hadn't seen Yasemin Avci in the line-up, then Cartwright had the wrong person.

Lena leaned forwards, putting her eyes even closer to the screen. But she already knew. Yasemin Avci was not there. Cartwright had arrested the wrong woman.

CHAPTER 5

The next day, Lena stepped out of her home into a London transformed by snow. She paused a moment, admiring the pristine whiteness. Snow always seemed to make the world quieter, calmer, as if the snow absorbed sound. And it was so clean: a protective coating, like a Marigold glove over the world.

Not for long, she told herself. It was early in the morning still. By the time commuters had trampled through, kids had fashioned snowballs and dogs had done their chilly business, it would be filthy. Not to mention slippery.

But for now, Lena decided to enjoy it. The satisfying crunch under her feet, the layer of protection from the dirty pavement underneath. And luckily, no snow had yet managed to penetrate her trainers and infiltrate her socks.

She hoped that the snow might just remain clean and crunchy until she met Cartwright that afternoon. It would be romantic, she decided, walking in Clissold Park next to the frozen lake. Cartwright had put on a brave face when she confirmed that none of the women were Yasemin. Lena had felt terrible, and for a second she'd even considered lying. Only for a second, though. There was very little that Lena was prepared to be dishonest about. He'd been so despondent she hadn't managed to discuss Terry with him: although she checked the internet regularly, she'd still found no information on his death.

41

Lena climbed aboard the bus and huddled next to the warm heater, watching the world trundle by through the window. Today would be a good day. Cleaning for Mrs Kingston, her favourite client. She couldn't tell her about Yasemin, of course, but she would talk about Terry's death. Then she'd treat herself to a hot bowl of soup at a café before meeting up with Cartwright. He would tell her that Terry had died of a heart attack and then she could dismiss the notes as the nonsense that they were and Sarika would be safe. And then perhaps they'd finally kiss again. She closed her eyes and enjoyed her thoughts.

'Oh yes, I've heard all about Terry Tibbs and his unsavoury demise. Would you like a Garibaldi biscuit?'

Mrs Kingston never failed to amaze Lena. She'd mentioned Terry and of course the ex-journalist was already in the loop. 'How did you know?' asked Lena, helping herself to a biscuit filled with sweet dark raisins. 'There was nothing online.'

'There will be any minute,' replied Mrs Kingston. 'It's the talk of the local newsroom. Even though I'm retired, I do keep abreast of the juicy stories. I still have my contacts, you know. Let's check again now. I'll fetch my laptop and take a look.'

'I will get it,' said Lena, watching Mrs Kingston strain to get up. Her arthritis was definitely getting worse. Lena wondered if she should stop by more often. She looked at Jasper, Mrs Kingston's rabbit. He stared back at her from under the coffee table, his mouth full of cabbage. He'd be no use at all if Mrs Kingston had a fall.

Lena handed her the laptop and Mrs Kingston snapped it open. 'Here we are,' she said. 'Not embargoed any more. If he hadn't been dead when he was found he'd have been high as a kite. And naked except for rather a tight collar round his neck.'

'Let me see,' said Lena, snatching back the laptop. 'Was it murder?' she asked, her heart sinking.

Terry Tibbs, 27, of *N1 Angels* fame, was found dead on Sunday morning wearing nothing but a leather dog collar at the Goswell Hotel in Angel, Islington. Cause of death is said to be heart failure prompted by a lethal cocktail of Ecstasy with a large dose of Rohypnol. Mr Tibbs was well known on the party scene and the police are not treating his death as suspicious.

'It sounds suspicious to me,' said Lena. 'Rohypnol, that is a rape drug.'

'Not always,' replied Mrs Kingston. 'People take Ecstasy to go up and then the Rohypnol to calm themselves down again. It's ten times more potent as a tranquilliser than Valium.' Lena shot her a surprised look. 'I ran a story on it – a while ago now,' Mrs Kingston added, in explanation. 'The collar makes sense too. ' She paused. 'Drugs and a little erotic asphyxiation. Quite a way to go.'

'I wonder who was with him.' Lena made a mental note to ask Cartwright.

'What a juicy story,' said Mrs Kingston. 'I expect they'll put the show back on catch-up now. Maybe even rerun it in a better time slot.' She popped another biscuit into her mouth and looked at Lena. 'Oh. He wasn't a friend of yours, was he?' she asked, with a spray of crumbs. 'I don't mean to be disrespectful.'

'I only met him once,' said Lena. 'But Sarika was dating him.'

'Really?' asked Mrs Kingston, looking surprised. 'I'm so sorry. Is she okay?'

'She is upset,' replied Lena.

'She wasn't, you know, his companion that night?' Jasper the rabbit turned and tried to look at them, his ears flopping over his eyes.

Lena brushed his ears back for him, and popped him on to her lap. He climbed up her chest and scrambled on to the windowsill behind the sofa. 'No,' she replied. 'He told her he had a party to go to.'

'Well that was certainly true,' said Mrs Kingston. 'A party to die for.'

Lena shivered and turned to stroke Jasper. He was staring out of the window, transfixed by the snow.

'I'm sorry,' said Mrs Kingston. 'That was crass of me. But Terry was a bit of a scoundrel. Always up to no good on *N1 Angels*.'

'You watched his programme?' asked Lena, incredulity filling her voice.

'I'm afraid so,' admitted Mrs Kingston. 'I had it on one day when my arthritis was playing up, then I got hooked. I'm putting it down to journalistic curiosity and I don't want anyone to tell me otherwise. I take it you haven't seen the show?'

Lena shook her head. 'Well,' said Mrs Kingston, warming to the subject. 'You've come to the right place. I'll fill you in.' She took another sip of her tea and her face filled with the same pleasure that must have come with breaking a news story. 'There were lots of characters: ad men, lawyers, bankers, you know the type; they will have moved here as Islington became more gentrified. Then there were some less affluent types, who have lived here forever in council flats. You know what the area is like.'

Lena nodded. Council flats with huge families squeezed into a single room bordering huge Georgian houses owned by a couple who might have a whole floor of their homes that they never even visited.

'The show followed a bunch of them around and we got to see all their dramas – fights, tears, romances, betrayals. But there was definitely one couple that were the stars of the show.'

'Terry and . . .' Lena struggled to remember the name.

'Marsela,' replied Mrs Kingston. 'Lovely Albanian girl. I thought they were still together actually, but if he was dating Sarika I suppose not.' She sighed. 'Terry and Marsela were like the Romeo and Juliet of North London,' she said. 'Marsela was a trainee lawyer, but not one of those smug people born with a silver spoon in their mouth. She was orphaned by the war in Kosovo and raised by her uncle in London. Such a clever girl. She had been dating a rich banker called Jack. Terry worked in his dad's pub, who'd raised him alone after his mum ran off. They were drawn to each other, clear as day. He worshipped her. She tried to resist but Terry pursued her intently. Everyone was rooting for them to get together. And of course they did. She broke up with Jack at the end of season one to be with Terry.'

'So Terry had a girlfriend?' said Lena. 'A real one.' She thought of the note. Perhaps it was from Marsela.

'Well, the show was semi-scripted,' admitted Mrs Kingston. Lena gave her a blank look. 'Real people,' she explained. 'And real relationships to some extent, but they put them in particular situations to make more drama when they are filmed. I always thought Terry and Marsela were real though,' she added. 'I can't believe they were good enough actors to fake that. And by the time season two began, they were living together.'

'Sarika thought that Terry really liked her. She was wrong.'

'Not so fast,' said Mrs Kingston. 'I haven't told you about what happened in season two yet.' She took another sip of tea, and Lena noticed a pained look in her eye as she rubbed her gnarled fingers. 'You'll never guess.' Mrs Kingston leaned in, full of excitement. Lena wondered how a sensible lady like Mrs Kingston could be so excited about something so silly.

'Terry changed, all of a sudden. It was like now he had Marsela, he didn't really want her. But Marsela was still smitten. Terry cheated on her, multiple times. By this point his dad had died and he co-owned the pub with his uncle. He thought he was quite the catch, it seemed.'

'They broke up?'

'Yes, early on in season two. But by the fourth episode they were back together. She just couldn't resist giving him chance after chance. Great viewing.'

'I did not think that you would like such a show,' said Lena, trying to be tactful.

'When you've got arthritis, your family live miles away and your only company is a rabbit, it's surprising what you'll watch to pass the time,' replied Mrs Kingston. Lena looked at her, making a mental note to visit more often.

'Don't look at me like that, Lena,' said the old woman. 'I'm just being maudlin. Actually I like watching the young men with their tops off.' She winked at Lena. 'Especially that Raz. If I were forty years younger . . .'

Lena decided not to mention her date with Raz. Mrs Kingston's heart might not take it. 'I must tell Sarika how he died,' she said, dreading it. Sarika was an eternal optimist, especially when it came to men. She'd be horrified at the manner of his death. But at least she would know the truth. Maybe it would help snap her out of the cycle of misery she'd been caught in.

'She's probably already seen it online, if we have,' said Mrs Kingston. 'And I doubt she'll be too surprised, if she's seen the show. Terry was always playing away. I really wanted Marsela to stand up for herself and dump him. But once you're in love it's hard to face the world alone again.' Lena watched as Mrs Kingston's eyes went to the mantelpiece. A black-and-white photo of a young man smiled back at them.

'I thought they were still a couple, actually, even now,' said Mrs Kingston, pulling herself together. 'I think there might have been talk of a wedding in the future – speculation was around some chateau in the South of France. I must be behind on the show gossip.' Mrs Kingston went back to the computer. 'Now I know what I'll be doing this evening,' she said. 'Jasper, make popcorn. We'll spend the night perusing the online gossip columns.' The rabbit ignored her, still transfixed by the snow. Lena wondered what he made of the white world outside the window. 'I'll make the popcorn myself, shall I?' scolded Mrs Kingston. 'Lazy rabbit.'

Lena got up to leave. She'd see Cartwright knowing far more than she thought she would, but at the moment she wasn't sure what to make of it. Was her cousin in danger or not?

Lena was right: Clissold Park was romantic today. It was still bitter out, but the sun was shining and the snow glistened like the quartz worktop in Mrs Ives's kitchen. She stood by the lake. The edges were still iced, but the centre was now liquid: dark and deep. A bird chirped a hungry song and Lena looked up at the nearby tree, its branches laden with heavy snow.

She'd slipped on her gloves and blew into her hands while she waited for Cartwright. Realising just how chilly she'd become, she glanced at her watch, trying not to let annoyance creep into her face. Three thirty. He was fifteen minutes late. *Milyen goromba*, she thought, hating lateness. She stamped her feet with cold and impatience. She had a job to get to soon and didn't have long. Snow was starting to seep in through the seams of her trainers, absorbed by her cotton socks. '*Szar*,' Lena cursed out loud. Nothing romantic would ever happen when her feet were cold and wet.

'I'm so sorry.' Cartwright's voice broke her reverie. 'I got caught up at work.' He handed her a paper cup of hot coffee, which promptly slipped through Lena's gloved hand. Some brown liquid splashed out, instantly melting the snow at her feet like an enchanted lily. They both bent to rescue it, banging heads. Cartwright laughed and Lena swore.

'You can have my tea,' said Cartwright, offering her his cup.

'There is still coffee here,' said Lena, wiping the snow from the lid and holding it more tightly. 'Thank you,' she added, as an afterthought.

'Let's walk,' said Cartwright. 'It's freezing.' He started a brisk pace, easily taking the snow in his police boots. Lena found herself scuttling along next to him, the grips on her trainers painfully inadequate.

'What do you know about Terry Tibbs?' asked Lena, a little breathless already. She had to stare at her feet in an attempt not to slip. She found herself getting even more annoyed. She wanted to be staring into Cartwright's eyes.

'What?' said Cartwright. 'The reality star who died recently?'

'Yes,' she said. 'Was it murder?'

'That's a funny thing for you to ask,' said Cartwright. 'I thought we were here to talk about Yasemin?'

'Okay,' said Lena, deciding to come back to Terry later. 'Who was the person you thought was her? The one you arrested?' asked Lena. Cartwright abruptly stopped. Lena skidded a little, righted herself and turned to look at him.

'We think she was a decoy,' he said. 'Apparently Yasemin is known for using them back home in Turkey when she thinks the police might be on to her.'

'And where does that leave your investigation?' asked Lena. 'You still have the decoy?'

'She will be no use,' said Cartwright. 'She's got a record a few years ago when she was picked up for soliciting, but the "drugs" she had was just a tiny bag of flour. There's not much we can do with that. Unless of course baking becomes a crime.'

'I am sorry,' said Lena. 'But I am sure you will catch Yasemin soon. You just need another plan.'

'I don't think anyone will be very interested in my plans again,' said Cartwright, with a laugh as cold as the snow. 'Or my CID application.'

He looked so miserable, tramping through the snow. Lena hurried to catch up with him and tried to take his hand, but he put it in his pocket just before she could. She grabbed cold air instead.

'Then maybe you can tell me about Terry?' asked Lena, trying to distract him from his misery. 'Terry Tibbs.'

'What's the interest?' Lena thought back to Sarika. The girl didn't want to be connected to him, so she couldn't mention her. Or the note Sarika had received.

'I am a fan,' declared Lena, hoping to keep things simple until she knew more.

'Really?' said Cartwright, walking even faster. 'I'm sorry but I can't discuss his case, it's confidential. I can only say what's been made public already. Looks to be an unfortunate accident. You'll have seen what he was up to: it's been covered online and probably the celebrity gossip magazines will pick it up too.'

'Was there anyone with him in the room?' asked Lena. 'Another woman?'

'I'm sorry, but I don't know,' said Cartwright. 'You really watch that show? It doesn't strike me as your sort of thing at all.'

Lena thought for a moment, concern for Sarika filling her mind. 'I have another question,' she said. 'If you thought someone was in danger, could the police offer them protection?'

'What do you mean?' asked Cartwright. He stopped dead again and turned to look at her. Lena skidded to a halt again, just about retaining her balance.

'Would the police need to know why the person was in danger?' she asked.

'Yasemin doesn't know that you came to the police station,' said Cartwright, his voice soft. 'I promise you. I would never put you in harm's way, Lena.'

'No, I did not mean . . .' Lena paused. She supposed that was as good an excuse to ask her question as any. 'But what proof would you need, if someone did need help?'

'Austerity has made it difficult,' said Cartwright. 'There'd need to be a very real threat, and even then we couldn't offer twenty-four-hour protection. There's the witness protection programme, of course, but that's very extreme.' He looked again at Lena, his eyes filling up with concern. 'Has something happened? If it has, you must tell me. I will find a way to help you. You know I will.'

'No,' replied Lena, thinking the notes were unlikely to get Sarika any help from the police, even if she hadn't been sworn to secrecy. She smiled at Cartwright. 'You must not worry about me,' she said. 'I can look after myself.'

She felt something hit her head. Hard. It took her a moment to register the familiar cold sensation that came with it. She turned around to see a gaggle of children running through the park, released from school. They were pelting each other with snowballs and one had hit her. 'Little rascals,' said Cartwright. Lena could feel snow dripping down inside her coat. Her neck was now as cold as her feet. She thought she could feel snow inside her ear. She glanced at her watch. She'd be late for her next job.

'I need to go,' she said to Cartwright, shivering. 'I have another cleaning job this afternoon. Thank you for meeting me.'

'Don't you want to walk a bit further? We've only been once round the lake.'

'I must get to work,' said Lena.

She trudged away from him, trying hard not to fall over while she was in his field of vision. She reached the main road. The snow here had already been turned to a dirty sludge by the grit that had been put down to melt it. She could see a pile of fresh dog poo sinking into the snow by the kerb. It made her sad, standing at the bus stop, thinking about how something as clean and beautiful as snow could turn bad so quickly.

Lena climbed the stairs feeling weary. After her walk with Cartwright, she'd had a particularly tough job cleaning wine stains after a very messy party thrown by one of her clients, and during which she'd missed a dozen calls from Sarika. But halfway up the staircase she paused. She could hear footsteps behind her. But when she looked back there was no one there. She must be over-tired, she thought to herself. Nothing a hot bath wouldn't fix.

Sarika had the door open and was shouting Hungarian at her before she'd reached the top flight. 'Have you seen the news online?' she said. 'It's all over the internet. The Terry I knew couldn't do that. It's a lie.'

'Yes,' said Lena. 'Let me get inside and we will talk.' She looked longingly at Sarika's feet, cosy in Lena's favourite slippers. 'I need to dry my feet,' she added.

Lena just had time to plant herself on the sofa and peel off her wet socks before Sarika started barking questions at her again. 'Was he with another woman? It didn't say online.'

'Cartwright could not tell me either.'

Sarika put her head in her hands. 'It doesn't make sense,' she said. 'He never seemed interested in that kind of thing. Why would he suddenly do drugs?'

'I am sorry,' said Lena.

'There's something else,' said Sarika, slowly. 'Something I did not tell you about before. Do not be angry.'

Lena watched Sarika as she got up and went to her room. When she came back she was holding a piece of office paper. 'Here,' said Sarika. 'Read this.'

I want you gone in one week. Or else.

'What do they mean, gone?' asked Sarika.

'I do not know,' said Lena, the icy feeling in her feet spreading through her whole body. 'But it is not good. We must take this note to the police.'

'I told you. No way,' exclaimed Sarika. 'But you have to help me. What if Terry was murdered and this same person is coming for me?'

'That is not likely,' said Lena, trying to keep the fear from her own voice. 'When did you get this note?'

'Saturday,' said Sarika.

'Saturday!' exclaimed Lena. 'Today is Wednesday. That leaves only a few days till the week is up. Why did you not show me this before?'

'You made such a fuss about the first note,' explained Sarika. 'I didn't want to worry you, and to be honest, I didn't want the hassle. And then with Terry disappearing, I forgot all about it. But now, with the way he's died . . .' Her voice trailed off.

'I will find out what happened to Terry,' said Lena. 'If this person who wrote the notes is involved in his death, we will have to go to the police. And if not, we will know that you are safe.'

Sarika began to sob. Lena enclosed her in a hug. 'I'm scared,' said Sarika.

'I know,' replied Lena.

CHAPTER 6

The cleaner found the body.

Those words, spoken by Terry's friend Raz, sent shivers down Lena's spine. She'd taken a few shifts cleaning hotels when she first came to London: it was exhausting. She'd be given an allocation of time to clean, but guests would often still be in their rooms and sleepily instruct her to come back later. And she would never know how messy each room would be. Some guests tidied up, maybe even more so than they did at home. Others would spread the contents of their suitcases across the floor, dirty every towel, sometimes even leave half-eaten slices of pizza between the sheets.

But a body?

She thought about the tired cleaner. Knocking on the door. Calling out 'housekeeping'. No answer. Swiping her key card and pushing the door open. Perhaps going straight to the bathroom to get started there. Coming out. The man on the bed. Undressed. Sleeping? Going up to him. A tentative prod. Cold and stiff. Maybe even staring back at her, with glassy eyes. Panic. Horror.

Lena shuddered again.

Then she pulled herself together. They still had a few days until the vague threat of 'or else' from the note writer. She found some comfort in the fact the note had been delivered on Saturday, before Terry died. Perhaps now Terry was out of the picture, whoever wrote the notes would leave Sarika alone. But she couldn't take that chance. She needed to know if someone else was involved in Terry's death.

The Goswell Hotel. It was local. She didn't know who cleaned there but it shouldn't be too difficult to find out. The world of cleaning was a small one, even in London. A phone call to her old cleaning agency and Lena had a name. Gloria Moreno. Through a friend of a friend at the agency, Lena managed to get a message to Gloria. They arranged to meet at 6.30 a.m. the next morning, just before Gloria's shift started at the hotel.

The Goswell Hotel was a smart, modern building on a busy road leading into Farringdon. Lena walked through the revolving door and was hit by a welcome blast of hot air. The hotel smelled like hot coffee and *kalács*, freshly baked cinnamon bread. What a lovely place for a meeting, she thought, wondering if she could stretch to a coffee and cinnamon bun in their café. Just the thing to warm her up on this cold Thursday morning. She smiled at a smartly dressed receptionist as she read her name tag. Maria Popescu. From her name, Lena guessed the receptionist was Romanian.

'I am here to meet Gloria Moreno,' Lena told Maria.

'No you certainly are not,' the woman replied. Lena looked at her curiously. How could she know better than Lena what she was here for? 'I mean you cannot come in here, right up to reception like a guest, when you are here to see the cleaner.'

'Where is she?' asked Lena, determined not to be brushed off.

'Gloria is round the back,' Maria added, after a quick enquiry to a colleague behind the desk. 'She is having a smoke in the car park.' Lena turned on her heels and walked back out through the front door, following the smell of smoke through the car park. She discovered a short middle-aged lady dressed in a white uniform shakily smoking a cigarette. 'Gloria?' she said. The woman nodded assent. 'Can I buy you a coffee back inside?' asked Lena, determined to ignore the uppity Maria. The snow was almost melted but it was still bitterly cold.

'No,' said Gloria. 'We talk here.' She dropped her cigarette, stamped it out and promptly rolled another, sprinkling tobacco into the paper with yellowed fingers. She lit it and took a deep puff. 'They don't like cleaner in guest café.'

Lena nodded, rubbing her hands together for warmth and wrapping her scarf more tightly around her neck. She should have bought them both a coffee from the local greasy spoon. Gloria was Colombian; if what Lena had heard was true, she would probably take her coffee even stronger than Lena. 'I only have five minutes,' added Gloria, sucking on her cigarette.

'Okay,' said Lena, wondering how to broach the subject.

'You have questions for me?' prompted Gloria.

Lena decided to get straight to it. Since neither of them was British, there was no need to discuss the weather at length before getting down to business. Sometimes it was a relief to talk to a fellow foreigner.

'You found the body of Terry Tibbs,' she said.

'How is that your business?' asked Gloria, her face suspicious.

Lena paused. 'He was a friend,' she said. 'Please, I just have a couple of questions then I will leave you alone.'

Gloria looked around, then nodded.

'Was there anyone else there in the room?'

'Like I tell police,' replied Gloria. 'Just him. Face down naked with collar. Like dog. Drugs everywhere.' She made a gesture to demonstrate all the drugs and a little ash flew from her cigarette on to Lena's trainer. 'Bottles, pills, powders. All alone. Like pervert.'

'Do you think there had been someone with him earlier?' asked Lena.

'How would I know?' Gloria almost spat out the words. 'He could say nothing. He was dead.'

'Is there CCTV?'

'Broken,' said Gloria. 'Management too mean to replace.'

'Any women's clothes in the room?'

'No.'

Lena thought. 'Was he drinking too?'

'Vodka and Coke,' she replied. 'Out of the toothbrush glasses.'

Lena found dread rising up through her. 'Glasses? More than one? How many?' she asked.

'I don't remember.'

'Any lipstick on the glass?'

'I don't know.' Gloria looked at her cigarette and then took another long drag. 'Maybe lipstick, maybe not. I am cleaner. Not detective.'

'But there were two glasses?' pushed Lena. 'When you went in.'

'Only one glass when the police arrived,' replied Gloria. 'Empty. No lipstick then.'

'Are you saying someone interfered with the room?' asked Lena. 'Before the police came?'

Gloria paused, and looked at Lena. 'I don't want trouble. The owners, they don't want more scandal here. Is bad enough there is body.' She threw her cigarette to the ground and stamped it out. 'I need this job,' she said. 'Maybe two glasses, maybe one. Ask the police. What they found is what they found.' She made to walk off.

'A man has died,' said Lena, grabbing her arm. 'If you know something you must go to the police. Or I could go for you, and tell them what you said.'

'I said nothing,' Gloria replied, shaking Lena's hand off. 'Leave me alone.'

Lena jumped on a bus back home. She could see the cars, buses and taxis stuck in rush hour going into the City, but she was going the opposite way and made good time. Hopefully she'd be able to have a pot of strong coffee, check on Sarika and make herself a *Szalonna* bacon sandwich before she had to head out again and start cleaning.

She hoped the sandwich would help her think. She couldn't work out what was the best thing to do with this new information. Should she go to the police? What would she say? That Gloria, the woman who found the body, told her that she may or may not have seen two glasses, but there was no point them talking to her because she'd lie? She couldn't say that to the police – they'd laugh her out of the station.

It was only Thursday. Lena would see what she could find out herself before the threatened week was up. She watched a group of people collectively shivering at a bus stop. If she didn't have anything to take to the police by then she'd think of another way to keep Sarika safe. Lena got off the bus and walked back to her flat. She'd go home, have her sandwich, then she had a house to clean in Barnsbury and after that she could investigate in earnest.

Lena heard a sound behind her and froze. She turned round but there was no one there. She shook her head at herself. So jumpy. Must be the empty stomach. She heard another sound, but realised this one came from her bag. A text. She got out her phone and a message popped up with an unknown number.

You do not know who you are dealing with. It's dangerous. Leave it.

Lena read the words again. The sensible part of her wondered if it was a wrong number, or a bizarre marketing campaign.

No, it was a warning. A warning to her.

But why? Who even knew what she was investigating?

She thought about who she'd spoken to so far. Raz, Cartwright, Sarika, Gloria. Could the cleaning lady be warning her off? She certainly hadn't been overly friendly.

Lena gritted her teeth. There was no way a little text message was going to stop her from helping her friend.

CHAPTER 7

Lena fished her keys out of her backpack for her first client that day: Mrs Ives. She liked this house – not too much mess and rarely anyone home. There was nothing more therapeutic, thought Lena, than undisturbed cleaning. In a way, she felt lucky that this was her job. Back in Debrecen, she'd worked in an office trying to sell subscriptions to a business magazine. She'd earned less than half the money she did here and had hated it. Cleaning might not be the most glamorous job in the world, but she was her own boss and she was useful. Plus it gave her time to think.

Lena put the key in the door. She'd made a quick call to Mrs Kingston who'd promised to try to find out Marsela's address through her network of contacts. Lena was hoping to pay Marsela a visit later that day and dusting was just the thing to help her plan what she'd say.

She pushed the door open and stepped inside, almost falling over a man crouched in the doorway. '*Szar*,' she cursed, and looked down. Mr Ives looked back up at her.

'How did you get my keys?' he said, cowering on the welcome mat.

'I am Lena Szarka,' she replied. 'Your cleaner. I come here every week and your wife gave me keys.' She looked at him curiously. 'No one is usually home,' she added.

Mr Ives smiled at her, his face relieved. 'Of course,' he said. 'Sorry.'

'What are you doing down there?' asked Lena.

'I'm not feeling too well today,' he said. 'So I thought I'd stay home. Sorry if I'm getting under your feet,' he said. 'Literally,' he added with a nervous laugh. He scrambled up.

Lena looked at him. He was shaking.

'You are not well,' she told him. 'Go to bed and I bring you hot tea.'

'That's very kind,' he replied. 'But I feel better here by the front door. I'm waiting for a very important letter. Tea would be lovely though.' He sank back down to the welcome mat.

Lena shrugged and made her way to the kitchen. She still wasn't used to the British and their strange ways. Popping the kettle on, she looked around her to see if anything other than Mr Ives was amiss. It seemed normal. Standard low levels of mess for this house: a few pots and pans to be soaked and washed up; the counters sprinkled with crumbs but otherwise clean; the odd piece of chopped vegetable that had escaped to the kitchen floor.

She brewed the tea, never quite sure if she was doing it right. Lena herself couldn't abide the insipid stuff. She opened the fridge, noting its contents. Plenty of milk, vegetables, fruit, two large steaks and a packet of fresh prawns. Half a pot of hummus that had seen better days. A large block of Cheddar and two rounds of Camembert.

Lena took the tea to Mr Ives, bending down to hand it to him. He smiled at her. 'You're a good sort, Leener,' he said.

'Lay-na,' she replied. She couldn't abide it when people rhymed her name with 'cleaner', although she supposed it was her own fault for calling her business Lena's Cleaners. The British, it seemed, couldn't resist a rhyme.

Mr Ives smiled weakly back at her in response and took a sip of tea. Lena left him to it. She decided to give him the run of downstairs and made her way up to the first floor to get started there.

Lena used the showerhead to rinse the bath. She wondered what Marsela was like. An orphan, according to Mrs Kingston. She'd had a search for *N1 Angels* on catch-up the previous evening, but there was still nothing there. Lena had to make do with watching a few clips on YouTube, and only had the sketchiest of ideas about what was going on. She certainly couldn't work out much about Marsela other than her penchant for red lipstick and Terry Tibbs.

She finished up in the bathroom and went to the bedroom. A suitcase was lying open on the bed. She went over to it. Had the Iveses been on a weekend away? She looked at the clothes, still folded in the special way she had to store clothes in drawers so they didn't wrinkle. So they were yet to go. It seemed odd to Lena, what with the fridge so full of fresh food. And they hadn't cancelled her clean the next week. Mrs Ives usually gave her plenty of notice. She moved the suitcase to the floor so she could change the sheets. As she did so she couldn't resist a quick rummage.

All the clothes were men's.

That explained it. Mr Ives must be going on a business trip alone, a long one by the looks of things.

Lena finished cleaning upstairs and made her way back down. 'Your laptop is under the bed,' she told Mr Ives, still sitting by the door. 'In case you were looking for it.'

'Why would I want my laptop?' he replied, looking bemused.

'For your business trip,' said Lena. 'I saw the suitcase.'

'I'm not going anywhere,' he replied. Lena looked at him. 'I'm just back,' he said quickly.

'Shall I unpack it for you?' offered Lena, not believing him for a second. No one else could fold clothes like she could. 'Put your clothes in the laundry?'

'No no,' he said. 'I'll do it later.'

'After your important letter gets here?' asked Lena.

'Exactly,' he said. Lena went into the kitchen and began running water to soak the pots and pans. Something was very off in the Ives household.

Even from the limited clips Lena found on YouTube, she knew *N1 Angels* was all about the glamorous lives of its cast. So she was surprised that when she went to Marsela and Terry's house, it was a very normal-looking 1930s semi on a very average cul-de-sac near Arsenal. Hardly where you'd expect a power couple of reality TV to live. She supposed it was filmed on sets and in locations, certainly not in this house. There was even a small gnome innocently fishing in the small front garden.

Lena walked up and rang the doorbell, noting its cheery tone. Nothing. She carefully stepped off the path and tried to peer through the window. It was sparkling clean, but completely obscured by the net curtain within. She stepped further into the garden, carefully avoiding the snowdrop flowers peeking up from the earth. She looked to see if there was a chink in the lacy armour, but to no avail.

'Oi,' said a voice. 'What do you think you're doing?'

Lena turned around to see a woman in her fifties in a navy tracksuit standing behind her, arms akimbo. 'Do you live here?' asked Lena. This woman was clearly not Marsela.

'I'm Neighbourhood Watch,' declared the woman, pride and menace mixing in her voice. 'And you need to leave these people alone. You women, nosing around here all the time. You won't even give Mars a drop of privacy to mourn.'

Lena smiled at the woman. This hadn't been her plan, but she felt it was the second-best thing. This lady clearly spent a lot of time watching what went on with her neighbours.

'My name is Lena Szarka,' she said, holding out her hand. The woman took it, looking a little surprised at her friendliness. 'And I am from Lena's Cleaners, a cleaning agency local to this area. This week I am offering a free clean to one lucky resident of this street. Since Mrs Tibbs is not home, could I offer you my services instead?' Lena hoped her deliberate mistake would get the woman talking. 'I have references here and am fully insured.'

'Margaret Hawthorne,' said the woman, looking Lena up and down, likely deciding whether to allow her into her home. 'And she's not Mrs Tibbs. They weren't married, you know.'

'You will not regret it,' said Lena. 'Which house is yours?'

'I'm not sure . . . the house isn't . . .'

'It will be the envy of your neighbours,' said Lena. 'And if you like the work I do, you can tell them all about me. Only you will be free though. Because you are the special one.'

That clinched it. Margaret beckoned her towards her front door.

Lena entered and took a quick look around. This was one of her least favourite types of houses to clean. Full of ugly little ornaments gathering dust and faded floral upholstery. Even when it was clean it would still look as though it were dirty.

'Would you like some tea?' asked Margaret. At least she was a polite client.

'Do you have coffee?' asked Lena. 'I can make it. Tea for you?' She went into the kitchen and looked out of the window, noticing the well-pruned hedge, allowing a good view of Terry and Marsela's garden next door. 'You sit down. I will bring it to you.'

Margaret perched on a chair in the kitchen and watched her curiously. Lena wiped the counter while the kettle boiled. 'You have a very nice home,' she said. 'And this is a nice place to live. A good neighbourhood.'

'Well you'd think, wouldn't you?' said Margaret, taking the bait like a fish to a worm. 'But there's all sorts going on here.'

'Really?' said Lena, opening the grill and inspecting it. Not too bad, but for a few cremated scraps of cheese. She went to the cupboard under the sink and looked for what she needed.

'Oh yes. Marsela next door. First all those antics with Terry fooling around and now this, god rest his soul.'

Lena turned from the cupboard, clutching a bottle of multi-purpose cleaner. 'How awful,' she said, trying not to sound too interested.

'At least he didn't croak at their house,' said Margaret, sounding a little disappointed. 'I don't think I could deal with a death next door. Poor Terry, in that hotel room.' She leaned forwards. 'He was found in a collar. Pretty kinky, apparently. Of course, it's all over the papers now, what with him being on the telly.'

'People are so nosy,' said Lena. 'Where was, what is her name, Marsela, that night?'

'At some showbiz party in town. She's inconsolable now. Soulmates they were. You saw the show?'

'No,' said Lena.

'The box set will be back on catch-up any day now, I expect,' said Margaret. 'Now he is all over the news. He loved her.' She leaned in. 'She was from Kosovo,' she whispered, as if it was a dirty secret. 'Albanian. But she spoke English perfectly because she had lived here since she was six. Her parents died in the war, poor heart.'

'And Terry loved her?' asked Lena.

'She was far too good for him,' declared Margaret. 'Clever, funny, ambitious. He worshipped her, then all of a sudden he didn't. Must have got bored. You know what men are like.' She tapped the side of her nose with her finger. 'He clearly didn't want to settle down, even though he'd never do better. It was really quite tragic, their relationship. That's what made it so gripping to watch.'

'She must have been very jealous,' said Lena. 'It sounds like Terry was hard to deal with.'

'I think she'd accepted that was what he was like,' said Margaret. 'She was used to it. I always told her he'd come back eventually, no matter who he ran around with.'

'You must be a very good judge of character,' said Lena, handing Margaret her tea.

'I am. Harold always used to say that about me.'

'What was he like?'

'Harold?' said Margaret. 'Well I married him back in . . .'

'No, Terry.' Lena looked at her. 'You must have known him very well. A good neighbour like you.'

Lena took a sip of her coffee. She'd used a full tablespoon of granules but they were stale and hadn't quite dissolved properly. It still tasted better than tea. She'd never understand why the British drank so much of that stuff.

'I never took to him,' said Margaret. 'But a lot of women did. He could be so charming. And he really used to worship Marsela, before he started playing away.'

'Their relationship was real?'

'Absolutely,' said Margaret. 'They lived together.'

'It's not just for the cameras?'

'Of course not. I've watched it on air and I've seen them together at home.' Through the gap in the fence, thought Lena. 'It's a tragedy that she's having to say goodbye to him. She's gone to stay with a friend for a few days. The funeral is next week. I always thought those two would work it out, settle down properly and have a couple of kids. That couple across the road have been trying for years. Five rounds of IVF they've had. Spent a fortune. More coffee?'

Lena declined. She sensed she'd got everything she could from Margaret and wanted to get started on the cleaning before the gossip began to spread to people not relevant to her enquiries. 'I must get on,' she said, squeezing out a sponge she found in the sink and giving it a tentative sniff. 'I am here to clean.'

'Of course,' said Margaret. 'I can tell you are a good worker.'

'Thank you,' said Lena, painfully aware that all she'd done so far was pump her for information and half-heartedly wipe a counter. 'When do you think Marsela will be back from her friend's? I would still like to offer her the free clean, especially after all she has been through.'

'The funeral is next Wednesday,' said Margaret. 'She'll probably be back at least the day before to get ready. She will want to put on a nice spread, I expect. For all his faults, there was only one Terry. It's only family and very close friends, but I know I'll be invited. I might even bake something myself.'

'Of course,' said Lena. 'You are a good person. I clean now.'

'I'll put in a word for you,' said Margaret, with a smile. 'For that free clean.' Lena smiled back. She got the sense that this was a woman who didn't get compliments very often. A little went a long way.

Lena managed to convince Sarika to join her on the next job that day, promising an update on what she'd discovered that morning. The house belonged to a nice couple who always tidied before she arrived. Not to the crazy extent that one of her old clients had, so that when she cleaned she couldn't help but make it dirtier, but enough so that she could vacuum, mop and scrub without going around the house picking up dirty socks first. No children or animals to make the place messy, just a bit of healthy dust on the mantel and the odd splatter of toothpaste on the bath-room mirror.

Her cousin sat on the sofa using the duster Lena had given her to dab at her eyes. Lena took a break from cleaning the kitchen and sat down next to her. She didn't even know where to start. It seemed all the news she had from the morning was bad.

'I went to Marsela and Terry's house,' she started.

'Did you see that *tehén*?' asked Sarika, putting down the duster. 'Was she even upset?'

'I did not,' said Lena. 'She has gone to stay with a friend. But I spoke to their neighbour.' Sarika looked at her, interested. 'I am sorry,' she continued, 'but the neighbour told me that they were a proper couple.'

Sarika laughed. 'That is just because they lived together for the show and Terry was such a good actor,' she said. 'He fooled everyone. But he loved me.'

Lena shrugged. She saw no point in pushing her argument, although she was sure Margaret was right. 'I think we need to find out more about Marsela. She could be the person who wrote the notes.'

'She might have been obsessed with Terry,' agreed Sarika.

'There is somewhere else that I went first,' said Lena. 'To the hotel.'

'The Goswell?' asked Sarika. 'It is so lovely there. I can't believe it is where—'

'I spoke to the cleaner, the one who found Terry's body,' continued Lena. 'She told me, well she did not tell me, but it sounds like there was someone else with Terry that night. A woman.'

Sarika looked at her for a moment, more tears welling up in her eyes. 'I am going to clean the bathroom,' she declared with a sob, and ran from the room.

Lena pottered about cleaning the kitchen for several minutes, but her heart wasn't in it. She made her way up to the bathroom.

Sarika was perched on the edge of the bath, her eyes fixed on the mirror, still lined with toothpaste splatters.

'The showerhead has limescale,' she said, attempting to break Sarika's reverie. 'But I have my own secret recipe.' She fished a bottle from her bag of cleaning supplies and shook her preparation, inside a plant sprayer for easy application. 'One day, if you are very good, I will pass on the formula to you.'

'I just don't believe he would be with someone else,' said Sarika, to her own reflection. 'He was into me. I'm sure he wouldn't do that.'

'Mrs Kingston said that on his show . . .'

'The show was made up,' said Sarika, turning to Lena. 'What happened on it wasn't real.'

'I thought it was reality TV,' said Lena.

'But it's still made up,' said Sarika. 'They are given storylines. He wasn't really with Marsela.' Sarika picked up the showerhead and admired her reflection through the grime. 'And he wasn't into that kind of stuff,' she continued. 'Nothing *perverz*. That's why I know that what they say about him is not true.'

'Men are strange creatures,' said Lena, taking the showerhead from Sarika and trying to unscrew it. 'They tell one girl one thing and another something else. Now, this preparation works best when we leave it to soak in for a little bit. Then the limescale will peel off like a lizard shedding its skin. Come and see.'

'If he'd wanted to do something like that he could have asked me,' said Sarika. 'One time, I—'

'This limescale is coming off in sheets now,' interrupted Lena, not keen to hear about her baby cousin's sex life. 'Come look.'

'But Terry was romantic,' said Sarika, coming to stand beside Lena. 'He was going to take me to Venice for the weekend in the spring. He promised.'

'That is nice,' said Lena, doubting he'd meant it. 'But you need to stop thinking about that. We need to work out if he was with someone else, and if so, who.'

Sarika ignored her. 'Perhaps he was going to propose,' she said. 'That is what people do in Venice.'

Lena looked at the girl, romanticising this man in her head. Building a relationship that hadn't happened. A future that they would never have. It wasn't healthy. And it wasn't going to keep her safe. 'Listen Sarika,' she said, taking the girl's hand. 'I am sorry that Terry is dead, but you did not know each other that well.'

'Why are you so down on our relationship?'

'I am sorry, Sarika, but I think the best way to deal with this is to see it how it was. A couple of months of dating.'

'No,' said Sarika. 'That was not how it was. He loved me.'

'Did he say that?'

'He didn't have to.'

'But he had a girlfriend,' said Lena. 'And it sounds like he was with another woman when he died.'

'I don't believe it,' said Sarika. 'Someone made it look like that. Terry would not have cheated on me. He was perfect.'

Lena turned her attention back to the showerhead. She peeled off the last shreds of limescale, getting the same satisfaction as from removing the remains of a scab. She gave it a quick wipe with her special cleaning loofah and looked at her reflection, pockmarked with water holes.

'What if he didn't want to cheat on me?' said Sarika. 'You said he was restrained in a collar. He could have been kept there against his will. Kidnapped.'

'It is possible,' said Lena, doubtfully. 'And it is why you need to be careful. Until we have found out the truth of what happened and why.'

'It is the only possibility,' declared Sarika.

'Not at all,' muttered Lena to the showerhead as she screwed it back in place.

'I heard that,' said Sarika.

'I am trying to help you,' said Lena. 'I just want us to keep our minds open.'

Lena lifted up the toilet seat and peered inside, thinking. The clients here had already put a splash of bleach in the bowl, unlike some people who allowed detritus to build up all week. She grabbed the loo cleaner and gave it another healthy squirt. She looked up. Sarika was gone already.

Lena grabbed the toilet brush and gave the bowl a thorough scrub before flushing the last of the mess away.

Back home, Lena put the coffee pot on to boil and dug out a box of her favourite chocolate-chip biscuits from the cupboard. They'd been opened. She reached inside, her heart sinking. None left, just crumbs. She knew Sarika was understandably emotional, but eating all the biscuits and putting the box back in the cupboard? There was no excuse for that sort of behaviour.

Sarika was in her room now, sulking. No, thought Lena to herself. She was being too hard on the girl. She was mourning.

Lena heard footsteps and a rustle at the door. She put the biscuit box in her small recycling tray and went to open the door. No one was there. It must have been a passing neighbour.

Lena took the coffee off the boil and grabbed a jacket. She'd pop to the local shop and get some more chocolate-chip cookies. Perhaps she'd even get some gingernuts too, Sarika's favourite.

Heading down the stairs, Lena wished she was going to fetch some *kiflis* her mother had baked instead. She was planning a trip home in March: to visit the place in the Transylvanian hills where she'd scattered her friend Timea's ashes. And to check on Timea's son Laszlo. Her mother said he was getting good at the violin now, even starting to show real talent. Apparently the screeching Lena remembered had been replaced by melodious tones reverberating around the expensive wooden instrument his father had bought him.

Lena pulled her coat around her at the cold assault of February air and hurried to the shop. Maybe her trip home should wait. Every time Lena went home her mother drove her just a little bit more insane. Not to mention added another few pounds to the scales in *kiflis*, *haluska* dumplings and *dobos torta*.

Thinking of extra pounds, Lena hesitated by the small selection of biscuits. Perhaps she should get some fruit instead? She'd stopped going running in the colder months and refused to pay gym membership fees to run on a ridiculous machine indoors like a hamster on a wheel, never getting anywhere. She was sure that cleaning all day was better exercise in any case.

She dismissed the idea. Everyone knew fruit did not go with coffee. Lena grabbed the biscuits – Maryland cookies for her and gingernuts for Sarika. She'd take the stairs back up to her fourth-floor flat. That would more than compensate.

Puffing a little from the staircase, Lena fumbled in her bag for her keys, dropping the biscuits in the process. The packets rolled away from her, making a bid for freedom down the staircase. Lena put her bag down and turned to give them chase.

Finally, both biscuit packets, keys and bag in hand, Lena attempted to open the door. It jammed, sending the biscuits to the floor once more. Cursing, Lena peered in, trying to figure out why the door wouldn't open properly. The mystery was solved: the chain was on.

Surely Sarika hadn't locked her out? Lena picked up her chocolate-chip biscuits and left the tube of gingernuts on the stairs.

'Open this door at once!' she commanded. She peered through again and caught a glimpse of Sarika waving a kitchen knife in the direction of the door. '*Mi a fene?*' Lena said, taking a step back. 'What the hell? Sarika, have you lost your mind?' She fished in her bag for her phone and took another step backwards.

Suddenly Lena was flying down the staircase. She landed with a painful thump, right on her bum. Lena felt a flash of panic and a pain in her shoulder. She realised her eyes were closed and forced them open. Sarika was standing over her.

Clutching the knife.

'Lena!' said Sarika.

'Put down the knife,' said Lena, as calmly as she could manage. 'I will not go to the police.'

'What do you mean?' said Sarika. She looked to the knife in her hand and surprise filled her face. She let go. It clattered to the floor. 'You didn't think . . . ?'

Lena tried to pull herself back to sitting and gave her body a quick check for injuries. Her coccyx was throbbing, extending its pain across her bum and lower back. Her shoulder was fine – it was her old bullet wound, joining in with sympathy pain. She hadn't been stabbed. But had she been pushed?

'Why did you do that?' she said, picking up the knife to get it away from Sarika's reach. 'You could have really hurt me?'

'I was scared,' said Sarika. 'Get up. We need to get back inside the flat.'

'I think I would rather stay here,' said Lena. 'Until you tell me what's going on. Why did you push me?'

'You fell,' said Sarika.

'I did not,' replied Lena, with dignity. 'I do not fall.'

'You don't think? I would never . . .'

Lena felt her bottom. There was something there. Something that felt crumbly, like damp sand. It rustled when she poked it. Eking herself further forwards, she discovered the offending weapon. A now squashed packet of gingernuts that had come out of all this much worse than she had. She must have slipped on them when she stepped backwards.

Despite herself, Lena let out a pained laugh. She handed Sarika the packet, crumbs sprayed over the stairs. 'The culprit,' she said.

'Now help me up and we'll get back inside. You can help me vacuum this up.'

Sarika hauled Lena to her feet and enclosed her in a quick hug. 'Let's get inside,' she said. 'And lock the door again. I have something I need to show you.'

CHAPTER 8

'*Szar*,' said Lena.

The women sat together on the sofa sipping the last of the Unicum and eating cookies. Lena had carefully placed a plastic bag on the sofa and a bag of frozen peas on top. She sat on them, feeling like the princess and the peas that she'd seen in one of Casper's storybooks. The peas numbed her coccyx as the Unicum warmed her throat and the biscuits filled her belly. But what was more chilling than the peas was the note that sat in front of them both on the table. The note to Sarika.

I know what you've done. It's your fault he's dead. You will be next.

'*Szar*,' said Lena, again. 'Terry is dead, but this person still threatens you.'

'I know,' replied Sarika. 'And there was no envelope, like before. Whoever it was came right to our door.'

Lena reached over and gave Sarika a hug, wincing at the pain at the base of her spine. 'We must take this to the police,' she said, releasing her. 'We need their help.'

'But look what it says. I can't go to the police,' said Sarika, stuffing another cookie into her mouth and sobbing crumbs on to Lena's lap.

'It says you are in danger,' said Lena.

'It says that I killed him,' replied Sarika.

Lena looked back at the note. She could see that it could

certainly be interpreted that way. 'The police will not take that seriously. You are innocent.'

'I was innocent of stealing that painting from the gallery too,' repeated Sarika. 'But they still arrested me. This is murder.'

'We do not know that it is murder,' said Lena.

'We do not know that it is not,' replied Sarika.

Lena nodded. 'That is true.' The more she found out about Terry's death, the more possible that looked. The threatening note that his uncle had burned. The drugs and the collar. The hint of a mysterious second guest in the hotel room who had vanished before the police arrived. And now this note. Terry was dead but the threats kept coming. Were they from his murderer? She shuddered.

Lena got up and went to grab their laptop. She flipped it open and began typing.

'What are you doing?' asked Sarika.

'Booking you a flight back to Hungary,' replied Lena. She'd use the money she'd been saving for her own trip: that could wait. 'For tomorrow. We need to get you away from whoever is sending these notes. And fast.'

While Sarika packed, Lena sat down in front of her trusty bulletin board. It was not the high-tech touchscreen suspect matrix that she'd seen in American TV shows, but it always helped her organise her thoughts. It was a large corkboard with a pine frame and had been covered in Post-it notes and photographs of her suspects while she was investigating Timea's death. Now it was empty.

Lena sought to rectify that. She pinned a picture of Terry that Sarika had cut from a magazine into the middle of the board and looked at him. He smiled back, unaware of what fate had in store.

She looked at the photo, from the same magazine, of his *N1 Angels* girlfriend Marsela. She was pale with dark hair that she wore in a messy bun. Her make-up was light, except for deep red lipstick. She was gorgeous, decided Lena. She hardly ever wore lipstick herself, disliking the mark it left behind on her coffee cups. Lena pinned up Marsela's picture next to Terry's.

She wrote down Barry, Terry's uncle's name, with a note next to it that said 'N1 Demons', the bar they ran together. It seemed an outside chance that Barry was involved, but she'd need to investigate.

She didn't have much to go on: the board was alarmingly empty still. She picked up the notes Sarika had received again and laid them down in front of her. The first one was stuck back together like chipped Herend porcelain.

He's not yours. He's mine. Do not touch him again. If you do you'll both regret it.

And then she put the second one next to it.

I want you gone in one week. Or else.

Then the third.

I know what you've done. It's your fault he's dead. You will be next.

She studied the three carefully. The handwriting was the same, quite elegant, no spelling mistakes that she could see. The same pen, a generic Biro from what she could tell, in a common shade of blue. The paper was always the same white copier paper.

Lena looked again. Why handwrite a note on printer paper? Surely if you wanted to remain anonymous it would be better to print a typed note? It would be an easy enough job to compare the handwriting here with a sample from someone Terry knew. If it was Marsela, the girlfriend and therefore a particularly likely candidate for the murder, she was setting herself up to be caught. Was she stupid, wondered Lena, or perhaps she thought the notes would never find their way to the police? She looked at them guiltily. So far she was right. Lena wondered if there was a way she could get the handwriting professionally checked, and still keep her word to Sarika.

Then there was the content of the notes themselves. In the first note, someone considered Terry to be theirs. Again, Marsela sprang to mind. Could there be anyone else he'd been with? Knowing what she knew about Terry, it would have to be an attractive woman. Probably in her twenties.

The second note was a threat, plain and simple.

The third note was less clear. What did it mean – what you've done? Did the writer just mean that Sarika had slept with Terry? In that case, a jealous ex, perhaps Marsela, would make sense. Or did the writer think that Sarika was the murderer? She could understand why it looked that way to Sarika. Lena sat back. If the writer thought Sarika had murdered Terry, it meant that they themselves were innocent. Or was that how the writer wanted it to look?

Whoever this person was, and whether they were a murderer or not, they were no friend to Sarika. At least in Hungary Sarika would be out of harm's way.

Lena had nowhere near enough information to figure out what had really happened. She had to find out more about the people in Terry's life. Luckily there was an event coming up where his family and friends would all be together. She just had to work out how to make sure she was there too.

Lena stood outside the funeral home the next day, looking at the selection of headstones tastefully arranged in front of a net curtain. She'd delivered Sarika to the airport and bundled her on to her overpriced, last-minute flight, and then rushed back to London to continue her investigations. Mrs Kingston had astonished her again, getting her the information she needed right away. But now, standing here, she wondered if she could make herself step inside.

Timea had had a very simple funeral, with a Catholic service, Lena's mother catering and only a few close friends in attendance, including Timea's son Laszlo, of course. It was what Timea would have wanted. What little money Timea had saved went directly to the boy instead of on flowers and fanfare. Later, Lena and Laszlo had taken her ashes to their favourite spot in the Transylvanian hills and scattered them there.

Lena prided herself on her control of emotions, but she could feel tears rising to her eyes just thinking about Timea being gone. For ever. Perhaps this wasn't such a good idea after all. There must be another way.

Lena turned to go. 'Can I help you?' asked a voice. Lena turned back around and looked at a small woman, perhaps five years younger than herself. 'It is a hard time,' said the woman, holding out her hand to shake. 'But we aim to make it easier. My name is Jane. Come inside and we'll have some tea.'

Lena allowed herself to be taken inside. It was a little dark, with the saccharine scent of lilies pervading the room. She took a seat in a well-worn armchair and tried to pull herself together. She reached into her bag for her flyers and portfolio. Taking a deep breath and a gulp of water from the bottle in her bag, she pushed her shoulders back and stood up.

'Do take a seat,' said the woman, handing her a cup of sweet tea. 'I'm sorry for your loss.' She smiled at Lena, and for a moment Lena found herself believing this woman knew everything she had been through. Knew how Timea had been taken from her. Knew how Laszlo would grow up without a mother. She took a sip of the tea and shook her head slightly. That was impossible. This woman was just a good sales lady. Selling an ineffectual antidote to grief.

'I have lost no one,' said Lena, trying to smile. 'I am here in a business capacity. Lena Szarka, of Lena's Cleaners. And caterers,' she added.

78

Jane looked at her in surprise. For a moment Lena wondered if she was going to wrench the teacup from her hand. 'I do apologise,' said Jane. 'I normally have a good radar for when people are in mourning. What can I do for you?'

Lena did her best to smile at the woman. 'We are a local business, like you are,' she said, putting down her teacup. 'We offer a full service for events. Cleaning is our history but we also provide delicious Italian food. We clean a venue or client's house before an event, provide the food and serving staff and clear up afterwards. I think that this is a very good service for a family in mourning.'

Jane nodded.

'We are a family company,' continued Lena, thinking of her cousin. 'And our rates are very reasonable, much lower than the larger catering companies. I have a portfolio of what we offer and I would like to give you an opportunity to try us.'

She paused, watching Jane's expression. 'It sounds very interesting,' said the woman, with a smile. She politely took the portfolio and began to flick through it. 'We do recommend a number of caterers to our clients that are tried and tested,' she added. 'So we would need a good reason to include you on our roster.'

'Let us prove it to you,' said Lena. 'I can offer you a discount of fifty per cent for the first job.' She hoped it would not be a large funeral, totting up some expensive calculations in her mind. Lucia would have to skimp on the usual bountiful helpings of mozzarella and prosciutto.

'And alcohol?' asked Jane, dropping her sympathetic face and putting her business hat on. 'That will be half price too?'

'We will do alcohol at cost,' said Lena, firmly. She couldn't afford to make a huge loss on this job. 'We are confident you will love the service we provide.'

'I don't think a client would be happy knowing that they were a guinea pig,' said Jane. Lena looked at her. Was this some kind of

79

bizarre pet funeral? Jane saw the confusion in her eyes. 'It is an important day for a client. No one wants to think that they are getting a test.'

'The client does not need to know about our arrangement,' said Lena, finally understanding. Jane wanted to pocket the savings. 'It is between us.'

'Then let's find a suitable occasion,' said Jane, getting out her iPad and swiping through appointments. 'Tuesday week? Mrs Hubbard? Lovely old lady, burying her husband.'

'We have a prior engagement that Tuesday,' said Lena, pretending to look through her diary. Terry's funeral was this Wednesday. 'But we are free Wednesday. We have had a cancellation.'

'That is short notice,' said Jane. She tapped her iPad. 'But we do have two that day.' She was likely looking at which one would be more lucrative. 'I think that Marsela Goga would be a good choice,' she said. 'The wake is for her boyfriend, Terry Tibbs. He was in the public eye, so discretion is of course required.'

'Of course,' replied Lena. She'd got the one she needed.

'The funeral service will be at twelve to one p.m. and the wake will follow at Ms Goga's home. I'll talk to her about the cleaning arrangements before and after. Fifty people expected.'

'Perfect,' said Lena. This was bigger than she'd imagined from what the neighbour Margaret had told her about an intimate event. She hoped her chef Lucia would be able to turn dried pasta and whatever vegetables were on special into mouth-watering cuisine.

On Monday, Lena let herself gingerly into her client Mrs Ives's house, making sure that Mr Ives was not squatting by the front door again. Instead she found a pile of mail on the doormat that had accumulated like a stack of sweet *palacsinta* pancakes. More post than usual, she thought, leafing through the pile as she went into the living room.

To her surprise, the room was shrouded in darkness. Lena went to open the curtains. Only then, when the room was flooded with light, did she notice Mrs Ives. The woman was curled up on the sofa with a blanket. She blinked and peered up at Lena through puffy eyes. She was surrounded by piles of crumpled white tissues, littering the room as though it were a graveyard for doves.

'What has happened?' exclaimed Lena. She barely knew Mrs Ives. The woman was usually at work on the two days a week when Lena cleaned and they communicated through scribbled notes left on the kitchen counter. Instructions on where cleaning products could be found didn't give much of a window into the soul.

'He's gone,' sniffed Mrs Ives. 'Rupert. He's left me.'

Lena sat down beside Mrs Ives and felt the soft sofa try to absorb her into its depths. She took her hand.

'I didn't even know he wasn't happy,' continued the woman. 'I thought he must be working late, then when he still wasn't home by midnight last Thursday I called the police. It wasn't till they got here that I realised most of his clothes were gone.'

'I am sorry,' said Lena.

'The bloody policeman found the note. It must have fallen off the fridge door on to the kitchen floor.' She opened her hand and showed Lena a crumpled Post-it note: *I'm sorry.*

'I've never been so humiliated,' she added.

'Is there someone I can call?' said Lena. 'Perhaps a friend . . .'

'No,' exclaimed Mrs Ives, her eyes a little crazed. 'I can't face anyone. You're the only person I've told.'

'So there was no business trip,' said Lena. It was making sense to her now.

'What business trip?' snapped Mrs Ives, looking suddenly more alert.

ELIZABETH MUNDY

'I saw him when I came to clean last week,' said Lena. 'He had a suitcase packed and told me he was just back from a trip.'

'That lying bastard,' said Mrs Ives, pushing the blanket off her and sitting up. 'What else did he say?'

Lena thought. 'He was waiting for the post to arrive,' she said.

'The post?' Mrs Ives spat out the words as if they had a foul taste.

'Yes,' said Lena. 'He was sitting right by the front door. I almost fell over him when I came in.'

'Nonsense,' declared Mrs Ives. 'He was probably waiting for some fancy woman.' Lena watched as she visibly deflated in front of her. Mrs Ives sat back again and pulled the blanket closer over her, as if it could shield her from the world. 'He always declared that he could never love anyone but me. Even after all these years. And I believed him. I must be some sort of idiot.'

'I am sorry,' said Lena again, patting her back awkwardly. The woman turned to her and began sobbing into Lena's shoulder. She could feel the tears beginning to soak through her jumper. Lena patted her again and looked around, wondering what the best course of action would be.

'I will make tea,' she declared, standing up. Tea was what British people seemed to want when upset. 'Then I will tidy up so you feel better.'

Mrs Ives grabbed a tissue from the floor and blew her nose into it then scrambled up and followed Lena into the kitchen. 'Fourteen years we've been married,' she said. 'And our son Oliver, he won't know what to think. Thank goodness he's away at boarding school.'

'What did your husband say?' asked Lena. She switched the kettle on and grabbed two clean mugs from the cupboard.

'Nothing,' said Mrs Ives. 'That's the worst part. Fourteen years and he cleared out and just left me that stupid note. Not even an explanation.'

'That is very strange,' agreed Lena, feeling her curiosity aroused. 'But he must have said something? Was there no clue before?'

'None,' declared Mrs Ives. 'He was busy at work, a few late nights. And now he is gone.'

Lena looked at Mrs Ives. She was mid-forties, and until her recent bout of crying had clearly looked after herself. Her hair was highlighted with expensive-looking honeyed tones and she kept herself in shape. Plus the dishes she left in the sink suggested she regularly cooked. She paid Lena on time, remembered a Christmas bonus and never forgot to buy Viakal when Lena requested it. She even said 'please' when she wrote Lena notes of specific cleaning tasks she wanted accomplished.

In simple terms, Lena could see no obvious reason anyone would be desperate to escape her. In Lena's experience, she bore all the traits of what Lena would consider A Good Wife. Lena handed her a mug of tea and a biscuit. Mrs Ives took a sip.

'I'm sorry to burden you with all this, Lena,' said Mrs Ives suddenly, as if the tea had awakened her sense of decorum. 'We barely know each other. It's just you're here and I haven't told anyone else . . . I feel ridiculous, being abandoned by my husband, and at my age. What will I do?'

'You are beautiful,' declared Lena. 'And strong and kind. He would have to be mad to leave you. And you do not want a mad husband. You are better off without him.'

'I don't feel better off,' said Mrs Ives, putting down the biscuit and covering her face with her hands.

'You will,' said Lena. She paused. 'My father . . . he left my mother, and me, when I was a teenager. I hated him for it then, but . . . now I think it was for the best. A *pártáruló*, a "rat" for a father is no father at all.'

'I'm sorry,' said the woman, through her hands.

'He stole all our savings before he left,' continued Lena, feeling the old bitterness creeping back. 'But it was a small price to pay to be rid of him.'

'My Rupert was a good husband,' said Mrs Ives, looking at Lena. 'That's why this seems so . . . out of character.'

'They all seem good,' said Lena. 'Until they betray you.' She got up. 'I am going to make this house sparkle for you,' she said. 'Everything feels better when your house is clean.'

'Oh damn it, Lena. I forgot to cancel you. Sorry.'

Lena stood in the hallway of Mr Quincy's house. He was her Monday afternoon client and a house-husband, so was often around when she came to clean. Lena liked him and couldn't work out why Sarika thought he was creepy. In her view, it took a strong man to take on the challenges of a role typically reserved for women. She certainly didn't want to spend her time looking after three little children. She'd much rather be at work.

'I'm really sorry but we don't need you today. We won't for . . .' The man paused, totting figures in his head. 'Two months.'

'Two months?' said Lena, her liking for the man evaporating. 'I need notice. You cannot just stop.'

'We're going away,' said Mr Quincy. 'It's sudden.' He paused, attempting to run his fingers through his curly hair. Lena looked at him. He was practically pulling it out.

'What is wrong?' Lena asked.

Mr Quincy looked past Lena's shoulder. Lena turned. She found herself looking at a photograph on the wall, staring into the eyes of an elderly woman with a deep leathery tan. 'It's Tina's mother,' Mr Quincy said quickly. 'She is very sick, in Cape Town. We're all going to look after her. We leave tomorrow.'

'I am sorry,' said Lena.

'Listen, I'll pay you for today, but that's all I can afford,' he said. 'The last-minute flights have really messed with our cash flow.'

'I understand,' said Lena, softening. 'You need to be with family.'

'Let me just grab my wallet.' Mr Quincy disappeared into the kitchen. The doorbell rang. 'Get that will you, Lena? I'm selling a few bits and pieces on eBay before we go. That must be one of the buyers.'

Lena opened the door. 'Where do you want it?' asked the man. He had three crates of food.

'I'm sorry,' said Lena to the man. 'He must have forgotten to cancel his Ocado delivery.'

'I'm from Morrisons,' said the man, grumpily. 'And it's too late to cancel.'

'Bring it on through,' said Mr Quincy.

'The food will all go off,' said Lena. 'You should send it back. Or I could take it to a homeless shelter?'

'Bring it through,' said Mr Quincy. 'Lena, don't give me that look. Our groceries are really none of your business. Here's forty pounds. I'll call you when we're back.'

'Okay,' said Lena, looking at him curiously. 'I hope your mother-in-law gets better.'

'What?' said Mr Quincy, already unloading various cheeses into the fridge. 'Oh right. Yes. Me too.'

Lena put her suspect board on the coffee table next to a notepad, a packet of chocolate-chip biscuits and a hot cup of coffee and turned on the television. Both seasons of *N1 Angels* were finally available on catch-up, albeit with a special black banner at the bottom in memory of Terry Tibbs. Made-up, semi-scripted or reality, it was possible the show held some clues to Terry's relationships. At the very least, she'd learn more about the people she'd meet at the wake on Wednesday.

CHAPTER 9

Lena was dreaming that she was sweeping up the fragments of a broken champagne bottle while Terry and Raz lifted weights and Marsela sobbed in the corner, when her phone rang. She looked around in confusion: the TV was still blaring out and she'd dribbled a little on to her sofa. She hurried to answer the phone. It took Lena's foggy head a moment to place the woman calling her. Maria Popescu, she said her name was. What was a Romanian lady doing calling her? It was halfway through the conversation that Lena realised she was the snooty receptionist from the Goswell Hotel. Maria wanted to meet with Lena that night. Lena hoped that the woman would shed more light on Terry's last night. Perhaps Maria had the key to the breakthrough she'd been waiting for.

It was late, bitterly cold, and the sky was hurling frozen balls of rain down like it was at war with the earth. Lena easily found the pub on Goswell Road but there was no sign of Maria. She ordered herself a cranberry juice and sat on a wobbly stool by the bar, watching the ice cubes melt into her drink. The toilet had spread its aroma over the whole pub: the air stank of urine, mould and bleach.

'Psst,' said a voice. Lena looked around and saw Maria peering around a door. 'In the back room,' she said, gesturing for Lena to join her. She obeyed. 'It's much quieter here and I do not want anyone to see us together,' said Maria. Lena was just about to give this ridiculously uppity lady a piece of her mind when the woman interjected. 'I have something to tell you about Mr Tibbs. In confidence.'

They sat down at a table in the otherwise empty room. The toilet smell was even stronger here, and Lena saw that there was a stain on the patterned carpet outside the gent's loo. There'd been a leak. By the musty stench of it, it had been leaking for some time. 'Thank you for contacting me,' said Lena, trying to ignore the smell.

'You are investigating the death of Mr Tibbs?' asked Maria. 'But you are not the police. The cleaning lady, Gloria, said you were a friend of his.'

'Yes,' replied Lena. 'I need to find out what happened to Terry. I do not believe he was on his own that night.'

Maria leaned forwards. Lena smelt her perfume, sweet and cloying as it mingled with the smell emanating from the carpet. 'He was not,' she said. 'He checked in with a woman.'

'Who?' asked Lena, her breath bated.

'I do not have a name,' said Maria. 'Mr Tibbs filled in the paperwork. He often has different ladies as his guest and we do not make him give us names. He is a good customer and we look after him.'

'Can you tell me what she looked like?' said Lena, pulling out her notebook. She'd got it from WHSmith a couple of days ago to help organise her investigations. It was black with a silver foil inlay that said 'Notes' and it made her feel like a real private eye.

'No notes,' said Maria, quickly. Lena put her notebook back in her bag, disappointed. 'And no. I did not see her properly. She kept her back to me.'

Lena looked at Maria doubtfully. 'The whole time?' she said. 'That does not seem likely.'

'Do you want my information or not?' replied Maria. 'I am taking a risk just telling you this.'

'How is it a risk?'

'None of your business,' said Maria, looking worried. 'Do you want my information or not?'

'Okay,' said Lena. 'Can you tell me hair colour?'

'No,' said Maria. 'She wore a hat.' Lena rolled her eyes. This was turning into a waste of time. Maria was clearly lying to her. 'The details do not matter,' continued Maria. 'I just want you to know that he was not alone in that hotel room.'

'Why have you come to me with this?' she asked.

'I liked Mr Tibbs,' she replied. 'I liked his show. And he was good to me. Polite, not like some of the guests we get. I want to help.'

Lena narrowed her eyes. 'Then why do you not give your information to the police?'

'Management do not want a scandal in their hotel,' Maria replied, just as Gloria had done. 'If I go to the police they will know.'

'You could go anonymously,' said Lena. 'The police would not say that it was you.'

'But what if they did?' replied Maria, with the paranoia typical of someone from a country with communism in its past. 'You are a much better person to tell.' Lena smiled, feeling an unlikely bond of trust between them. 'If you say I told you, I can just say you are lying. No one will believe a Hungarian cleaner.' Lena took a sip of her cranberry juice. That was why Maria wouldn't give her details of the woman's appearance. It would give Lena's story veracity if she went to the police and it matched any CCTV footage they might have on the street.

'You must be able to tell me something about this woman,' she said, keen to wrap this interview up.

'She had an accent,' said Maria.

'She spoke?'

'A little. She was foreign. Not Romanian, I would recognise that. But maybe she was Russian.' Maria paused. 'Or Hungarian.' Lena raised an eyebrow. Was Maria trying to implicate Sarika?

'Anything else?' she asked.

'Yes,' said Maria. She leaned in, so close that Lena could see a couple of errant hairs sprouting from the woman's chin. 'I've seen her before in the hotel. Several times. And with a different man each time.'

'She was a prostitute?'

Maria got up to go. 'Not a word to anyone,' she said. 'I have told you more than I should. My last favour to Mr Tibbs.' Maria left.

Lena sat for a moment, absent-mindedly scratching the layer of dried-in alcohol on the table with her fingernail. A woman with a Hungarian accent who went to a hotel room with Terry. She didn't like what she was thinking.

'Of course, Sarika is above suspicion,' said Mrs Kingston. They were sitting in her living room the next day.

'Of course,' agreed Lena.

'She was in her room all night,' said Mrs Kingston.

'That is what she told me,' replied Lena. They sat in silence for a moment. 'It was not Sarika in that hotel,' said Lena. She picked up a biscuit, then put it down again and stood up. 'I need to clean,' she said. 'It will help me think.' Lena went to the kitchen and grabbed a rag she'd made from a pair of Tomek's old socks. Her ex-boyfriend had left them behind when he moved out, and the cotton worked very well in combination with the organic polish she'd made from coconut oil, white vinegar, lemon juice and rosemary. She rubbed a little of it on the mantelpiece and let the scent of the rosemary waft over her. Already her mind felt clearer.

'If the girl was a prostitute,' she said, thinking aloud. 'Then someone hired her.'

'Agreed,' said Mrs Kingston.

'And it could have been Terry,' she said.

'I don't think so,' said Mrs Kingston. Lena looked at her. 'He had an ego the size of this room,' the lady continued. 'I don't think he'd think that he should have to pay for what so many women were happy to give him for free.'

Lena began to dust off the photos on the mantel. A black-and-white photo of a handsome young man looked back at her, his smile memorialised for ever. 'If Terry didn't hire her, someone else must have done,' said Lena. She thought about her suspect board, covered in women's photos. 'I always thought it must have been a woman who wanted Terry dead,' she continued. 'What if it was a man?' In her mind, the suspect board was filling up again.

It was Mrs Kingston's turn to look thoughtful. 'Let's assume for a moment that it was murder,' she said. 'We are saying an unknown man hired a prostitute to kill Terry?'

'It does sound far-fetched,' said Lena, seeing the men disappearing from the board again.

'Not necessarily,' said Mrs Kingston. 'He did have enemies. Marsela's ex, Jack, for one. He was desperate to be with Marsela again.'

'In the show,' said Lena, feeling everything was coming back to a work of fiction.

'Of course, it's perfectly possible that I'm wrong about Terry not hiring a prostitute,' said Mrs Kingston, breaking Lena's reverie. 'Maybe he wanted to do something kinky that he didn't think any of his girlfriends would be up for. He was trussed up in a leather collar, after all.'

Lena thought. She was pretty sure Sarika would have indulged whatever fantasy Terry could dream up. She tried to blink the image of her baby cousin and Terry in a latexed tryst out of her eyes. 'Maybe,' she said. 'But prostitutes do not normally murder their clients.'

'That is true,' said Mrs Kingston. 'You don't often hear about prostitutes who double up as hit women. But it doesn't make it impossible.'

'But it still might not be murder,' said Lena. 'He could have taken too many drugs himself, and the woman ran away instead of helping or calling an ambulance.'

'The drugs never seemed right to me,' said Mrs Kingston, thoughtfully. 'He's a party boy, sure, but he always struck me as one of those people who will drink ten pints and a Jägerbomb on a Friday night, but would never touch drugs.'

'But drugs killed him,' Lena replied. 'Somehow they got into his system.'

Lena went back to the kitchen and began to fill the sink with hot water to soak Mrs Kingston's pans. She squirted in washing-up liquid and admired the iridescent bubbles that foamed up. Even now, having been a cleaner for almost four years, she was as entranced as a baby by the beauty of bubbles. Her mind went back to the task in hand. If it was a man, paying a prostitute to administer an overdose to Terry would cost a lot of money. 'I still think if someone killed him, Jack was involved,' she heard Mrs Kingston say, when she turned off the tap. 'He's always had it in for Terry.'

'And he was jealous?' said Lena, coming back to the living room. She knew how dangerous jealousy could be.

'He's in love with Marsela,' replied Mrs Kingston. 'They've been vying for her attention from the start. Marsela dumped the wealthy banker Jack for bad boy Terry.' She smiled. 'I remember what it was to be young. The allure of the scoundrel. It's a very powerful pull.'

Lena nodded. She'd heard such things, but had never applied it to herself. She liked nice men who treated her well.

'Tell me more about Marsela and Jack's relationship on the show,' she said. 'I have only watched a few episodes.'

'They were a couple when the show started,' said Mrs Kingston. 'They even dated for a bit again in season two, after Terry dumped Marsela. But when Terry clicked his fingers she dropped Jack in a flash.'

'And what is Jack like?'

'Plenty to say for himself,' said Mrs Kingston. 'Always talking about his job and money. I think he's a bit of a . . .' Mrs Kingston broke off, looking for the right word. 'Dick,' she said in the end. Lena laughed at the old lady using that word so decisively. 'He thinks a lot of himself. I believe he worked for a Chinese bank, then started up his own firm when he got some investors after the show. Hand me the laptop and we'll look it up.'

Lena stepped over Jasper and grabbed the laptop. The power cable was only a little chewed by the rabbit. She opened it up and placed it on a cushion on Mrs Kingston's lap. 'Now,' said Mrs Kingston, painfully stretching her gnarled fingers. 'Let's find it.'

Lena left her to it and grabbed a broom to sweep up the worst of the rabbit's food that was littering the floor, as always. Jasper rescued a piece of carrot from her clutches and hopped under the sofa to enjoy it in peace. 'Here we are, Lena,' Mrs Kingston announced. 'Gosh, I must be losing my touch. The whole website just sounds like financial clichés, I can't get any sense out of it.' The old lady peered at the screen. 'Still, I suppose all these trendy little investment shops spout this type of rubbish these days. They've lost the art of plain speaking. Grab a Post-it note and I'll give you the address.'

'I have a notebook now,' said Lena, with pride. 'Write the address in there,' she said, passing it to Mrs Kingston.

'I'll read it out and you can write it,' said Mrs Kingston. 'Pens are a bit tricky with my arthritis these days.' She sighed. 'And I used to have the fastest shorthand in London.'

Lena took down the address and began cleaning again. Jasper had found the pile she'd made sweeping up his food and was eating it as quickly as his little teeth could manage as she approached with the dustpan and brush. Lena decided to leave him to his feast and went into the kitchen to do the dishes.

'There are less likely motives for murder than jealousy,' called out Lena, thinking of her past cases. 'But I am still suspicious of Marsela.' She thought back to what Margaret had told her. 'I wonder if she was really at that showbiz party all night.'

'Only one way to find out,' said Mrs Kingston. 'Saturday night, correct? Let's see where it was. You can go talk to them. Here we are. A bar called Macaques in Chelsea.'

Lena scribbled it down in her notebook. 'I know you like Marsela,' she called out. 'But she might be a better actress that we give her credit for.'

Lena came back into the living room, but Mrs Kingston had closed her eyes. Sitting there, Lena noticed how frail she looked. Lena carefully tucked a blanket around her shoulders and removed the teacup from her hand. She'd clean quietly today.

That afternoon, Lena stood outside Macaques on the King's Road. Two giant wooden carvings of monkeys stared back at her, guarding the door. One was baring its teeth in a snarl, the other appeared to be laughing. Lena didn't really enjoy either reaction to her attempt to dress as if she belonged in this bar. With her charity-shop dress and the faux sheepskin coat she'd bought in a cheap shop last year outside the Hunyadi Square Market in Budapest, she felt like an imposter in this world. 'That's what I am,' she told herself. 'But I don't need to fool them for long.' She pushed the heavy door open and stepped inside.

It was a Tuesday and she'd timed her visit for four p.m., hoping to catch the bar staff while they had time to chat. She blinked for a while inside, her eyes gradually acclimatising to the darkness. It was more like a forest than a bar, with what she presumed must be fake trees growing from the floor to the ceiling. As she got used to the light, she spotted more monkeys dotted all over the place. Some stone, some wood, some furry and unnervingly lifelike.

Lena walked up to the bar, eyeing the extremely thin and ridiculously beautiful waitress. She was preparing herself to order an expensive cocktail, tip the bartender generously and then see what she could discover about the party Marsela had been at the night Terry was murdered.

'Nice coat,' said the waitress, looking Lena up and down. Lena looked back at her. Her hair was dyed a Marilyn Monroe shade of blonde and she was wearing heavy eyeliner and pulling both off expertly. This was all Lena needed, some attractive waitress giving her attitude before she'd even started her attempt at charm. 'I have the same one,' the woman continued, with a smile. 'You have been to Hungary?' she asked.

Lena grinned and answered in her native tongue. 'You are Hungarian too,' she said, wondering how she could have mistaken the girl's distinctive Budapest style.

'*Természetesen*,' said the waitress, bursting into Hungarian. 'I am Ana, it is a pleasure to meet you. All day I'm surrounded by the English. They are lovely, but I miss my people. And some of the people in this bar are so snobby they might as well be Austrian!' They both smiled, on safe Hungarian territory. 'Let me get you a drink,' said Ana. 'On the house. My boss doesn't come in till six p.m. A Monkey Puzzle? It's vodka, lime, coconut milk and lemongrass. Of course it's not a patch on the cocktails at the Bar Pharma in Budapest, but it's pretty tasty.'

'Sure,' said Lena. 'Thank you.' She watched Ana prepare the drink.

'So what are you doing here?' asked Ana.

'In London or in this bar?'

'Either,' said Ana. 'Me, I came over here for an Englishman I met in Budapest when he was on holiday. We fell desperately in love. Then when I arrived, it turned out he was married. *Fattyú!* But I got this job and decided to stay. I can't believe what they pay! I was a nurse in Budapest and I am earning four times what I was there. And no bedpans to empty. A few years here and I'll be able to buy myself a nice flat overlooking the Danube back home. Pay is so good!'

'Wealthy clientele?' said Lena.

'Ridiculous,' replied Ana. She leaned forwards as she passed Lena her drink. 'We even get royals in here sometimes. And politicians,' she whispered, even though they were still talking in Hungarian. 'Not that they tip much.'

Lena laughed and sniffed her cocktail. It smelled like a Thai green curry. She took a sip. Actually it was pretty good. She decided to jump right in with her questions while things were going well.

'A girl I know was in here,' she began. 'Saturday the second of February. Marsela Goga, from *N1 Angels*. Were you working?'

'I remember her,' said Ana. Lena took another sip of her drink, letting the heavy coconut soothe her disappointment. She had been hoping the alibi was false. 'I've seen the show a couple of times. Raz is cute.'

'Was she here all night? It's just . . .' She tried to figure out why she'd need to know that. 'Someone told me she'd seen her with my boyfriend, later on, in . . . Shoreditch. I want to find out if it's true.'

'If your boyfriend is English then it probably is,' sympathised Ana. 'Dirty cheaters. Though it's not like Hungarian boys are much better. Spoilt by their mothers and still expecting their girlfriends to do their laundry at thirty.'

'I went out with a Pole,' said Lena, allowing herself to be drawn into the topic. 'He didn't even know washing machines existed. Thought laundry was done by the enchanted hedgehog!' They both laughed. 'I've heard she was here all night?' said Lena.

'I don't know who you heard that from, but unless it was staff I wouldn't trust them,' said Ana. 'That was the most extreme party I've ever seen, and I've seen plenty. Most of that crowd wouldn't have known their own name after nine p.m., much less who was here and who wasn't. Marsela seemed pretty sober though.'

'When did she leave?'

'I'm not sure,' confessed Ana. 'But she certainly wasn't still here at two a.m. There was a hard-core group of them doing unspeakable things to dear Donald there.' She gestured to a red-faced, blond-haired monkey in one of the trees, glaring down at Lena with vitriol in his eyes. 'So she was gone by then.' Lena took another sip of her drink. It was near the bottom and she could really taste the vodka. 'Another?' offered Ana.

'I don't want to get you in trouble,' said Lena, hopping off her bar stool and wobbling. 'Or myself,' she added. 'But take my number. It would be nice to have a new Hungarian friend in London.'

'I was hoping you'd say that,' replied Ana. 'We must go to The Rosemary, they have the best *töltött káposzta* in town.'

Innocent people did not lie about where they were. Lena knew that. She also knew a lie was not enough for the police to change their minds about an accidental death and assign a murder to a popular reality TV actress. And Marsela could very well just have gone home to bed earlier than she said. But still, that was not what she had told the police. It was suspicious.

CHAPTER 10

Lena was starting to get nervous. It was half an hour till the wake started and her chef Lucia had not arrived. Sarika had called her the day before, desperate to come back for the funeral, but Lena insisted she remained in Hungary. It was not safe for Sarika in London, and certainly not at this wake.

Lena inspected her handiwork with pleasure: the house was immaculate. Although it had been tidy when Lena arrived, her eagle eye had picked up multiple pockets of dust and grime overlooked by the usual cleaner. The skirting boards now shone, the bathroom downstairs was free from mould and the light shades looked as though they were brand new. She'd had a good snoop around the ground floor but hadn't found anything of interest. Tidying upstairs wasn't part of the arrangement, but Lena hoped she'd have time to have a look up there as well. And even if she didn't find anything more on Marsela, the wake was the perfect opportunity to widen her suspect net.

The house inside was as expected from the outside: very normal. From her viewing on Monday night, she'd been expecting it to transform into something much more glamorous once she opened the door. But clearly nothing had been filmed here: most of the action took place at Terry's bar, on the streets of Islington and at other local businesses. In fact, the house was tasteful and homely with overflowing bookshelves the only clutter.

Lena put that down to Marsela: Terry did not have the air of a well-read man.

Just as Lena decided to take a look upstairs, the bell rang. When Lena opened the door she was greeted by a staggering tower of Tupperware. '*Incubo!*' it said. 'A nightmare. Help.'

Lena grabbed the top five boxes to reveal a flustered-looking Lucia. 'I am so sorry I am late,' she said. 'Can you bring the rest in from the car while I get started cooking? If we hurry I'll still have time to do the *calamari fritti*.'

Lena went to the car and gathered a huge armful of Tupperware boxes containing Lucia's carefully prepared food. She bit her tongue. Lucia wasn't like Sarika, she told herself. It was not like her to be late. Something must have happened.

'I know you must hate me,' said Lucia as Lena entered the kitchen. 'But pass me that bunch of basil. In fact, tear it for me, will you? I know you are not normally allowed to help in the kitchen but this is an emergency. No, not like that. Gently. It is not the basil's fault.'

Lena continued to rip the basil leaves, more carefully now. 'Whose fault is it?' she said.

'Irina!' declared Lucia. 'That girl is not much use when she is here but even less when she is not. She quit this morning. She has a new job, apparently. Something more glamorous on double the money. She could at least have worked today, but she flat out refused to help with Mr Tibbs's wake.' Lena nodded and Lucia continued. 'The cheek of her. She even told me if I lost twenty pounds she could hook me up with some work. Doing god knows what.' She shivered.

'Some jobs are dirtier than cleaning,' said Lena.

Lucia turned the stove on and began to heat vegetable oil for the *calamari*. 'I know she had a second job too, but you'd think after all I'd done for her she wouldn't just leave me in the lurch like this.' Lucia put the *calamari* in the oil and listened to it sizzle.

Lena breathed in deeply. Basil and seafood. She loved the smell of Lucia's cooking, so much lighter than her mother's rich stews. 'At least she won't somehow manage to burn my *insalata verde*. Again,' she said. 'I didn't even know lettuce could catch fire.'

'Maybe it is for the best that she is not here,' said Lena.

'Maybe,' agreed Lucia. 'Now, do you think you can chop some garlic without causing chaos?'

Lucia had done herself proud on the food. With a relatively small budget, she'd cooked up a mouth-watering selection of Italian antipasti: *arancini*, *gamberetti* fried with garlic, *calamari*, olives and *bruschette* covered with tiny chopped tomatoes and basil. Even the pesto that Lucia declared ruined by Irina the previous day wasn't too bad. The girl had accidentally put gorgonzola in it instead of pecorino. It had a distinctive taste, but Lena rather liked it. They decided to serve it anyway on a pasta salad, just this once.

Lena left her chef putting the finishing touches together in the kitchen and inspected the ground floor. She placed the flowers that had been delivered tastefully around the room. Glancing at her watch she decided there was time to have a quick snoop upstairs before the guests arrived for the wake.

The bedroom was surprisingly small and fairly ordinary. Until Lena flung open the cupboards and discovered much of the bedroom had been annexed to allow for an enormous walk-in wardrobe. There was a large bookshelf in the corner, weighed down by heavy tomes of law. The soft carpet was littered with a selection of rejected black outfits like dead ravens.

Lena made her way downstairs. Just in time. She heard the key in the lock. A woman in black slipped in and shut the door behind her with a sigh of relief.

'I am Lena Szarka, you must be Marsela Goga,' said Lena, recognising her chief suspect. The woman held up her finger, in a gesture of silence, and leaned back against the door, shutting her eyes.

Lena took the opportunity to inspect Marsela. She had dark hair and pale skin with a dramatic flash of red adorning her lips, just as in the photo pinned to Lena's board. She was on the short side and, although she was slender, her dress was stretched at the seams in a way that suggested recent weight gain. She had bags under her eyes that her make-up couldn't hide.

'I needed a minute,' she said apologetically, eventually opening her eyes. They were a vivid blue, like Terry's. 'It has been a long day already. Maybe serving food wasn't such a good idea. Hungry people don't linger.'

'It is just close relatives and friends?' asked Lena.

'That's what I wanted,' said Marsela. 'But we'll probably end up with a circus of fame-hungry acquaintances looking to cash in on the event. I'm not letting press in, but it's hard to keep everyone out.' She went up to the mirror and adjusted her hair. 'I look like I've been crying,' she said. 'Don't I?'

'Yes,' replied Lena honestly.

'Good,' said Marsela. 'I have. Get me a drink, will you? Vodka tonic. Hold the tonic.'

The doorbell rang as Lena delivered Marsela's drink. 'You might as well let them in,' she said, going upstairs. 'Call me if anyone looks like they are stealing. And please bring me up another drink.'

Lena pushed her shoulders back and picked up a tray of Lucia's *arancini*, delicious fried risotto balls with a small bowl of *pomodoro* sauce. She looked around the room, determined to identify people who could have designs on Terry and therefore might be the author of the notes. They must be female, which ruled out about half the mourners in the room. They would most likely be young if they'd been involved with Terry: probably under thirty. That ruled out another large component of the guests. And knowing Terry, they would be glamorous. Lena spotted the neighbour Margaret, clutching a tray of what must be her homemade biscuits. She'd try to avoid her.

Lena saw a group of women who matched her profile perfectly. She approached them with her tray out and her ears open.

'He was a right sort,' said a lady with blonde hair, orange skin and lips so plump she looked as though she'd been stung by a bee, as she reached out to take a canapé. 'I don't know how I'll ever get over him.'

'I know what you mean, Livs,' said a redhead with breasts so large her back must ache, swigging her wine like it was a Jägerbomb. She put her glass down and then took an *arancini* in each hand, popping one into her mouth. 'I don't think I'll be able to cope,' she declared, her mouth still full.

Livs blew her nose loudly. 'Becs, it's one hundred per cent disaster,' she said. 'Ooh, is that tomato sauce?'

Lena nodded. 'With fresh basil and balsamic vinegar,' she said. She offered the platter to a lady who was standing with them. She looked different to the other two, surgically unenhanced and more natural. Lena took another look at her. She was dark-skinned, with long black hair. She shook her head, a tear rolling down her cheek. 'I'll never eat again,' she said.

'You shouldn't try to diet now, Rubilla,' said Livs. 'Give yourself a day off.'

'It's because she's upset,' said Becs. 'You silly moo.'

'Oh,' replied Livs, putting her arm around the girl. 'You're lucky. I eat like a pig when I'm sad. When our Dave died I gained two stone. Had to live on ciggies and skinny pasta for three weeks before my shoot for the *Sun*.'

Rubilla began to sob and disappeared from Lena's view as the woman encircled her in silicone hugs.

Lena looked at the three of them, trying to memorise the names. The blonde was Livs, the redhead Becs, the dark girl Rubilla. They all matched her profile.

The hug came to an end. Lena handed Rubilla a serviette and she blew her nose loudly.

'You all dated Terry?' said Lena. She knew she was just meant to be serving canapés but couldn't resist the urge to find out more.

'Are you press?' whispered Becs. 'Marsela was so strict about letting them in.' She smiled at Lena and winked. 'Great cover, serving the food.'

'Yes, we all dated him,' added Livs, barging forwards and grinning at Lena. '*Ciao* magazine did a piece on it. Becs and I did a photo-shoot together. Wish we could have got you in too, Rubilla. We'd have been like Charlie's Angels. You could be the Chinese one, since you're Indian.'

'Pakistani,' muttered Rubilla, through her tears.

'What about Marsela?' Lena asked.

'She had a picture too. Wouldn't have it with us though, stuck-up cow. An inset of her looking sad. That was the angle. Love-rat Terry and his bevvy of beauties break the heart of foreign lawyer Marsela.'

'She was upset?' asked Lena

'Not really,' dismissed Becs. 'It's all made up.'

'Marsela and Terry were purely for the cameras,' explained Rubilla. 'He told us that. And you can see what an odd couple they'd be. It's what he did in his own time that matters.'

'And he did us,' said Livs, with a laugh. 'What mag are you from? I'll do topless. I can show you my portfolio. I have it in my bag, I left it over here somewhere . . .'

Lena thought a minute. 'I cannot look now,' she said. She lowered her voice to a whisper. 'It would blow my cover,' she said. 'Write down your names and contact details,' she said, pleased with herself. She'd be able to track the women down again, investigate them online and also see if any of their handwriting matched the notes.

'Here's my card,' said Becs. Lena frowned.

'And mine,' said Livs. Lena looked at the cards in front of her. Both had photographs of themselves in low-cut tops gazing seductively at the camera. She looked back at the women.

'Where is Rubilla?' she said, noticing the girl had disappeared while she'd been inspecting the cards.

'She's always running off like that,' said Becs.

'Bit of a weirdo,' added Livs, who had fished a mirror out of her bag and was reapplying lipstick. 'Hasn't even had her tits done.'

Lena looked around the room. She saw a familiar face in the crowd.

Sarika.

Dressed in black. Tears streaming down her face. Lena shoved the platter of canapés at Becs and made a beeline for her cousin.

'What are you doing here?' she said, pulling her to the privacy of the kitchen.

'I could not miss this,' replied Sarika. 'I had to pay my respects to Terry. I crept into the back of the funeral service and now I am here.'

'You are meant to be in Hungary. It is not safe.'

'It doesn't matter,' replied Sarika. 'I owe it to Terry to be at his funeral. It is what he would have wanted.'

'Well, you are going straight back to Hungary,' said Lena. But Sarika had already walked into the living room. Lena followed her.

'Who are all these women?' Sarika asked, looking around. 'What did they have to do with Terry?'

'They're on the circuit,' Raz appeared and gave a dazed Lena a kiss on each cheek. 'When you said you did events, I didn't realise you meant funerals.'

'My first,' said Lena.

Raz watched Livs sashay by. 'Great work.'

'Terry knew so many people,' said Sarika, looking around. 'These could have been the guests at our wedding.'

'Be careful,' said Lena to Sarika, drawing her out of Raz's earshot. 'Marsela is upstairs. Those girls over there all dated Terry too. One of them could have written the notes.'

Sarika turned to look at them. 'The redhead is beautiful,' she said. 'But Terry chose me over her.'

Raz joined them again. 'So, Lena,' he said, allowing her to refill his glass. She was watching Sarika. The girl was embracing Terry's uncle Barry. 'This is kind of like our third date.' Lena looked at him in surprise. 'You know what happens on third dates,' he added, with a wink.

'You can fill glasses,' she said, handing Raz the bottle. 'I need to keep an eye on Sarika. Not too full as Marsela wants people to start leaving soon.' Raz took the bottle, confusion clouding his face. 'Think you can handle that?'

'I can handle anything,' said Raz. Lena was already out of earshot.

'Oh Lena,' said Sarika. 'I was just telling Uncle Barry how much I miss Terry.' Barry had removed a hipflask from his pocket and was taking a swig. 'It's the little things, you know,' said Sarika. 'Like how he sneezed.'

'And you miss your nephew?' asked Lena, watching Barry. He was swaying slightly.

'Of course I do,' he replied. 'He's my brother's boy. But I have to admit,' he leaned closer to the women, 'takings are up since he stopped giving free drinks to all and sundry.'

'My Terry was so generous,' agreed Sarika.

'Your Terry!' said Barry with a laugh.

'Yes, my Terry,' said Sarika, bristling.

'He was Marsela's if he was anyone's,' said Barry. He dropped his voice to a loud whisper. 'If she did pop him off I wouldn't blame her. He treated that girl like dirt.'

Lena filled a champagne glass and handed it to him. 'The police must have investigated that possibility,' she said, trying to sound casual. 'They always look to the partners.'

'Terry's death was an accident,' said Barry, his voice sharp. 'And anyway, she was at some fancy showbiz party,' he said. 'Terry wasn't even invited. Livid, he was. Apparently some of the younger royals turned up, I heard. He couldn't believe they'd invite Marsela and not him. But she's classy, you know.'

'She says that she was there all night?'

'Why are you so interested?' asked Barry, narrowing his eyes at her. 'I saw you at the bar with Terry, and now you are serving drinks at his wake and asking all sorts. Terry was on his own that night; it's not like it was murder. Who are you?'

'No one,' said Lena hurriedly. 'I will bring more food. Come on, Sàrika.'

Lena ran the hot tap and washed up in the kitchen. She'd paid a deposit to borrow the glasses for the occasion and didn't want to risk them getting cloudy in the dishwasher. The guests had finally gone, she'd put Sarika in a taxi with instructions to go straight home, double-lock the door and call her if anything happened. Marsela ventured back downstairs. Lena reached into the fridge and removed the last of the wine from the wake.

'Would you like a top-up?' asked Lena, stepping into the living room. There were still remnants of food to be cleaned away and she wanted to vacuum, but thought Marsela might want a moment to reflect before Lena made too much noise. Catering funerals and negotiating emotions was a messier job than she'd anticipated.

'Good idea,' Marsela replied. Lena filled her glass. 'This has been a hard day,' she said. 'Fame-hungry women flocked around Terry when he was alive and I can't even get rid of them now he's dead.'

'I am sorry,' said Lena. 'Mourning should be private.'

Marsela took a deep swig from her glass. 'Perhaps you'd like to join me? I don't feel like drinking alone. Not today. But I do feel like drinking.'

Lena hesitated for a split second, looking at the mess in the kitchen. She didn't clean as well after a drink. But finding out more about Terry and Marsela was what she was here for, and there could be no better opportunity. 'Thank you,' she replied, topping up Marsela's glass and taking a modest amount for herself. They sat together in silence for a moment.

'You're Hungarian?' asked Marsela.

'How did you guess?'

'I picked up a little of the language from a friend at law school,' said Marsela. '*Szarka*. That means magpie, correct?'

'Correct,' said Lena, impressed.

'I am from Kosovo originally,' said Marsela. 'Myself and the Hungarian, we were the only ones in our class from Eastern Europe. And the only ones who could not afford the textbooks.'

Lena looked at her. 'Your English is so good . . .' she began.

'I moved here when I was six,' explained Marsela. 'When my parents died I came to live with an uncle in the UK. I was very lucky to have the opportunity. But he was not a kind man.' An awkward silence fell.

'A lot of people were at the wake,' ventured Lena. 'Terry was . . . very much loved.'

Marsela emitted a harsh laugh. 'That's a nice way of putting it. Yes, he was what you'd call a player. Lots of girls always on the go.'

'That is hard for you?' said Lena. 'You must get so jealous.' She thought of the note.

'He wasn't like that at the beginning. He was devoted to me.'

'What happened?'

Marsela looked at her, and took a large swig of her wine. 'Let's just say things changed.'

There was a knock on the door. 'Can you answer it?' said Marsela. 'If it's another of his women, get rid of her. I've had my fill for today of his crazy flings.'

Lena opened the door. A man stared back at her: a man she recognised from *N1 Angels*. He wore an expensive-looking suit and was clutching a bottle of vodka.

'The wake is over,' said Lena. 'I am sorry, but you must leave.'

'Marsela, I'm here,' he called out, ignoring Lena. 'Jack is here.' He pushed past Lena into the house.

'Jack,' said Marsela, standing up and walking over to him. 'I missed you at the funeral,' she added.

'I was busy in the office,' said Jack. 'Shares don't just buy and sell themselves. And Terry and I weren't exactly mates. But I'm here to support you now.' Lena watched as they embraced.

Marsela glanced at Lena. 'Let's go upstairs,' she said. 'We can talk there, out of Lena's way.'

Lena watched them climb the stairs, Jack still holding the vodka bottle. So despite what Marsela had said about Terry, she was still close with her ex-boyfriend. That was an interesting development.

'Those deluded girls,' said Sarika, making herself comfortable on Lena's bed. Lena sat on the floor and leaned her corkboard against the bedside table. So far only Barry's name was written up there, with Terry and Marsela's photos smiling back at her. She gathered a collection of Post-it notes and a marker pen, and the business cards the two women had given her, ready to go up. 'They think that Terry cared about them. When clearly it was only me he liked. Loved. Don't you think, Lena?'

'Sarika, we need to focus,' answered Lena. She was finding it frustrating that Sarika seemed more interested in Terry's fidelity than in her own danger. 'I need to add more suspects to the board. People who might have written the notes, maybe even murdered Terry. You need to book your flight back to Hungary.'

'There's snowstorms in Debrecen,' replied Sarika, looking up from the laptop. 'All the flights are grounded.'

'What?' exclaimed Lena. 'You cannot stay here. It is not safe.'

'I don't have anywhere else to go,' replied Sarika. She sat back. 'And I think I know who sent the notes. It has to be Marsela. She was jealous.'

'She does not seem jealous,' said Lena, thinking of Marsela. She had a quiet dignity to her, despite all the cheating.

'I bet she murdered him too,' continued Sarika. 'She lured him to the hotel to talk about the show, then drugged him and took all his clothes off.'

'But why?' asked Lena.

'She's unhinged,' replied Sarika, with a shrug.

Lena handed her a Post-it, despairing at Sarika's sloppy motive ideas. Cartwright was a much better partner in detection. 'Okay. Put it all on there,' she said, to keep her quiet. 'We will put your suspicions on the board.'

'Really?' said Sarika. 'Brilliant.' She grabbed the pen and began scribbling.

Lena looked at the board. She pinned up the two women's business cards and wrote down Rubilla's name too. She didn't even have a surname for her, but perhaps she could get more details from the others. Any one of them could have been more serious with Terry than they let on, and any one of them might have been the woman Terry was with that evening.

She paused, then looked again at Uncle Barry's name. She wasn't sure what the motive would be. Surely, if it was murder, it wouldn't be over a few free drinks? There could be more to it than that – she knew business partnerships could get ugly.

Lena glanced at Sarika. She'd turned over the Post-it and was scribbling more on the reverse.

She wrote down Jack's name too. He seemed unlikely to have been naked with Terry in a dog collar in the hotel room that night, but she didn't want to rule anyone out too soon just because of their gender. She shouldn't make assumptions. Jack used to be with Marsela, and here he was again, cosying up to her now Terry was dead. Still, if Terry was with someone in that room, his past history suggested it was a woman. And if Maria was right, it could have been a prostitute.

And the notes, of course. She looked at them, enclosed in their plastic bags and pinned to the board. Malice still leaked from them.

Sarika put her Post-it note on the board and then stopped to stare at the bags.

'Don't worry,' said Lena. 'We will find out who sent these notes to you. And stop them.'

'Thank you, Lena,' said Sarika.

'It has been a big day,' said Lena. 'I think we both need to get some rest before we work out what to do with you tomorrow.'

'I will be in the living room,' said Sarika. 'I want to remember the good times with Terry for a while. My mother told me that I should light a candle for him and pray.'

Lena smiled at her. It had been a long time since either of them had been to church, but a Catholic upbringing never left you completely. 'That is a good idea,' she said. 'Just make sure the door is double-bolted.'

'I will have a drink for him too,' said Sarika. 'My mother gave me a bottle to bring back with me. She always says a fiery shot of Palinka is good for everything, from indigestion to grief.'

★ ★ ★

109

Lena dreamed of lettuces on fire and Jasper, Mrs Kingston's rabbit, grown to giant proportions and jumping around her living room making the most awful screeching sound. She woke and opened her eyes but the noise didn't disappear. It wasn't a giant rabbit. It was her smoke alarm.

She jumped out of bed, coughing, and ran to the door. It was cool to the touch so she flung it open. 'Sarika,' she shouted, as smoke flooded into her room. She ran to Sarika's bedroom but the girl wasn't there. Coughing some more, Lena came back to the living room. It was hard to see with the smoke stinging her eyes, but she could tell the light of the fire was near the front door. Filling a saucepan with water, Lena flung it in the right direction. It hissed like an angry cat. She refilled the pan and repeated the exercise several times.

The orange flames hissed to black, the fire extinguished. Lena opened the windows and waved out the smoke. Only then did she see Sarika, curled up on the sofa. Absolutely still. She pulled the girl up and dragged her to the cold fresh air of the open window.

Sarika began to cough. Lena breathed a sigh of relief. 'What's happening?' asked Sarika, conscious but groggy.

'A fire,' said Lena. 'A small one,' she added, seeing Sarika's look of fear. 'And I have put it out.' She climbed on the sofa and reached up, removing the batteries from the alarm. Finally there was peace.

'My candle!' said Sarika. 'But I blew it out. I think I did.'

Through the smoke, Lena could still smell alcohol, likely from Sarika's breath. That must be why she hadn't been woken by the smoke or the alarm. 'You are okay,' she said. 'That is the main thing. But I think we should go to the hospital to be sure.'

There was a knock on the door.

'We'll get kicked out of the building,' said Sarika.

'It will be fine,' said Lena. 'Wrap up warm, I'll deal with the neighbours.'

Lena went to the door, stepping carefully around the burnt patch on the floor. It was surprisingly small for that much smoke. She found the sleepy-looking building manager standing in his dressing gown. He looked at the blackened floor. 'A little accident,' explained Lena.

'You need the fire brigade?' he asked, rubbing his eyes.

'It's all out now,' said Lena. 'And do not worry, I will repair the damage.'

'You'd better,' he replied. 'The landlord won't be pleased.'

'It will be good as new,' said Lena, closing the door.

CHAPTER 11

Lena spent most of the night in A&E with Sarika, who had finally been seen by the doctor as dawn broke. Sarika was given the all-clear and a lecture. It turned out that candles, tissues and alcohol, though a good combination to help with grief, were a bad combination for fire safety. Lena tucked her up in bed, assuring her that a little scrubbing, a few more hours with the window open and replacing a small area of laminate and everything would be back to normal.

She thought where Sarika should go as she scrubbed the floor. It was Thursday morning now: almost two weeks after Terry's death and the threatening note. Nothing had happened after a week as the note threatened, but then again, Sarika hadn't been here.

Her phone rang. It was Cartwright, and he wanted to meet for lunch between his shifts. Perfect. She must keep her promise to Sarika, but perhaps there was a way to get his advice.

Lena bit into her chicken and bacon baguette and smiled at PC Cartwright, who was tucking into a gravelly-looking lentil super-food salad bowl.

'Were you out last night?' he asked her.
'Why?'

'Your eyes look a little red,' he said. 'It's not like you.'

For a moment Lena considered telling him she'd been out on a date to make him jealous. She dismissed Sarika's voice in her head, thinking that maybe she spent too much time with her cousin. 'There was a fire at my flat last night,' she said. 'I spent much of the night at the hospital with Sarika.' She looked at his face, filled with alarm. 'Do not worry,' she added. 'We are both fine.'

'A fire? How did it start?'

'Sarika was burning a candle,' began Lena. 'Because . . .' She couldn't tell him that Sarika was mourning Terry. 'She often does,' she added. 'And she had strong Hungarian liquor and there were some tissues. It is okay, the fire was small. Little harm done.'

'Almost two thousand house fires are started by candles each year,' said Cartwright sternly. 'Two hundred in London alone.' Lena smiled at him. She loved it when he spouted statistics. His face was so earnest. 'She should be more careful.'

'I know. She does too now,' she said. 'So, what is happening with Yasemin?'

Cartwright chewed his food and swallowed. 'There's not the resources there was on it, after what happened,' he said. 'And I'm not as involved.'

'That is not fair,' said Lena. 'You got closer to catching Yasemin than anyone else ever has.'

'Not close enough,' replied Cartwright. He leaned forwards, almost knocking over his bowl of lentils. Lena leaned in too, hoping her breath didn't smell of bacon. 'But there is a new lead,' he said. 'A potential informant I've managed to track down.'

'Tell me,' whispered Lena.

'I can't say much about it,' said Cartwright. 'Even to you. It's very confidential. And in fact, I've not mentioned it to my superiors yet. I want to make sure it's genuine. But it has been very helpful so far.' He leaned in and began to whisper. 'Apparently, Yasemin has a new business venture. She's still up to her usual roster of street gangs, muggings and drugs, but there's something new. My source reckons it's a gold mine for her.'

'What is it?' asked Lena.

'I wish I knew,' replied Cartwright. 'I'm building up the relationship in the hope he'll tell me more. And even if he does, I'll need something to corroborate it against before I go further. I don't think my career could take another knock like the one it had after your video line-up fiasco.'

Lena sat right back and shoved in a huge mouthful of her sandwich. She'd been enjoying it until now, but the chicken was suddenly dry and the crusty baguette scraped the roof of her palate. She chewed for what seemed like hours, then, determined to defend herself, swallowed it with effort. 'You cannot blame me,' she declared.

Cartwright almost spat out the pomegranate seed he'd just popped into his mouth. 'Oh god, no,' he said. 'Did it sound like that? I suppose it did. Lena, it is not your fault, it is mine. All mine. I just hope that I don't lose my job.' He reached out a hand and put it on Lena's, trapping her sandwich underneath.

Lena extracted her hand, too cross at what had happened to enjoy his touch. 'There is something I need,' she told him. She couldn't fight the urge to talk about her case any longer. 'Do you remember we were talking about Terry Tibbs?' she said. Cartwright frowned back at her, but she put it down to the large kale leaf he'd just put in his mouth. 'I do not think he was alone in that hotel room.' She'd decided now that two people at the hotel had told her this, it was time she shared it with her favourite policeman.

'Why are you so interested?' asked Cartwright. 'It is the accidental death of someone you don't know.'

'I know the cleaner who found the body,' said Lena, feeling like this was a stroke of genius. A reason to be interested, and a link to the information she had. 'She was obviously very upset.'

'Why didn't you say before?' asked Cartwright, his face softening.

'She is shy of the police,' said Lena, honestly. 'But I know I can trust you with what she told me.'

'Carry on,' said Cartwright.

'She said that there were two glasses out when she cleaned the hotel room. And then I spoke to the receptionist. She said that there was a woman who was with Terry when he checked into the hotel.' Lena leaned in. She could smell the sweet potato in Cartwright's salad. 'And she hinted that the woman was a prostitute.'

Cartwright looked excited. 'I took a sneak peek at the case notes,' he said. 'After you were so interested before. The officer in charge believes that Terry was in the room on his own. They put his death down to an accidental, self-administered drug overdose, probably with an auto-erotic motive, judging from what he was wearing. But if he was with someone, that all changes. Of course, that could still be the case, but this needs to be investigated before the inquest. Great work, Lena.'

Lena smiled and shrugged, pleased. She polished off the last bite of her baguette and opened the chocolate brownie packet, offering a piece to Cartwright. 'When can you get the cleaner and receptionist to the station?' he asked, waving away the brownie.

'They will not talk to the police,' said Lena, chewing merrily. 'They both told me that they would deny all knowledge.'

Cartwright almost choked on his quinoa. 'So this is just hearsay?' he said.

'Yes,' said Lena. 'I heard them say it.'

'You don't understand,' said Cartwright. 'There's nothing we can do on this information. There's no hard evidence that there were two people in the room?'

'No,' said Lena. 'It has all been cleaned up. And the CCTV was broken.'

'And the witnesses will not bear witness. Not even to the police, let alone in court.'

'That is right,' said Lena.

Cartwright sighed. 'I'm sorry, Lena, then there's nothing we can do.'

'But she is still out there. What if she hurts someone else?' Like Sarika, thought Lena.

'Don't worry, Lena,' said Cartwright, placing his hand on hers again. 'Even if there was someone there, it still looks like a party gone wrong. Not a serial killer.' He laughed and Lena snatched her hand away, feeling patronised. She took another bite of brownie and relented a bit, watching Cartwright chase the final pomegranate seeds around his bowl with a plastic fork. She hadn't given him all the information, so how could he know why she was worried? She found the urge to tell him about the notes, then remembered Sarika, crying on the sofa. She'd keep her promise.

She was enjoying a final bite of brownie when her phone beeped. She looked at the message and her mouth froze mid-chew. An unknown number.

Leave it alone or worse will happen.

'What's the matter?' asked Cartwright, reading her face. 'Was the message bad news?'

Lena swallowed the rest of her mouthful but the brownie stuck in her throat. She turned the screen to him. 'I had a message like this before,' she said, after he'd read it. She scrolled up and showed it to him. 'I thought it was a wrong number.'

'What does it mean, "worse will happen"?' he asked.

'I do not know,' said Lena.

Cartwright looked at her, his face a picture of concern. 'That fire,' he said. 'You are sure it was the candle?'

'Yes, of course,' said Lena.

116

'Where did it start?'

'In the living room. By where Sarika was sleeping.'

'Was it near the front door?'

'It is a small room,' said Lena. 'Everything is near the front door.'

'I don't want to alarm you,' began Cartwright, 'but whenever a fire starts near the door it should be investigated, just in case it is arson.'

'Arson?' exclaimed Lena. 'But it was a candle!'

'It could well have been, but let's get a fire investigation team down there and check for accelerants just in case.'

'I've cleaned,' said Lena. 'Thoroughly. There will be nothing.'

Cartwright looked at her. 'Do you know any reason someone might try to hurt you?'

Lena felt a burning more intense than the one on her laminate floor to tell him everything. But she remembered her promise to Sarika. 'It is probably nothing,' she brushed off. 'A wrong number and a candle with too many tissues.'

It was Cartwright's turn for his phone to sound. 'I need to get back,' he said. 'But Lena, I'm worried about you. Is there somewhere you can go, somewhere safe?'

'I am fine,' said Lena.

'Maybe you should come and stay with me? You'd be very welcome.'

Lena felt an initial rush of excitement at the thought. Living with Cartwright. Spending their evenings together, cuddled on the sofa. And their nights . . .

But what about Sarika? She couldn't leave her alone. Not when she was the one who might really be in danger. 'I am fine,' she repeated. 'But thank you.'

Lena thought she registered disappointment on Cartwright's face. 'At least let me check that number and see if we can get a trace,' he said.

Lena nodded and he took it down. 'Take care, Lena,' he said, and kissed her on the cheek as he left.

Lena's mind was already racing as she left the café. Walking along the road, she tried to make sense of this. She was pretty sure the fire was an accident. But who were the messages from? The first text had come after she'd spoken to Gloria. Since then, she'd talked to all those people at the funeral, including Marsela. But no one seemed worried.

No one except Maria, the hotel receptionist. She had shared her information, but had not liked Lena investigating.

Lena stopped in her tracks. She wasn't going home. She was going to the Goswell Hotel.

Lena almost laughed when she saw Maria's face. The receptionist looked as though she'd had too much sour calf's-foot soup at the sight of Lena at her front desk. 'I told you not to come here,' hissed Maria.

'I want to talk to the management,' replied Lena.

'There's no way that is happening,' replied Maria. 'Get out or I'll call security.'

Lena looked at her a moment, then screamed. 'A mouse,' she shouted, pointing at the floor. 'There is a mouse in this hotel.' The guests queueing to check in quickly disbanded.

'Be quiet,' said Maria. 'There is no mouse.'

'You're right,' replied Lena. She raised her voice again. 'It is too big for a mouse,' she said. 'I think it is a rat.' One of the guests screamed. 'And there is another one!'

'Make this stop,' said Maria.

'There it is,' said Lena. 'Under the desk.'

'You can see the manager,' hissed Maria.

Lena crept forwards and peered under the desk. 'My mistake,' she said loudly, reaching under the desk. 'It is a glove.' She held it up and then chucked it to Maria. The guests laughed and the check-in queue re-formed.

'Come with me,' said Maria. 'The office is in the back.'

The manager did not strike Lena as a man who was worried about scandal. Or about anything. He was in his fifties, dark, around six foot four, two hundred and fifty pounds and smoking. Lena felt her fingers itching to clean the office: towers of paperwork leaned at dangerous angles, ashtrays littered the remainder of the desk and the floor looked like it had never been vacuumed. An over-flowing bin released an odour of ageing kebab and garlic sauce. Lena decided her imaginary rat could live quite happily here. This room was clearly not in Gloria's cleaning remit.

'Mr Moustafa,' began Maria, hesitantly. He didn't look up from the paper he was studying. 'This lady is asking questions about Terry Tibbs.' He dropped the paper immediately and sprang to his feet in a more spritely manner than Lena would have thought he could manage. Both women took a step back.

He looked at Lena. 'Who are you?' he demanded. 'Police?'

Lena decided to go with that assumption. 'I just have a few questions,' she said, neither confirming nor denying her identity. 'About the night of Terry Tibbs's death.'

'I told them everything already,' he replied. He took a deep drag from his cigarette. 'It is a very sad accident.' He smiled at her. 'Sorry I cannot be more helpful,' he added, his voice saccharine and dripping with sarcasm.

'I have reason to believe there was a woman in the room with Mr Tibbs,' said Lena. Mr Moustafa's eyes swung to Maria. 'She is not my source,' said Lena quickly. 'I have seen footage that shows Mr Tibbs entering the hotel with a woman,' she lied.

'Unfortunately our CCTV was faulty that night,' said Mr Moustafa. 'But the woman did not come into the hotel. Did she?'

119

'No, Mr Moustafa,' said Maria, quickly.

'Then we are done here,' he said. 'I have a call to make and cannot keep the lady waiting.'

'Thank you for your time,' said Lena. Maria led her out, but she lingered for a moment outside the door and glanced back inside. Mr Moustafa had picked up the telephone and was dialling. He looked nervous.

'Get out,' said Maria.

Lena obeyed. She took a deep breath of the cold February air and walked back towards Angel. Although he had put on a front, Mr Moustafa was clearly terrified. But why?

CHAPTER 12

Lena pounced, just in time to catch her client Penelope's child Casper as he leapt from the dining table. She didn't normally clean here on a Friday, but Penelope had begged. Apparently her in-laws were coming to stay at the weekend and they judged Penelope harshly if there was mess. Of course, Penelope had shot out of the door as soon as Lena had arrived, and she was left resentfully cleaning and caring for the children. The dog barked at her, jumping up on to the table himself. He clearly thought table diving was a great new game. 'Sarika!' shouted Lena. 'Come here.'

'I was feeding Crispin his milk,' said Sarika, coming into the dining room holding the squirming toddler. She put him down and he tottered off on his chubby legs. The dog jumped from the table and flattened him. The child burst into a laughter so manic it bordered on tears as the dog covered him in saliva with his huge pink tongue.

'We need to talk,' said Lena. 'We need to plan how to keep you safe. I wish we had a quieter job today. Cleaning for Penelope is like working in the monkey enclosure at Debrecen Zoo.'

'I love it here,' said Sarika. 'The kids, the dog. It's what I want one day.' She smiled at Lena. 'Penelope is lucky,' she said.

'Penelope is tired,' said Lena.

'Can we play in the garden?' asked Casper. 'Please.'

Lena looked out of the kitchen window. It was grey and overcast, but the snow had melted. 'Wrap up warm,' she said. 'And look after your brother.' After they had both put on hats, coats and scarves, Lena opened the door to the small garden. With all the barking and screaming, she felt like she was releasing them into the wild.

Lena bent down to pick up a stray toy car and grimaced in pain. The hours spent scrubbing the floor yesterday to try to get rid of the signs of the fire had taken their toll on her back. She tried to reach the painful area to massage it, but found her arms were just not designed to accomplish that task.

'I will do that for you,' said Sarika, seeing her struggling. 'Sit down.'

Lena collapsed on to the sofa, still clutching the toy car. It beeped at her impatiently. Sarika jumped up behind her and began pummelling her back. 'Ouch,' exclaimed Lena.

'You are very tight,' said Sarika, jabbing her finger into Lena's spine. 'Maybe we should treat ourselves to a nice massage at a spa? Terry used to get a massage every week. Swore by them, especially with all the football he played. He was picked for the under-twelves at Arsenal. Did you know that? He could have been a footballer.' Her voice trailed off, likely thinking of what might have been.

Lena decided to keep her text and suspicions about the fire to herself. Sarika had plenty to worry about already. 'I have to wait for a massage till I go back to Hungary,' she said, moving the subject from Terry. 'It is so expensive in this country.' She thought longingly of the swimming baths back home. Pools of every temperature, from scalding hot to bracingly cold. Nothing felt better than catching the train to Debrecen and spending the day sitting in steaming hot water in the outside pool in the middle of winter, watching the snow melt around you. The old men would sit there for hours playing chess. Mihaly gave the best massages.

He was a beefy man in his fifties and grunted as he rubbed her, digging his hairy hands right to the root of her tension. Not like the wimpy girl who had tickled her back on the one occasion she had sought treatment in this country. All her tension came back as soon as she received the bill.

'I have some painkillers if you would like one,' said Sarika, giving up on Lena's back. 'I keep them in case I have a hangover . . . or, you know, a headache from working too hard.'

Lena laughed. 'That is very organised for you,' she said. 'I am impressed. And yes please.'

Sarika reached into her bag, unzipping the back compartment. 'Ouch,' she said, drawing her hand away.

'What is it?' asked Lena.

'I have a paper cut,' said Sarika, looking at her hand in concern. 'Which is weird. I don't carry paper around with me.' She reached back into her bag and withdrew the offending paper. She emitted a small scream and dropped it on to the floor as if it were on fire. 'It's another note,' she said to Lena.

Lena bent to pick it up, trying to ignore the pain as her back objected.

You will pay for what you have done.

Lena stood and paced the room as she studied the note. 'It is different,' she said, finally.

'Someone else is threatening me now?' said Sarika. 'Great.'

'No, it is the same person,' said Lena. 'The handwriting is the same. But the paper is different. Usually it's on copier paper, but this is a page ripped from a little notebook. Look, you can see where it has been torn.'

'So she ran out of paper,' said Sarika. 'What are we going to do?'

'You cannot stay in my flat any longer,' said Lena. 'This person knows where you live. And if you cannot get back to Hungary then we need to go to the police.'

'No way,' replied Sarika. 'I've told you no. And look what it says again. "You will pay for what you have done." Whoever wrote this makes it look as if I murdered Terry. Just like the last note.'

'It could just mean that she thinks you stole her boyfriend.' Lena turned the note over, and peered at it more closely. There was a small green and blue smudge in the corner. Lena thought, racking her brains for what it could be. Finally, she lifted the note to her face and gave it a sniff.

'You have lost it now,' said Sarika, watching her. 'My only hope for being rescued and she has gone as mad as Al Hrabosky.'

'Smell this,' said Lena, thrusting the paper towards her.

'No,' said Sarika. 'You need help.'

Lena looked at the paper again, then lifted it up to her face. She stuck out her tongue and licked the page. 'It's as I thought,' she told the horrified Sarika. 'It's Lucia's pesto.'

'You are saying Lucia wrote this? Why? Did she have the hots for Terry? She's pretty, in a curvy sort of way, but Terry would never have gone for her.'

'No,' dismissed Lena, keen to stop her cousin babbling. 'It is the batch of pesto that she brought to the funeral. I can taste the garlic, the basil, the pine nuts. But also the gorgonzola. She made it before Irina quit, and told her to add pecorino, but you know what that girl is like. She put in blue cheese instead. She used it for the funeral because we were desperate, but never before, never after. You know what that means?'

Sarika looked at her. 'I hate blue cheese,' she said. 'It is disgusting.'

'That means that someone who was at the funeral must have written this note,' said Lena, with a smile. 'It is what we thought, but now there is proof. They probably saw you and wrote it on whatever was available. From what the notes say we know it is someone who considers Terry to be hers so it must be someone he had some kind of relationship with. So it will be a woman, likely youngish, and attractive . . .' she paused and tried to censor herself, but couldn't resist a dig, 'because he is shallow.'

'It wasn't definitely a girlfriend,' said Sarika, breaking Lena's train of thought. 'It could have been a crazy fan.'

'Well, we'll start with the people who match our profile at the funeral,' said Lena, pleased with her use of profiling. Cartwright would be impressed. 'And work from there. But first I'll make sure that Lucia didn't use that pesto anywhere else. Now, you couldn't have got that pesto on it yourself?'

'I haven't even opened that pocket of my bag for ages,' said Sarika. 'Look, the painkillers are out of date. You can still have one though, I'm sure they are fine.'

'No thanks,' said Lena, deciding to live with her pain. 'So who are our key suspects?' She got her own notebook from her bag. Both children came running back into the house, closely followed by the puppy. All trailed mud. Casper pulled himself up on to the sofa and sat next to Lena, staring intently at her notebook.

'Livs and Becs,' said Lena, trying to ignore the boy. She passed a toy car to his brother who promptly put it in his mouth. The puppy barked, wanting a treat. 'They are already on the suspect board but we can prioritise them now.'

'What about that Indian girl?' asked Sarika, getting up to fetch the tin of dog biscuits. 'She looked at me funny.'

'Rubilla, she was Pakistani,' said Lena. Casper wrestled the pen from her hand and began drawing on her notebook. 'She didn't have a card, but I'll see if the others know where she is. They seemed like friends.'

'Marsela,' said Sarika. 'I still think it is her. What a beautiful dinosaur, Casper.' The puppy jumped up and Casper offered the notebook to him to lick before Lena could snatch it away.

'That would make sense,' agreed Lena, looking in despair at her previously professional notebook, now covered in slobber and dinosaurs. 'She is someone I need to find out more about. And quickly. I will go there, as soon as we are finished.'

'I will stay with the kids,' said Sarika. 'You can go now.'

'Good idea,' said Lena, feeling delighted to escape. 'The sooner we find out the truth, the sooner you will be safe again in London.'

CHAPTER 13

Marsela opened the door; it was past noon but she was still in her dressing gown. Lena could see make-up smudged over her face. It appeared to be left over from a few days ago. 'I lost my necklace at the funeral,' said Lena, in explanation. 'It was my grandmother's. Can I look for it?'

Marsela shrugged, standing aside so Lena could enter.

'I am sorry for the intrusion,' said Lena. 'I can clean while I am here if you like. No charge.'

'Do as you please,' said Marsela. 'I'm going back to bed.' Lena followed her into the kitchen and watched as Marsela rummaged in the cupboard. She heard glass clinking before Marsela pulled out a bottle of something clear. She held it away from her and squinted at it. 'Last year's raki from Mykonos is all that's left,' she said. 'I need to go shopping.'

'I can do it,' said Lena, spotting a golden opportunity to check Marsela's handwriting. 'Write me a list.'

'Vodka,' replied Marsela. 'Keep it simple.' She trudged up the stairs with the bottle.

Lena stood in the kitchen and thought about what she was looking for. Handwriting, to check against the note. She fished it out of her backpack and read it again.

You will pay for what you have done.

It was harder than she thought. There was an iPad, locked, on the kitchen table. No handwriting there. She opened and closed various drawers. Nothing written. She wondered if Marsela was someone who would deface books with scribbles. The bookshelves were full of thick volumes, some in English and others in Albanian. She pulled out a couple and flicked through. They were pristine. Marsela didn't even fold down the edges, let alone write in any of them. Lena couldn't help but respect her for that, unhelpful as it was to her investigations.

Never mind, she'd keep an eye out while she looked for other evidence.

Lena went back to the kitchen and looked at the dirty dishes. A bowl with the remnants of what looked to be tinned tomato soup. A plate with a few toast crumbs. A couple of half-drunk cups of coffee. Had Jack been staying: were the cups for two?

Lena looked more carefully at the old milky coffee and gave each a sniff. One smelt much more sour than the other. From different days. So no obvious signs Marsela had had a guest, and no handwriting for her to check. This was turning out to be a waste of time.

She gathered the dishes and loaded up the dishwasher, and gave the counters a quick wipe. For a moment she got excited when she saw splatters of something red on the floor, before she realised it was drops of the tomato soup. She grabbed a mop and gave the floor a quick wipe. Then she realised it was clinging more stubbornly to the floor than a quick wipe would remove. She ran the hot tap and filled a bucket, deciding to give the floor a proper clean. At least then her trip would have accomplished something.

Afterwards, Lena decided to investigate the interior of the sofa. Perhaps there was a clue lurking under the cushions. She pulled them off, one by one, and found the usual detritus of crumbs, coins and a couple of hairclips. Nothing more telling than that. She picked up the coins and popped them on the coffee table and went to fetch the vacuum cleaner. She couldn't bring herself to leave the inside of the sofa like that. Giving the cushions a good thump to get the dust out of them, she turned on the vacuum cleaner, enjoying its comforting purr.

She put the sofa back together and took the vacuum into the kitchen. It was a Dyson and filled with remnants of dust. She emptied it into the bin, noticing a foul smell as she did so. It hadn't been long since the funeral, but Marsela had managed to create a large amount of waste. She must have cleared out the cupboards and fridge. Lena heaved the bag out and popped it on to the kitchen floor. It promptly split, sending stinky rubbish over the nice clean tiles.

'*Szar*,' said Lena, feeling herself fill with hatred for people who overloaded their cheap bin bags. The bane of her life. Nonetheless, she went to find a new bag and gather up the mess.

There were several empty tins of tomato soup, she noticed. These could have gone into the recycling. Lena decided that maybe Marsela was the murderer: people who didn't recycle were capable of anything, in her book. She began to sort through the debris, putting it into piles of recycling, organic waste and proper rubbish. The kitchen floor was a write-off anyway; she'd need to mop it again when she was finished.

A crumpled piece of paper caught her eye. It looked familiar. She straightened it out and set it on the lino in front of her.

The same paper. The same ink. The same handwriting.

You didn't deserve him. That's why I took him from you. Forever.

Lena didn't hesitate. She got out her phone and dialled.

'What is it, Lena? Whose house is this? What are you doing here?'

Lena forgot the note. She forgot the reality TV star upstairs. She even forgot the pile of rubbish festering on the kitchen floor.

Cartwright was standing at Marsela's front door in tight running trousers and a Lycra top that clung to his body with sweet,

sweet sweat. She could see the details of his abs, his pecs, even the silhouette of his gorgeous belly button, deep and inviting.

'Lena!' said Cartwright. 'What's wrong? Are you injured?'

'*Istenem*,' said Lena. Cartwright wiped the sweat from his brow. 'My god.'

'What?' he replied.

'I was not expecting you to be so . . .'

'I'm a bit sweaty,' said Cartwright. 'Sorry.' He put his arms across himself self-consciously and Lena felt her heart melt. 'I was on a run around Clissold Park when you called, you know, that track around the lake . . .' He trailed off. 'I hope I don't smell,' he added. 'It sounded important so I ran straight here.'

'Come in,' replied Lena, taking his hand to lead him. His hand was damp and cold but the contact made her feel warm. 'I am sorry to cause you inconvenience,' she said, taking charge of herself again. 'But I need you to see this. I have touched nothing since I found it.'

Cartwright followed her into the kitchen. 'Was there a burglary here?' he asked, looking at the rubbish on the floor. 'Looks like the foxes have been at it,' he added.

'Look,' commanded Lena, pointing at the note. 'I left it where it fell in case there is evidence. DNA evidence,' she elaborated, pleased with her knowledge.

Cartwright winced a little as he got down on one knee to examine the mess. 'Bit stiff from the run,' he said. 'What am I looking at?'

'That paper,' said Lena. 'Read what it says.'

'*You didn't deserve him. That's why I took him from you. Forever.*' He looked back at Lena. 'Whose house are we in?'

'Mine,' said Marsela. She'd come downstairs at the sound of the doorbell. 'What the hell is going on here?'

Cartwright stood up and turned to her.

'Oh,' said Marsela, even though he hadn't spoken. Her hands went to her hair and she began to detangle it with her fingers.

'I am PC Cartwright,' said Cartwright, holding out his hand to Marsela. She took it and smiled at him. The handshake lasted longer than Lena deemed necessary.

Lena produced the note Sarika had received. She handed it to him, forcing him to drop Marsela's hand to take it. Now she had evidence against Marsela, she felt justified in revealing Sarika's connection. 'Sarika received this,' she said.

'*You will pay for what you have done,*' Cartwright read.

He paused. 'Lena, what does Sarika have to do with Terry Tibbs?'

'They were dating.'

'Not another one,' said Marsela.

'But you didn't say,' said Cartwright.

Lena looked back at him but didn't reply. 'When did she get these notes?' asked Cartwright.

'This was put into her bag on the day of Terry's funeral,' said Lena. 'The first one came a few days before Terry died.'

'Why didn't you tell me about this?'

'I wanted to,' said Lena. 'But after what happened at the gallery . . . she was afraid . . .'

'Who the hell is Sarika?' interjected Marsela. She'd managed to wipe away some of the mascara under her eyes with her finger while Cartwright quizzed Lena.

'There are more too, back at our flat.'

He put the note down and turned to Lena. 'I don't understand.'

'We are in Terry Tibbs's house,' she said. 'This is Marsela Goga, Terry's girlfriend. This note was in her kitchen,' she said. She read the note again, aloud.

'*You didn't deserve him. That's why I took him from you. Forever.* It's different to the others,' she said. 'This note is a confession.'

★ ★ ★

131

Marsela came back down the stairs. Lena had wanted to drag her to the station in her dressing gown, but Cartwright had insisted that she be allowed to dress. She looked much better now, Lena noticed, dressed simply in jeans and a cashmere jumper. All traces of old make-up were gone and she'd painted her lips their trademark red. She looked fresh and pretty. Too pretty, Lena decided, looking with concern at Cartwright. He was watching Marsela come down the stairs.

'I'm ready,' she announced.

'I'd like to talk to you both here for a moment first,' said Cartwright. He and Lena had exchanged few words while Marsela had been upstairs, other than recriminations on both sides about why she hadn't brought the notes to him earlier. 'We need to establish a few facts before we bring this to official channels.' He turned to Marsela. 'I'm off duty,' he explained. 'And this isn't my case. I want to make sure we're not going to waste anyone's time.'

Lena wasn't standing for that. 'It is a confession note!' she said. 'To a recent murder. There is just one question.' She turned to Marsela. 'Why did you do it?'

'Hold on,' said Cartwright. 'There are more questions than that.'

'Anything I can do to help,' purred Marsela. 'I've spoken to DI Damper already of course,' she added. 'I'm not sure what you think I've done,' she said to Lena. 'But I'm more than happy to talk to this charming officer.' She smiled and Cartwright blushed.

'Terry was your onscreen partner,' said Cartwright, getting out his iPad and tapping in notes.

'And offscreen,' said Marsela. 'It was a reality show. The relationship was real. For me.'

'Okay,' said Cartwright. 'And . . .'

'Why did you not send that note?' said Lena, impatient. 'What was it doing in the bin?'

Marsela looked at them both.

'Lena, please,' said Cartwright. 'I need to establish the facts.'

'The note just appeared on my doorstep,' said Marsela. 'Kind of like you did,' she added, looking at Lena.

'So you didn't write the note?' asked Cartwright.

'Of course she did,' said Lena, feeling the tide turning.

'And you threw the note away?' said Cartwright. 'You weren't worried?'

'I get these things all the time,' said Marsela, with a shrug. 'Although usually people just post this rubbish on Twitter. They don't hand-deliver them.'

'We have to check her handwriting,' said Lena. 'Cartwright, make her write something.'

'I'd be happy to,' said Marsela. 'However, I know my rights,' she added. 'I'm a lawyer. But I've got no problem cooperating with this lovely policeman as long as it's informal.' She smiled at Cartwright. 'I'm not under arrest, am I, officer?'

'Of course not,' said Cartwright. 'But I would like to flag this to the officers in charge of the investigation,' said Cartwright. 'If that's all right with you, Mrs Tibbs?'

'Oh, Terry and I weren't married,' said Marsela. 'Call me Mars.'

'Perhaps you'd like to accompany me now, Mars, and get this sorted out. Lena, you need to fetch the other notes. And your cousin Sarika.'

Lena sat in the police waiting room, tapping her foot. It was busy on a Friday afternoon and an unsavoury-smelling man was sweating next to her. She tried politely to cover her nose with her scarf, but the stink was beginning to sneak through. Lena had been home and had the notes with her, still in their plastic bags. But she didn't have Sarika. The girl wasn't back from Penelope's house and Lena was glad. This was her chance to present all the information she'd gathered to the police. It would be much better without Sarika there to confuse matters.

Eventually Cartwright emerged into the waiting room and Lena leapt up. 'This is DI Damper's case,' said Cartwright. He'd got changed into his uniform but still looked slightly flushed. He stepped aside to reveal a frowning man in his forties. 'So I think it makes sense for you to relay your information directly to him. I really shouldn't be involved.'

'But can you be there too?' asked Lena. 'It would be better.'

'If you feel that is necessary,' said Damper, without a smile. 'Please, come through. We'll talk in the interview room.'

Lena was sick of this police station. It felt like nothing ever went her way here. It was where she wasn't taken seriously when her friend Timea was missing. It was where Sarika was arrested when she was accused of stealing a painting. She caught Cartwright's eye and felt better. It was also where he worked.

'Yes, it is necessary,' said Lena, belatedly. 'He is a very good policeman that I trust.'

'Good to hear,' replied Damper, unenthusiastically. They took their seats in the room.

'This is Lena Szarka,' said Cartwright. 'She is—'

'PC Gullins filled me in,' said Damper, his voice gruff. 'I know who you are.' Lena looked back at him. After Timea's murder, PC Gullins wasn't exactly her biggest fan, and now it seemed DI Damper wasn't either. At least she wasn't trying to be a reality star, she thought. Popularity had never been her strong suit.

'I have information about Terry Tibbs's death,' she told them. 'I found the note that Marsela wrote, but there is more that I need to tell you. Much more.' DI Damper raised an eyebrow, pushed a button on the tape recorder and announced the time, date and attendees for its benefit.

'What was your relationship to Mr Tibbs?' he began.

'He was dating my cousin, Sarika Toth. They both received threatening notes, like the one that was in Marsela's rubbish.'

'And Sarika has not spoken to the police, or raised any concerns?'

'She was scared,' said Lena. 'I think that Marsela has been threatening her, and might be involved in Terry's death.'

'Not another one,' said DI Damper, rolling his eyes. 'The number of calls we've had from people who've watched the show and think Marsela was within her rights to murder him. Only equalled by the number who suspect Jack. Reality telly should be prosecuted for creating a public nuisance.' He started to his feet.

'Let's hear what Lena has to say,' said Cartwright, stepping in. He smiled at Lena. 'She has helped the police before.'

Lena thought that was rather an understatement, after the two cases she had solved for them, but at least Cartwright was trying to help. Damper sat down. 'Go on,' he said. 'But I don't want to hear anything about *N1 Angels.*'

'Of course not,' she said. Lena took another breath and tried to ignore Damper's bored expression. She'd be as factual as she could and keep things straight for them. It was all she could do. 'On Tuesday the fifth of February, I found a note to Terry in his bar, N1 Demons. It said "You've hurt me so much Terry. Now I will hurt you." As Terry had died only days earlier, this made me suspicious.'

'Do you have this note?' interjected Damper.

'Unfortunately it was destroyed by Terry's uncle, Barry Tibbs,' replied Lena. 'He threw it in to the fire pit at the bar without reading it.' Cartwright raised an eyebrow and made a note but Damper continued to look unimpressed.

'So I did a few more investigations,' continued Lena. 'On Thursday the seventh of February I met with the cleaner who found Terry's body. She told me that there might have been two glasses and one might have had lipstick on it.'

'Might?' queried Damper. 'And that is not what she told us.'

Lena pressed on. 'The receptionist at the hotel, Maria Popescu, told me that Terry did not check in alone that evening. He had a woman with him.'

'Again, not what she told us. What did this woman look like?'

'Maria could not say,' confessed Lena. She hurried to continue, realising that was the weak part of her story. 'And then I discovered that Marsela was not at the party at Macaques when she said she was. I spoke to the barmaid, Ana, who told me that she left before two a.m. And I read online that the murder happened between one a.m. and four a.m. It would take twenty minutes in a taxi at that time of night to get from Chelsea to Angel,' she continued. 'Half an hour maximum.'

Damper smiled at her. 'I have multiple witnesses, some of the UK's most esteemed celebrities, who say she was there till four a.m.,' he answered. 'Are you telling me they are lying?'

'I am telling you they were too drunk to know what time it was,' replied Lena. 'My source was rock-cold sober,' she added.

'That's a good point,' said Cartwright. 'Sir, bar staff are usually reliable witnesses.'

'The bar was busy,' snapped Damper. 'And this is my case. Now, I understand that your cousin Sarika was involved with Mr Tibbs. But she is not here?'

'She is working,' said Lena. 'But here are the notes.' She laid them out with a flourish on the table. It felt good to share them finally with the police, like she'd wanted to from the start. 'I have kept them in plastic bags to preserve fingerprints,' she told them. Lena sat back to watch their reactions. Cartwright read the notes with interest. Damper frowned.

Lena told them when each note was received, but hesitated to mention the blue cheese pesto. She was already feeling that Damper was not taking her seriously. 'Like I said,' she continued, 'it looks as if Terry was with a woman in his hotel room when he died. Marsela lied about her alibi. Terry received very similar notes to my cousin, including threats, and he is dead. I think that whoever sent those notes could have killed him and plans to harm my cousin. And today I discovered one of the notes in Marsela Goga's bin.' Lena paused for a moment. 'She is the writer,' she told them. 'And perhaps she was involved in Terry's death as well.'

'We need to speak to your cousin,' said Damper. 'It sounds like she should have come forward a long time ago.'

'But you will arrest Marsela?'

'Thank you for your time,' said Damper, getting to his feet. 'We'll be in touch if we need anything more.'

Lena turned the key in the lock. Sarika was back, and sitting on the sofa wiping her eyes. 'I was watching old episodes of *N1 Angels*,' she told Lena. 'Look how beautiful Terry was.'

Lena looked. 'What's going on in this episode?' she asked.

'This is the episode where Terry comes back from Ibiza and discovers Jack and Marsela having dinner together,' Sarika said. 'He's fuming. At the end of the episode, Raz reveals that Terry had a threesome in Ibiza and Marsela throws her drink at him.'

'Sounds eventful,' said Lena.

Sarika blew her nose. 'It is a good show,' she agreed.

Lena thought for a moment, wondering how to tell Sarika what had happened. 'I think I know who sent the note,' she said. 'I found one in Marsela's rubbish.'

'She's been writing the notes? She's the one threatening me? I knew it.'

'That's not been confirmed yet,' admitted Lena. 'She claims she just received the note. She is at the police station now.'

Sarika pressed pause on the remote and turned to Lena, eyes expectant. 'What did it say?'

'Same kind of thing as yours,' she said.

'That is great,' said Sarika. 'Either they've found the culprit and can sort it out, or at worst they have the clue and I don't need to be involved.'

'Not exactly,' said Lena, looking to the freeze-frame on the television. Terry was staring back at them mid-shout, his brow furrowed and his mouth wide with anger. He reminded Lena of a perch she'd caught at Lake Balaton on a family holiday years ago.

'You gave PC Cartwright my notes too, didn't you?' said Sarika, getting to her feet. 'Lena, how could you?' She left the living room and went into her bedroom. Lena followed her. She was kneeling down by the bed, tugging a dusty suitcase out from under it.

'You cannot run away,' said Lena. 'Where would you go?'

'I'll hide out until the flights to Debrecen open again.'

'You cannot go. Not now. The police want to speak to you.'

'I'm not going back to prison,' replied Sarika. She flung open the suitcase and screamed.

A large spider was scuttling towards her, wakened from its slumber. Sarika leapt backwards. Lena closed the suitcase, trapping the spider inside.

'Do not go,' said Lena. 'The only thing that will make you a real suspect is if you disappear again. Stay here and help the police. Help them find out what really happened to Terry. Marsela is in custody now. She cannot hurt you.'

She looked at her cousin, whose eyes remained fixed on the closed suitcase. 'It is what Terry would have wanted,' she continued, determined that her cousin must not flee and incriminate herself. 'You owe it to him.'

Finally Sarika's eyes met hers. 'Okay,' she conceded. 'I will stay for Terry. And I will go to the police tomorrow. But on one condition.'

Lena smiled at her cousin. 'Do not worry,' she said. 'I will get rid of the spider.'

CHAPTER 14

It was the kind of Saturday designed for staying inside, thought Lena. It was a pity the police didn't agree. The rain was fierce, but the wind had already mangled the umbrella Lena had been holding over herself and Sarika and they'd had to abandon it in a bin. Lena clutched the base of her hood under her chin: the gusts were even trying to rip that from her.

'What will the police ask me?' asked Sarika, for the umpteenth time. 'What do they think I have done?'

'It is routine,' replied Lena. 'You were important to Terry,' she added, generously. 'So they need to see what you know.'

'They didn't know I had anything to do with Terry until you got involved,' said Sarika. 'Now what is going to happen?'

Lena pulled her hood tighter around her face, as if to insulate her from Sarika's worries. 'It is not a reason to be upset,' she said. 'Because you got the note you are involved.' She peered round her hood and caught Sarika's expression of fear. 'Involved,' she said again. 'In danger maybe. But not a suspect.' She pushed open the police-station door and felt a welcome blast of warm air.

DI Damper led Sarika away and Lena leaned back in the plastic chair, affixed to the floor to stop it being used as a weapon. She breathed in the warm air and smelt the rainwater evaporating from her coat. Even the rain smelt different in London to that in her village back home. More like traffic, she decided. And less like pigs.

'I'm sorry Lena, I'm not allowed to talk about it,' said Cartwright. They had nipped out to grab a hot drink and were queuing in the café across the road while Sarika spoke to Damper. 'It's an open investigation.'

'You helped with Timea.'

'I was assigned to that case,' countered Cartwright. 'That was different.' They reached the front of the line and Cartwright ordered an Earl Grey. 'Hot chocolate?' he offered.

'Okay,' said Lena, feeling the need for some comfort.

'But I have looked into that text message you received,' said Cartwright, handing Lena her drink. She took the paper cup and sipped, burning her mouth. 'Dead end I'm afraid. It was an unregistered pay-as-you-go phone. We can't trace it.'

Lena thought for a moment, her mind still on Sarika. 'You always say that the partner is the most likely person to murder someone.'

'Of course,' he replied. 'Forty-four per cent of women who are murdered are killed by a current or ex-lover. ' He took a sip of his own drink. 'Ouch,' he said. 'This tea is hotter than molten lava. Let's head back.'

They stepped into the cold day, the rain and wind still battling it out to create more misery. 'So statistically,' said Lena, 'Marsela is the most likely suspect, if it was murder?'

'Only six per cent of male murder victims are killed by their partners,' said Cartwright. 'Very different statistics. And we do not know that it was murder.'

They hurried back into the shelter of the police station. 'At least tell me one thing,' said Lena. 'Did Marsela's handwriting match the notes?'

Cartwright looked around. 'No,' he said quietly. 'She didn't write them.'

Lena could barely believe it. 'But her alibi? She lied.'

'And it turns out that the alibi for Marsela Goga is absolutely watertight, unlike this police station,' he said, gesturing to a bucket in reception collecting water. 'The officers have interviewed the barmaid and she was mistaken. Marsela was definitely there all night.'

'No she was not,' said Lena, taking another sip of her hot chocolate and burning her tongue again. 'Talk to Ana.'

'The officers have spoken to Ana Horváth,' said Cartwright. 'And she was mistaken,' he repeated. 'The alibi really is solid.'

Lena tutted. 'The alibi is nonsense,' she said. 'I do not know why DI Damper is lying.' She thought. 'You could investigate him, see what he has to gain . . . ?'

'Lena, no,' he said, looking around him. 'I'm sorry Lena, I've told you all I can.'

The hot chocolate was just reaching drinkable temperature when Sarika came charging up to Lena, almost knocking it from her hands.

'We need to get out of here.'

Lena got up, grabbed her backpack, and Sarika bundled her out into the rain.

'What happened?' asked Lena, hurriedly doing up her coat again. She put her hood up and enjoyed its cosy insulation. Then she realised she couldn't hear Sarika's response. Reluctantly she pulled it back down and felt the rain assault her scalp.

'You had to meddle!' said Sarika. 'You had to get me involved.'

'You asked me to!' said Lena. 'You asked for my help.'

'Never again,' said Sarika. 'You make everything worse. And there goes our bus.' Both women watched it zoom past, spraying water from the kerbside over a small group of schoolchildren who squealed in objection.

'Come on,' said Lena. 'The next one will not be for half an hour. I will buy you a coffee.'

'You'll buy me a vodka and Coke,' replied Sarika. 'After what I have just been through.'

To Lena's dismay, Sarika led them to N1 Demons. She felt as if she was starting to be a regular there. She steeled herself for the assault of the thumping music when the door opened, but there was none. Sarika looked confused too. The lights were brighter than usual, so you could see where you were going. The banging of bass was replaced by the sound of couples munching on crisps and a group of men playing darts. 'It's busy,' remarked Sarika in surprise.

Barry grinned out at them from behind the bar. 'Ale is on tap now,' he said. 'None of that bottled cat's piss. I can't afford a refurb until the insurance money comes through, but I've brought in an old sofa and put it where those daft stools were, if you ladies would like a comfy seat? No cocktails fancier than a G&T, and we've got cheese and onion crisps instead of wasabi peas.' He smiled again, looking satisfied. 'The devil's own food, wasabi peas,' he said. 'Why turn an innocent pea into a torture device like that? The Japanese have no business making snacks.'

Sarika sank into the sofa without a word of objection and Lena bought her a vodka and Coke and herself a coffee. 'Tell me what happened,' said Lena, handing Sarika her drink. 'What went wrong at the police station?'

'I told them all about how happy Terry and I were together,' began Sarika. 'How we were boyfriend and girlfriend and that I thought he was about to tell me he loved me.' Lena took a sip of coffee in an attempt to mask her eye roll. 'The officer seemed very interested, so I told him how we were meant to meet on Sunday evening, but that Terry didn't show up. He was even more interested in the night before. You remember? We watched that film and then I went to bed. He was very interested in the fact I was in bed, alone, the night Terry died.' Lena looked up, starting to worry.

'What did they say about Marsela?' she asked, nerves seeping into her voice.

'He was also interested in my criminal record,' continued Sarika. 'You remember, that time I was arrested for shoplifting when I was a teenager? Well, he seemed very excited about that.'

'And Marsela?' pushed Lena.

'Of course they couldn't pin the stolen painting on me, here in London,' said Sarika. 'But they knew that I'd gone missing for a while. And they were very interested in why I hadn't come forward before, when I received the notes. Suspicious, they called it. Uncooperative.'

'Another?' Lena heard Barry call out.

'No,' she said.

'Yes,' said Sarika.

'I'll bring it over,' said Barry.

'So that means . . .' began Lena.

'They know all about my past, about me and Terry, and they know I have no alibi. This is all your fault, Lena. If you'd let me keep quiet they wouldn't even know I existed. Now they are poking around in my life. Again.'

Lena hardly felt that was fair, but she did feel sympathy welling up inside her for her young cousin. It was bad enough when she'd been accused of stealing a painting the previous summer. Now to have even a hint of suspicion on her for Terry's death? It was too much.

'But what about the notes you received? The threats?'

'They didn't seem very interested, certainly not concerned. Maybe I should just get away. They told me not to leave the country, but I saw this morning that the storm over Debrecen has passed – it's a sign. I will book my flight.'

'You must not go. They will think you have something to hide.'

'You are the one who made me go before!'

'That was different,' said Lena. 'Give me a few more days,' she pleaded. 'I will find out the truth. In the meantime, you cannot stay. Whoever is threatening you knows you live here.'

'You just told me not to leave.'

Lena thought. 'You cannot leave the country but you must go somewhere. Perhaps you can stay with Lucia for a few days?'

'And Kat?' spat Sarika. 'I would rather take my chances with the note writer.'

Lena thought. She was sure Mrs Kingston would take Sarika in, but it was too much to ask of the old lady. She thought of her bank balance. There was not much there after she'd paid for Sarika's last flight home, but there was some. 'You must stay in a hotel,' said Lena. Sarika grinned at her. 'A cheap one,' she warned. 'And you must be careful.'

CHAPTER 15

'I have to say, I agree with the police,' said Mrs Kingston, as Lena cleaned for her that afternoon. 'I can't believe Marsela would do something like that.'

'You do not know her,' said Lena. She passed Mrs Kingston her cup of tea and bent down to collect the scraps of carrot that Jasper the rabbit had abandoned.

'I do know her.'

'You have never met!' said Lena. 'All you know is what the show wants you to.'

'I may be old,' replied Mrs Kingston. 'But I'm not an idiot. I know that *N1 Angels* is not completely real. But I have watched every episode. I know what she is like. I know that she would not threaten anyone. She is clever and she is driven but she is not violent. It's not her style.'

'I think she is hiding something,' said Lena. 'She is too perfect.'

'The only mystery is why Terry went off her,' said Mrs Kingston.

Lena stopped picking up the carrot scraps and looked at her. 'That is a good question,' she said. 'Why?'

'The show never really explains it,' said Mrs Kingston. 'It looks like Terry just got bored. Men do that.'

Lena nodded her agreement, but at the same time found herself thinking. Could there be more to it? She remembered something

Irina, Lucia's assistant chef, had said. 'Apparently Marsela knows Kat,' she said.

'Kat?' said Mrs Kingston. 'Isn't she Sarika's old flatmate?'

'Yes,' replied Lena. 'Until Sarika stole Kat's boyfriend. She lives with Lucia.'

'She worked on an internet sex chat room, if my memory serves me right. How would someone like that know Marsela?'

'That is what I will find out,' said Lena. She picked up the carrots again and carried them into the kitchen, with Jasper trailing hopefully behind her.

'At the beginning of series one,' said Mrs Kingston, her voice carrying to the kitchen, 'Marsela was with Jack. And whenever she and Terry split up, he was the one she would go to for comfort.'

'And they went upstairs together after the funeral,' said Lena, coming back to the living room, the rabbit hopping along after her. She thought a moment. 'Do you think they could have had an affair?'

'If Marsela cheated on Terry, that would certainly explain his change of behaviour,' said Mrs Kingston. 'And to be honest, I've never really warmed to Jack. He was always boasting about that investment management business of his. He liked to rub how much money he had in people's faces. I'm surprised Marsela was interested in him at all. But then she did love Terry too. There's no accounting for taste.'

'I wonder if they are together now,' said Lena. 'If when Terry died, Jack finally got what he wanted.'

'Ah, you're coming round to Jack as a suspect!' surmised Mrs Kingston. 'You know I've always been suspicious of him. I expect I can find out if they are together.' She typed something into her keyboard. 'I remember when the internet was invented,' she added. 'I was already well into my career. The first time I "dialled up" as they used to call it, I thought that this internet thing would never take off. So slow. And so much information no one cared about. Full of chat rooms with lonely people scattered all over the world, spelling badly and swearing at each other.' She chuckled. 'How wrong I was. We'd have to rely on library archives in the old days, but now everything is at your fingertips.'

'What have you found?' asked Lena, feeling concern for her friend. It wasn't like Mrs Kingston to ramble like this.

The old lady turned the laptop so Lena could see. 'There are plenty of pictures of the two of them together,' she said. 'Which is what you'd expect; after all, they used to date. But here,' she said, typing again. 'I've limited the date range to after Terry's death. Look, there is one evening that they went out together.' Mrs Kingston pointed to a series of photos clearly taken on one night. Marsela was wearing black and Jack was staring into her eyes. 'That seems pretty cosy,' she added. 'No kissing shots though. And oh, look at that one – he's not Jack. She's out with what *Internet Star Spies* dubs 'A Mystery Hunk'.

Lena looked. She shut her eyes then opened them again. There was no mistaking it. That was Cartwright.

Cartwright had never met Mrs Kingston, and Lena couldn't bring herself to tell the old lady it was him. 'Let me have a look,' she said, grabbing the machine.

She studied the picture. Cartwright and Marsela were walking side by side down an Islington street in the daytime. They were looking at each other and laughing, clearly sharing a joke. She looked more closely and smiled. Cartwright was wearing his running clothes, and she recognised Marsela's outfit too. This was no date. It was from yesterday: when Cartwright took Marsela to the police station.

'What's wrong?' asked Mrs Kingston. 'You've gone very quiet.'

'Nothing,' replied Lena. 'That is not romantic.'

'It certainly looks like there's some chemistry there to me,' said Mrs Kingston. 'Look at the way he's looking at her . . .'

'No,' barked Lena, too quickly. 'Okay,' she continued, collecting herself. 'I will investigate Jack and Marsela more to see what is happening with them. But what about the other girls I met at the funeral? There must be a way to find out more about them.'

Mrs Kingston looked thoughtful. Lena glanced back at the screen, then flicked the laptop closed. 'They already think you are a journalist, correct?'

'That is what I told them,' said Lena.

'Then you have a perfect excuse to ask them whatever questions you want,' said Mrs Kingston.

'But I know nothing about how to do an interview,' said Lena. 'Or show business.'

'I'm afraid I can't go with you,' said Mrs Kingston. 'It just wouldn't be believable. There're not many showbiz reporters who match my demographic, unfortunately. Do you know anyone else who could help? You just need someone to add legitimacy so they don't suspect you. Then you can quiz them about their movements on the night that Terry died.'

Lena smiled. She knew the perfect person.

'When you called for a date I didn't think you'd be inviting other women along too,' said Raz. It was Sunday lunchtime and they were sitting in a bustling N1 Demons. 'Not that I'm complaining.' He winked at her.

'You understand this is not a date,' said Lena. 'We are working.'

'Sure, sure,' said Raz. 'You told me. You think a fit bird knocked off Terry and is going to get Sarika next.'

'Maybe,' she replied.

'You want to pretend to be a showbiz journo and I'm here to help. Kind of like your knight in shining armour,' he added.

'Okay,' conceded Lena, glad he understood the plan at least. 'And we want to find out how well these women know Terry and what they were doing on Saturday the second of February between one a.m. and four a.m.'

'When Terry died.'

'Exactly,' said Lena.

'Show me their cards again.' Lena handed them over. Livs was Olivia Winslow; Becs was Rebecca Scott. Both stated their profession as 'Model/Actress'.

'I saw them at the funeral,' said Raz. 'That Livs girl had great . . . eyes. I think I've seen her around before as well. Not sure where.'

'You do not remember when Terry dated them?' she asked.

'I doubt if Terry remembered,' said Raz. 'Dated is probably not the right word. Shagged after a night out, I expect. And they've been dining out on it ever since.'

Lena couldn't help but shake her head a little at that. She knew she was a bit old-fashioned, but she couldn't imagine wanting to share her bed with a man she hardly knew. And certainly not wanting to become famous for it.

'I'm not like that, you know,' said Raz, looking at her earnestly. 'Don't get me wrong, I've had my fun. But I respect women. Strong women, that is, like you. I'm not looking for a one-night thing.'

Lena wasn't listening. 'There they are,' she said. Raz turned to look. They were more flamboyantly dressed today than they had been at the funeral. Livs was wearing a fitted short red dress with stiletto boots that came over her knees. Becs had opted for a leopard-print jumpsuit with a plunging neckline and strappy sandals. They probably would have fitted in well with the old-style, dark and noisy N1 Demons when Terry was in charge, but with the new relaxed decor they looked dissonant, like peacocks strutting through the Blackwall Tunnel.

'Raz,' shrieked Livs, grabbing him in a hug that suggested they had known each other for years. 'I love you on *N1 Angels*. You're one hundred per cent my fave.'

'After Terry,' corrected Becs, doing something with her hands that vaguely resembled a cross over her ample bosom. 'May he RPI.'

Lena frowned. Even with her limited English, she was pretty sure it was RIP.

'Of course, after Terry,' said Livs, releasing Raz and enclosing Lena in a suffocating embrace. 'Thank you so much for calling.' She looked around. 'Where is the photographer?'

'I am doing a written interview,' said Lena.

'But you need a picture,' said Livs. 'Or what's the point?'

'I've sent her one of me from my portfolio,' said Raz. 'She wants something sexy but sad.'

'That is right,' said Lena, glad she had brought Raz along. 'No smiling.'

Livs looked crestfallen. 'I'm always smiling,' she said. 'It shows off my cheek fillers.'

'A pout maybe?' suggested Raz. Livs grinned at him.

'That is sorted out then,' said Lena, keen to move the conversation on. 'I am interviewing the three of you about your feelings on the death of Terry Tibbs.'

'Devastated,' said Becs. Lena scribbled down the word in her notebook. She'd wiped the dog slobber from it, but it still didn't smell as fresh as it used to.

'Heartbroken,' added Livs. 'One hundred per cent.'

'I'll miss him down the gym,' said Raz.

'Excellent,' said Lena, still writing. She hoped people could muster up more genuine sadness when she passed away. 'Now, can each of you tell me about your relationship with Terry?'

'Love of my life,' said Becs, before Livs could get a word in. 'That night we spent together after the party at Cleopatra's Rug was magic. The first time was over pretty quick, I think he was too excited. But then the second, my, he knew where my hotspots were, if you know what I mean. And that tongue of his . . .'

'I do not need those details,' said Lena, quickly. 'It is not that kind of article.'

Becs laughed. 'You should spice it up a bit,' she said. 'It's what the readers want.'

'I think I know what my readers want,' said Lena, stiffly. 'And you?' she said, turning to Livs. 'What was your relationship?'

'Same,' said Livs. 'He was a god. I can't believe he's gone. I'm heartbroken.'

'We were good mates,' added Raz. 'Top bloke. Great in the gym. Could dead-lift a hundred kilos, no problem.'

Lena was still scribbling what Livs and Becs had told her. Both had spent one night with Terry and, despite their protestations, didn't seem to know him that well. She couldn't imagine either bothering to write Sarika those notes, let alone murder Terry through jealousy. Still, appearances could be deceptive. She needed to be thorough.

'And I expect you can all remember what you were doing the night that Terry Tibbs passed away?' she said. Livs and Becs looked at her blankly. 'It was the second of February,' she said. 'Late at night. It was two weeks ago yesterday.'

'I'll never forget it,' said Becs. 'I was in Tenerife filming *Lust Battle*.'

'You got on that?' interjected Raz. 'Congrats.' Lena just listened. She'd ask Mrs Kingston to look it up later.

'And I was doing a guest appearance on *Maid in Manchester*,' said Livs. 'I'm one of the girls dancing in the nightclub, then I catch Gary the barman's eye and go home with him.'

Raz nodded respectfully. 'You girls are getting good gigs,' he said, impressed. 'I was at home getting my beauty sleep.'

'Your skin looks great,' commented Livs, flashing him the smile she was so proud of.

'Thanks,' said Raz. 'It's the kale smoothies.'

'I have most of what I need now,' said Lena. 'One more thing. Is there anyone else close to Terry who I should speak to, that you know of? Marsela, obviously. But maybe your Pakistani friend from the funeral? She left without giving me her card.'

'You mean Rubilla,' said Livs. 'Sweet girl.'

'Not as close to him as us, obvs,' said Becs. 'But you could do. They had a one-night fling and it got papped. Lucky thing. Rubilla Patel she is.'

'Do you have her number?'

'No, she's funny about that. She's not even on Facebook.'

'Then how can I find her?'

'Oh she's around,' said Livs. 'We'll look out for her.'

Lena had to be satisfied with that, for now. Her curiosity about this girl was aroused. 'Thank you for your time,' she said. 'You can go now.'

'But we haven't even had a Pornstar Martini yet!' objected Livs.

'Barry doesn't do them here any more,' Raz told them regretfully. 'Let's go to Ladykillers. I'll get them in. Lena?'

'I have to write my article,' said Lena. 'Deadlines. Have fun.'

She watched them leave and then looked back at her notes. She didn't think she'd found her suspects here, but she'd check their alibis anyway. Just in case.

'I'm impressed you pulled it off, Lena,' said Mrs Kingston. Lena had popped over to update her that afternoon. 'Well done.'

'It was not so hard,' replied Lena, feeling pleased with herself nonetheless. 'It was good to have Raz there.'

'I still can't believe you know *Raz98gunsout* and haven't introduced me,' scolded Mrs Kingston. 'He's gorgeous.'

'I will bring him here,' she promised. 'After we have found Terry's murderer.'

'Right, let's get on with it then,' said Mrs Kingston. 'Livs checks out. Here she is, Olivia Winslow, on the cast list for *Lust Battle*. According to this, "Sexy singles battle in the sand to be crowned king and queen of this resort in paradise. Each week, the winners of the week's challenge couple up to spend a night in the tree bed together, with only the cameras for company. The girl the viewers vote as the lustiest will win £20,000, but will only keep the money if she can identify her partner in lust in a blind kissing competition."'

Lena rolled her eyes. 'Even I wouldn't watch that,' said Mrs Kingston. 'But filming only finished a week ago and it was shot on location in Tenerife. She would have been there on the day Terry died.'

'So she could not have committed a murder,' said Lena. 'That is a much better alibi than Marsela claims.'

'True,' said Mrs Kingston. 'Then Becs. I know the show she mentioned, and here she is. Rebecca Scott, appearing in *Maid in Manchester*, filmed when she said. You might like that show, Lena. It's not bad: they follow a group of waitresses, bartenders and cleaners around the city. They wait on everyone else until after their shifts, then they have crazy parties and sleep with each other.'

'So Becs couldn't have murdered Terry either,' said Lena, deciding to sell her television.

'No. Who is the other girl you mentioned? From the funeral.'

'Rubilla Patel,' said Lena. 'I have no other details.'

'That makes things tricky,' said Mrs Kingston. 'Any clues?'

'Livs told me she had one night with Terry and that it got . . .' Lena struggled to think of the word Livs had used. 'Papered?' she offered, tentatively.

'Papped?' suggested Mrs Kingston. Lena nodded. Mrs Kingston typed for a moment, then turned the screen to Lena. 'It's not a very good picture, but I think this must be her.'

Lena peered into the computer screen. She could see Terry in a tight embrace with a dark-haired girl outside what seemed to be a nightclub. She couldn't make out Rubilla's face, as her lips were locked with Terry's. 'Maybe,' she said.

Mrs Kingston groaned a little as she shifted in her seat so that they could both see the screen at once. 'Let's see if I can do any better,' she said. 'Ah, here you go. The morning after.'

This image was clearly Rubilla. Lena also recognised the main entrance to the Goswell Hotel. Rubilla was wearing a tight black dress and was barefoot, clutching her heels in her hands. She was looking directly into the camera. Terror filled her eyes. 'Yes,' said Lena. 'That is her.'

Mrs Kingston clicked on the image. 'It happened about three months ago,' said Mrs Kingston. 'Judging from the article. She was one of a string of girls Terry bedded, apparently.'

'Just before he met Sarika,' said Lena.

'Let's see if we can find anything else out about her,' said Mrs Kingston. 'She might have been filming with one of the other girls that night.' She began typing again. 'Oh,' she said.

'What?'

'That's her again, isn't it?'

Lena looked at a smiling girl in a sari. 'Yes,' she said.

'Are you sure?' she said. 'This link doesn't take you to a show-biz site.'

'Yes,' said Lena, leaning in. 'What is it?'

'She's missing,' said Mrs Kingston. 'This post is from her family. They are trying to track her down.'

CHAPTER 16

Lena rang the bell and waited. No answer. She fished in her back-pack for the keys to Mrs Ives's house. Lena put the key in the lock. It had been over a week since she'd last been here – the lady had cancelled her Thursday appointment.

'Mrs Ives,' she called, thinking she could be asleep, or too miserable to come to the door. There was no answer.

Lena paused. Her mind went back to Terry's body. Found by the cleaner.

She listened. There was a faint noise, an occasional pitter-patter, like mice tap-dancing. Or rats, nibbling a body. She stopped her-self. She was being ridiculous.

Lena went to the kitchen. 'Mrs Ives?' she said, looking at the woman in front of her.

Mrs Ives didn't look up, but was definitely alive. Her fingers hovered over a keyboard and she was hunched forwards over her breakfast bar, peering intently into a screen. She was wearing a tired nightgown, her hair was unbrushed and there were bags under her eyes. Occasionally her right hand reached out to grab a cup of coffee and put it to her lips.

'How long have you been here like this?' asked Lena, walking up to her and placing her hand gently on the woman's shoulder.

'Oh, Lena,' she said, looking briefly up. 'I didn't hear you come in. Put the kettle on for more coffee, will you?'

'I think you need sleep more than coffee,' said Lena, watching the woman's hands shake even as she typed. 'What are you doing?' She put the kettle on all the same.

Mrs Ives stopped what she was doing and looked at Lena, blinking. 'Maybe I have been here rather a long time,' she admitted, stretching her neck. It clicked in objection. 'I've been doing some research online. I've managed to hack Rupert's dating accounts – thanks to a few YouTube "How To" videos. That bastard.'

Lena came and stood behind her. 'What do you mean?' she said, looking at the screen. An attractive girl with heavy lipstick pouted back.

'He's been on Victoriamatthison.com,' she said. 'And Bienvenue.com. And hookupcentral and even the charmingly named fckbuddezislington,' she spat. 'And he's been chatting to these women. Screwing them too, no doubt.'

'You need more than a coffee,' said Lena. 'I will get you a brandy. Come, have a break.' Lena felt as though she should work in a bar, the amount of alcohol and sympathy she'd been dishing out recently. Men certainly seemed to have a detrimental effect on women's livers.

'No, I need my wits about me,' replied Mrs Ives. 'I've found my way into all those accounts, but I haven't got access to his text messages yet. There's one girl he's been chatting to more than the others online, some girl from Bienvenue. I can't even see a picture of her face; she's just posted a photo of her body in trashy underwear.'

Lena made her a strong coffee. 'I am sorry,' she said.

'Sounds like they were planning a trip, him and Wonderbra. Then it all stops, a few days before he disappeared: that's when they must have started texting and that's who he must be with. If only I'd activated the tracker on his phone, it would all be much easier.'

'You do not deserve this.'

'He's going to deserve what's coming to him,' said Mrs Ives. 'Ten grand has disappeared from our joint account. I bet that bought him quite a party.' She took the coffee and turned from the screen to look at Lena. 'It wasn't real,' she said, her voice distressed. 'I thought we were happy, living this wonderful life together, but it was all in my head. He wanted more and he wanted out. Why didn't he just say?'

'Maybe he did not want to hurt you,' said Lena. 'Because he loved you.'

'Yes, well, it doesn't look like it,' said Mrs Ives, her focus back on the screen. 'Let's see if I can hack into his Facebook Messenger. That's a good start.'

It had been a long time since Lena had been ice skating.

And yet here she was, wearing two pairs of socks, thick gloves and clutching her trainers in her hands, waiting in the queue for ice skates at the rather beautiful pop-up rink in Somerset House. All at Cartwright's invitation for his Monday afternoon off.

'We had ice-skating lessons at school,' Cartwright told her. 'There's nothing like it, for forgetting your problems. Gliding along the ice like a . . .' he thought a moment, '. . . duck on water,' he finished, somewhat lamely.

Lena laughed and exchanged her trainers for a mismatched pair of red and blue ice skates. They were not the elegant white boots she'd been hoping for, and were much heavier than she was expecting. Cartwright was already towering over her in his own skates, a fetching pair of sandy-coloured boots that he'd claimed to have owned for years. She settled down on a hard bench and struggled to pull the boots over her socks.

'There was no ice rink in the village,' Lena told him. 'But we used to go out on the frozen pond some winters. Until Tobias fell through the ice one year.'

'Oh,' said Cartwright. 'Was he okay?'

'Eventually,' said Lena. 'But he ruined it for the rest of us. I have not been on the ice since I was eight.' She looked at the rink. It hadn't been that hard then, and there were plenty of small children whizzing around today. She'd be fine.

'Of course if you ski then ice skating is easy,' said Cartwright. 'It's the same distribution of balance. You need to lean forwards, not back.'

Lena nodded. Of course she'd never been skiing in her life. She loved the Transylvanian hills in the summer, when the mountains were covered in flowers and you could trek for hours with only the birds, the cows and the odd mountain goat for company. But why anyone would choose to spend their holidays and hard-earned cash bombing head first down a mountain on cold slippery snow completely eluded her.

Finally, Lena managed to jam her foot into the boot. She smiled, already feeling victorious. The other foot went in much more easily and she tied her laces with aplomb. Cartwright helped her to her feet, and with only a small amount of wobbling on the rubbery flooring, they made their way to the ice.

Lena stood at the side for a moment, feeling the ground slip away from her. 'Come on, Lena,' said Cartwright, holding out his hands.

'I get my balance. One moment,' said Lena, clutching the sides. Cartwright glided off, looking as if he had been born on the ice. A small child also holding the side tugged at her trouser leg, wanting to get by. Lena let go of the side and pushed herself away a little, cursing the child under her breath. He had a lot less far to fall. Realising she could not reach the side and couldn't seem to get herself back, she promptly fell to the floor with a cold bump.

'Takes a while to get used to, doesn't it?' said Cartwright, skating up to her backwards. He reached his hands and Lena allowed him to pull her to standing. 'Let's go together,' he said. 'We can use each other for balance.'

It was much easier with Cartwright's hand in her own, realised Lena. He went slowly, pulling her along. She leaned forwards, occasionally lifting one foot to give herself a little push and a bit more speed. Finally taking her eyes off the ice, Lena allowed herself to look around and realised she was having fun.

'Look at that girl, she's amazing,' said Cartwright, gesturing to the middle of the ice. Lena looked. A short, pretty girl in a figure-hugging onesie was pirouetting in the centre of the rink. She stopped spinning and glided over to an uncomfortable older man, clutching the sides of the rink like Lena had been. 'No guesses who chose their date venue,' said Cartwright with a laugh.

Lena looked more closely at the girl as she whizzed past them. 'I know her,' she said. 'That's Irina.' The girl was already gone, back to showing off in the middle of the rink. 'She used to be Lucia's assistant chef,' said Lena. 'She's Russian,' she added.

'That explains it,' said Cartwright. 'Great skaters, the Russians. I still remember the routine Ekaterina Gordeeva and Sergei Grinkov did to win the figure-skating winter Olympics back in 1994. Stunning.'

A small child crashed into Lena's legs, sending both of them flying. Even Cartwright went over. The child began to cry and an indignant-looking mother stormed in, shot an angry glance at the two of them and rescued him from the ice. Lena sat a moment longer, feeling her trousers absorbing melting ice. Cartwright was on his feet again, and hauled her back up to standing. 'These children are a bit of a hazard,' he said. 'How about we take a break and grab a drink? There's something I want to tell you.'

★ ★ ★

Lena felt stiff already and blisters had formed on her feet. She didn't dare peel her socks off, certain they would take the skin off with them. So she did up her trainers loosely and took a sip of the mulled wine Cartwright handed her from the bar over-looking the rink, enjoying the feeling of sitting down on something that was not icy cold and very hard.

'It's Yasemin,' said Cartwright. 'I told you I had another lead?'

'Yes,' said Lena.

'I think we're going to get her this time,' he said. He looked around. 'I've had reliable information about another drugs deal. With the Albanians this time. And on the next sting, we'll have my source with us. Someone who can identify Yasemin without a shadow of a doubt, before we've even arrested her. Finally, things are looking up.'

'I am pleased for you,' said Lena, taking a warming sip of mulled wine. She considered telling Cartwright about the progress of her investigations, but decided against it. She wanted to see what more she could find out about Rubilla before she spoke to the police again.

'Did you clean there yesterday?' asked Sarika. 'He's a Monday client, right?'

They were walking past Mr Quincy's house: the house-husband who said he had gone back to South Africa to visit his sick mother-in-law. Sarika had her arm through Lena's. She'd received no more notes, had had no more hassle from the police and was enjoying her stay in the hotel. Lena was back in her good books.

'Not now,' said Lena. 'When I went there last week, Mr Quincy said he did not need me for a few months.'

'Good,' said Sarika. 'He always creeped me out.'

'I liked him,' said Lena. 'He was a very modern man, staying home looking after the children while Mrs Quincy went to work.'

'He was weird,' said Sarika, decisively. 'And I didn't like the way he always looked at my chest.'

'You think everyone fancies you,' said Lena, with a laugh. 'He was devoted to Mrs Quincy.'

'No he wasn't,' said Sarika. 'I saw his profile on a dating site. Bienvenue.com.'

Lena stopped in her tracks. 'Really?' she said. They both turned and looked at the house. 'I did not think that he was like that.'

'Well, he was,' said Sarika. 'You were wrong about someone, for once.'

'It was strange the way he cancelled me, all of a sudden,' said Lena, thinking. 'And he had that grocery delivery, right before they left.' She looked at the house again, then blinked and looked more closely. 'There is a light on,' said Lena. 'But they are meant to be abroad.'

'Maybe they left it on to stop burglars,' suggested Sarika. But Lena was already walking up to the house. She peered through the window.

'People are living here,' she said. 'There is fresh fruit in the bowl.'

Sarika laughed. 'He was just trying to get rid of you, Lena,' she said. 'The modern man you liked so much.'

Lena scowled. 'Why would he lie?'

'You are always saying that most men are liars,' said Sarika, enjoying this a little too much for Lena's liking.

'Perhaps he had less money to spend,' said Lena. She thought a moment. 'Something else. Normally they get their groceries from Ocado, but this last time the delivery was Morrisons. Perhaps he is economising.'

'That wife of his is loaded,' said Sarika. 'She works in the City and gives him an allowance.'

'Maybe you are right,' conceded Lena. 'He is up to something.

161

Perhaps he is not so lovely, after all.' She shot the house another look as they walked past. She couldn't make sense of it.

Sarika had gone to another cleaning job, and Lena stood outside the Patel house in Barnes. It was a semi-detached 1930s building, like so many in London. For once, she wasn't pretending to be a cleaner as she went to meet them. She'd phoned ahead to arrange. The Patels wanted to know that their daughter was okay and Lena knew that, on the day of the funeral, she was. Lena smiled for a moment. How much she would have liked that information when Timea was missing. Of course, it didn't happen.

She rang the doorbell. A glamorous woman in a sari opened it. The spicy scent of curry lingered in the air. 'You have more news on my daughter?' she said, holding her hand and pressing it a moment. 'I am Sunita Patel, her mother. Come in.'

Lena entered. The carpet felt soft and deep beneath her feet. She reached out and touched the sumptuous wall, discovering it to be covered in a silky wallpaper. She followed Sunita through to a large open-plan lounge, furnished with a leather three-piece suite and an elaborate mahogany shelf system, dominated by a flat-screen television.

Sunita grabbed one of the many framed photographs that lived on the mantelpiece. 'Here, this is my Rubilla. You saw her? When? How was she? Will she come home?'

'Don't pester her.' A man somewhat older than Sunita lumbered in from the next room. 'Get me a drink, woman,' he said to his wife, sinking into the leather sofa.

'Get it yourself,' said Sunita. 'Sorry about my husband, Lena. He always tries to make me get him things when we have company. Only chance he gets. But he makes a good point. Would you like tea?'

'No,' said Lena. 'Thank you.'

'See,' said Sunita. 'She doesn't want anything. So be quiet, Bilal.' He harrumphed in reply and turned the television on. Sunita snatched the remote and turned it off again. 'Don't pretend not to be interested in where you daughter is,' she said. 'You know you miss her too.'

'She's brought shame on our family,' he replied. He reached for the remote again but Sunita had hidden it within the folds of her sari.

'A moment of madness,' said Sunita. 'That is all. We can forgive her. Did she say when she was coming home?'

'You are her friend?' asked Bilal, before Lena could respond. 'We haven't met you before. She never spoke about you.'

'We are new friends,' replied Lena. 'How long has she been missing?' She wanted to get a sense of whether Rubilla might have an alibi as well.

'We haven't seen our girl for three months,' said Sunita. 'We reported it to the police, of course, when she first went, but then she started calling, every now and again, to let us know that she is safe.'

'Do you know why she left?' asked Lena.

'It was after those terrible photographs.'

'When she spent the night with Terry?' asked Lena. Sunita nodded. 'I saw her at Terry's funeral,' added Lena. 'That was six days ago and she was okay then. Upset for Terry, but okay.'

Even Bilal smiled at that news. 'It is good,' he said, his face softer. His wife took his hand. He frowned. 'But why would she go to the funeral after that man ruined her life?'

'Ruined her life?' repeated Lena.

'Ruined her reputation,' explained Sunita.

'And her marriage,' continued Bilal.

Lena looked at them in surprise. 'Rubilla was married?' she asked.

'You can't be much of a friend if you don't know that,' said Bilal.

'Her marriage was a joke,' said Sunita. 'No wonder she doesn't talk about it. She doesn't even use her married name any more.'

'Her wedding cost me fifty thousand pounds,' interjected Bilal. 'My life savings. Over nine hundred guests.'

'And you declared it to be the happiest three days of your life,' snapped Sunita. 'And worth every penny. She never asked for a fancy wedding, so stop complaining.'

'Who was her husband?' asked Lena. Could this be another suspect? 'She did not mention him.'

'I'm not surprised,' said Sunita. 'It was not a happy marriage.' She turned to her husband. 'I don't know what I was thinking, letting you marry her to that man.' She sounded as if she was starting an argument they'd had many times before.

'Vikram is from a good family,' replied Bilal. 'He was a good match for her.'

'I should have insisted on vetting him myself, not trusting that mother of yours to just send him over from Pakistan like that.' She turned back to Lena. 'Rubilla was always so lonely,' she explained. 'She had a good job in an office and she worked hard, but she had no luck with men. She had boyfriend after boyfriend, but none of them nice Muslim boys. We thought we were doing the right thing, finding her a good husband to settle down with. My marriage was arranged and, despite how it looks, we've been pretty happy.'

'We make the best of it,' said Bilal, with a smile. Sunita threw the remote at him with a laugh.

'Rubilla agreed, though now I think it was just to please us. But Vikram seemed such a nice boy. He'd been to university in Lahore and had a good job at Unilever back in Pakistan. His family have a business here, a restaurant where he could work while he looked for another job like the one he had left. It all made sense. They met, seemed to get on and the wedding went ahead.'

'Nine hundred guests,' muttered Bilal. 'The shame.'

'But then it all went wrong. Vikram was not the modern man we'd been led to believe. He did not like Rubilla working at all, and she loved her job. His views on women were, as it turned out, rather backwards.'

'He was fine,' insisted Bilal. 'He liked cricket.'

'If he was fine our daughter wouldn't have been driven to an affair with a TV star and run away and we wouldn't be meeting strangers in our house to find out how she is,' snapped his wife. 'Vikram tried to get her to quit her job; it seemed he expected her to stay at home cleaning and making him samosas all day. She was desperately unhappy. He was miserable too; I think he took it out on her that he couldn't find a job in London like the one he had back home. He was stuck waiting tables in the restaurant. I said to get a divorce but no one else in the family would hear of it. So here we are. No daughter.'

'Is she coming home?' asked Bilal.

'I do not know,' said Lena.

'What kind of friend are you?' he asked. 'Meeting at funerals and knowing nothing about her?' Suspicion was filling his face. 'How did you find us?'

'I saw online—' started Lena.

'Is it money you're after?' asked Bilal, looking at her in a way that made Lena feel like dirt. 'Or are you another journalist?'

Sunita put a hand on her husband's arm. 'Bilal. She saw our daughter. She is telling us she is safe, or at least was safe six days ago. She did not have to do that.' She turned to Lena. 'Thank you,' she said.

'When I see her again I will ask her to get in touch,' said Lena.

'Tell her to come home,' said her father. 'We miss her.'

'Her husband,' began Lena. 'Where can I find him? In case she wants to talk to him?'

'Where he always is,' said Bilal. 'Lahore Spice on Blackstock Road.'

'We will not make her go back to that man,' said Sunita, giving Bilal a stern look. 'We just want her to be safe. And home.'

Lena walked back to the bus stop, lost in thought. She was adding up in her head all the things that had happened recently. Terry's death. Sarika threatened. The warning texts. The fire in her flat. The suspects. The note in Marsela's bin. The runaway.

She still felt suspicious of Marsela: it seemed to her that she must be hiding something. Were the notes really from her after all? Perhaps she had disguised her handwriting. But Marsela had been so convincing when she'd said that she'd received the note too – even the police believed her. Surely she wasn't capable of that level of deception?

Lena stopped herself. If anyone was capable of deception it would be Marsela. She was clever: a trained lawyer. Now she was a reality TV actress, blurring the lines between what is real and what is fake for a living.

The bus arrived just as Lena got to the stop. She jumped on board. She'd take down Livs and Becs from her suspect board when she got home; their alibis were sound. But she would leave Rubilla. She couldn't help but hope that Rubilla was not guilty. It would devastate her parents.

Lena stopped herself again. There were few parents who wouldn't be devastated by their child committing a crime. Just because she'd met these ones didn't make Rubilla any less likely a suspect. She'd been miserable in her marriage, had a fling with Terry that had caused public shame, and now she was missing. She had to be a suspect – for the notes, and perhaps for the murder too.

She should consider the husband as well. If he was the traditional Pakistani man the Patels had told her about, the shame of his wife cheating on him could be unbearable. But enough to drive him to kill Terry? She'd pay Lahore Spice a visit and see what else she could find out.

Then there was Jack. She still knew very little about him, other than Mrs Kingston's impressions from the show. He was some kind of investment guru. But more importantly, he was – if *N1 Angels* was to be believed – in love with Marsela. Did he have an alibi for that evening? It was unlikely that he'd written the notes – and even less likely he'd sent one to Marsela. Or was it? Was he interfering in Terry's love life, like Terry had stolen Marsela from him? Lena didn't have the answers but she felt that he was definitely worth investigating.

Lena got off the bus, crossed to the centre of the road and waited on the pedestrian crossing at the middle. She stepped out. A van, from nowhere, screeched towards her. She jumped back. It was speeding and Lena felt a gust of air as it whizzed past, narrowly missing her. Her heart raced as she watched it disappear around a corner. It seemed like the van had been aiming straight for her.

CHAPTER 17

For once, Lena was pleased she'd made an effort to be nice to Veronika, one of her fellow cleaners at Prontaclean, her old agency. She had never liked her and had always felt that the girl was greedy; Veronika would pride herself on managing to do a five-hour job in three. It didn't matter to her that corners were left dusty; ovens unopened; cutlery drawers in disarray. She did the minimal amount she could get away with, so she could fit in more clients and make more money.

But when Lena opened her own agency, Veronika had come to her asking for work. At a higher rate, of course, for a reason Lena couldn't fathom. She'd politely put her off, claiming not enough work to go around yet. But she'd sworn to herself that that girl would never work for Lena's Cleaners.

Lena wasn't sure what it was that had stopped her from telling the girl what she really thought of her. There was something ruthless about Veronika that made Lena nervous. And also made her think that one day this cleaner could be powerful.

It wasn't today.

But she was useful. Lena had looked in more detail at Jack's website and discovered his office was in Angel Heights. That building was covered by her old agency; not much of a coincidence, as recently they'd won a contract for one of the largest serviced office companies in the borough. And Veronika worked at Angel Heights. She'd love it there, thought Lena. Offices were much better suited to her style of cleaning. It was no one's home; no one really cared how clean the place got as long as dirty mugs were collected and bins emptied.

Veronika was more than happy to give Lena one of her shifts, and didn't even ask why. Apparently there was a security guard she'd been wanting to spend time with for a while, and Lena's offer meant they finally had an evening free together.

Jack's office was on the second floor, but Lena had to clean the whole building. She decided that she would do as Veronika would, just this once. The bare minimum. Maybe a little extra dusting, she decided, and a quick vacuum. But nothing too flashy. She'd start in Jack's office and see what she could find out about him first. Mrs Kingston had found his website fishy. Was his business in trouble?

The second floor housed about twenty companies, as far as Lena could make out. Each was separated from the next with barriers of frosted glass, giving the whole place the feeling of being in a beehive. Lena found the sign for Jack Husky Capital and peered through the glass.

It was seven in the evening. A few businesses still had people sitting at their desks, peering into their screens. Jack's area was tiny and deserted. Lena stepped inside. Then outside again, to check the sign. This was the right place.

She stepped in again. There was a single desk and a leather swivel chair, still in its plastic wrap. A large cardboard box sat on the desk. She read the print on it and discovered it was a computer. Never unpacked. There was a small pile of unopened mail on the desk and a phone, its red light suggested unanswered voicemails.

Lena didn't really know what to expect from a small investment company, but she was thinking she'd find more than this. She peered into a neighbouring cubicle. A slight man in a suit was typing, but looked up and met her gaze. Lena took that as an invitation to enter his office.

'I'm still drinking my coffee,' the man told her. 'I'll put the cup in the kitchen when I'm done.'

'There are no cups next door,' Lena told him, unsure of the best way to start the conversation.

He grunted, and began typing again. Lena lingered. 'Has the company just moved in?' she asked.

'Nope,' he replied. 'It's been like that for months.'

'Does anyone do any work there?'

The man looked at her, then stretched his arms up and circled his wrists. Lena listened to them click. 'I've been here since seven a.m.,' he told her. 'An hour before the London markets open. That guy pops in once a week, collects his mail, listens to his messages and then sods off again. He hasn't even unpacked his bloody computer. But guess who's got more AUM?' Lena looked at him blankly. 'His assets under management,' the man explained. 'I've been doing this for ten years and have half what he's got. And I get results. Great results, sometimes. My fund is top quartile three years running. His fund barely meets inflation.' He picked up his coffee cup and took a swig. 'Just because he is on some pile-of-rubbish reality show, the investors come running. Well, they are a bunch of mugs.'

'It must be frustrating,' said Lena, keen to find out more.

'Damn right it is,' said the man. He leaned forwards in his chair. 'I'm not sure he even knows what a derivative is,' he said, with a laugh. Lena joined in, as if she were as familiar with derivatives as she was with Marigold gloves. 'Flaming buffoon,' he said. 'Still,' he leaned back again. 'People get the investment managers they deserve. They'd do better with a bank account.' He took another swig and held out his cup. 'I'm done with this now,' he told her. 'You take it. And would you mind wiping my desk? I spilled some mustard from my steak sandwich at lunch two weeks ago and there's still some residue.'

Lena obliged. What was Jack up to?

'He did it then,' said Sarika. 'He must have murdered my darling Terry.'

'Not so fast,' said Mrs Kingston. 'It is quite a leap from being a bad investment manager to being a murderer.'

Lena reached for another gingernut, pleased that she'd invited Sarika to clean for Mrs Kingston with her today. It gave the old lady someone else to talk to, and meant Lena didn't need to battle Sarika's wild assumptions on her own. And although she knew her cousin was safer in a hotel than staying with her, she always felt better when she could keep an eye on her.

'He doesn't even have a computer on his desk,' said Sarika. 'He is up to no good.'

'To be fair, he does have a computer,' said Lena. 'But it is still in the box.'

'That in itself is not too damning,' said Mrs Kingston. 'But he does have a motive.'

'Marsela,' said Lena. 'Marsela was with Terry and you told me that Jack loved her.'

'He did,' said Mrs Kingston.

'Marsela and Terry were not together,' objected Sarika, again. 'How many times? It's not real.'

'I think that was,' said Mrs Kingston. 'Did you even watch the show?'

'I sometimes fast-forward the bits without Terry,' admitted Sarika.

'So we have a possible motive,' said Lena. 'But I am not sure what his work situation has to do with it.'

171

Mrs Kingston dunked her biscuit in her tea and then pulled herself up to go to her computer. 'Something about his website didn't feel right,' she said. 'I'm going to send the link to one of my old colleagues who covered financial news. Perhaps he can help us with what's going on.'

'How does that get us any closer to finding out what happened to Terry?' complained Sarika.

Lena was inclined to agree. 'We see what they say,' she said, to be polite to Mrs Kingston. 'But I will talk to this Jack man as well. See if I can flush him down.'

'Out,' said Mrs Kingston, with a suppressed laugh.

'Exactly,' said Lena. 'Now Sarika, we have had enough coffee. It is time to clean for Mrs Kingston.'

'Oh you don't need to bother,' said the woman. 'It's really not that dirty.'

'It is not Lena's Cleaners clean,' replied Lena. 'We'll get to work. Sarika, think while you polish. Cleaning is the best time to solve crimes. It frees up your mind to new possibilities.'

'I think best drinking vodka and Coke,' said Sarika, hopefully. 'Everyone is different.'

'I think I have some vodka somewhere,' said Mrs Kingston. 'I certainly have gin.'

'We clean,' said Lena firmly. 'And we think.'

'Maybe we don't need to,' said Mrs Kingston.

'I do need to clean,' insisted Lena.

'No, we don't need to think,' said Mrs Kingston. 'Because I have a plan already.' She strained to stand up, then batted off Lena as she tried to help her. 'I don't think I'm up to it,' she said. 'But I can tell you how. Does Jack know what you look like? Either of you?'

'I saw him after the wake,' said Lena. 'But I don't think he even looked at me.'

172

'He wouldn't have noticed the staff,' said Mrs Kingston. 'Excellent. Time for my stint as an investigative journalist to be useful again.'

Sarika skipped off to go shopping straight after they'd hatched their plan. Lena hadn't seen Sarika so excited in a while, and was pleased that she was involving her in the investigation. She supposed, in a way, it was making Sarika feel empowered again, as though she had some control over what happened to her. She deserved it; life had been hard for her cousin recently.

Lena crossed Highbury Fields. Though it was still cold, Lena felt as if she could smell spring in the air. Crocuses were starting to spread their purple and white blossoms across the field, and she could see daffodil stems poking up hopefully through the grass. Lena carried on through Highbury Barn. She paused at Little Highness, thinking she could hear the distinctive shriek of her client's toddler Casper coming from the soft play. Another toddler she didn't recognise came charging up to the door and pressed his face to the glass like a suckerfish. Lena continued down the hill to Blackstock Road.

There was Lahore Spice. It had a red sign with gold lettering, and a poster in the window that promised all you could eat on a Sunday for £7.95. She could smell fried onions, garlic and spices from the street. Her ex, Tomek, would love it here, she decided, and wondered for a minute if he'd eaten there with his new girlfriend Emma.

Lena batted the thought away, pushed open the door and stepped inside. It was dark, with red carpets, sitar music and an even more intense smell of spices. It was early for dinner and there was only one couple inside, assiduously munching their way through a tower of poppadums.

A man approached her, his black hair slicked back. 'I am looking for Vikram,' she told him.

'And you have found him,' he said, flashing her a smile. 'To what do I owe this pleasure?'

'I have information about your wife,' she said. The smile faded from his lips.

'Come in the back.' Lena followed him to a small table at the back of the restaurant, on which stood an open bag of Bombay mix and a bottle of tonic water. 'What do you want?' he asked.

'I wanted to let you know that she is safe,' said Lena. 'I saw her, not long ago. I have told her parents already, but I thought I should tell you as well.'

'She spoke about me?' asked Vikram.

Lena wondered what to say. 'Of course,' she lied. 'You are her husband.'

'What did she tell you?'

Lena thought again. Really what she wanted was to find out his attitude to Terry, and what he was doing the night he was murdered. 'She is sorry for what she has done,' said Lena. 'With Terry Tibbs.'

Vikram laughed sharply. 'She had a good husband,' he said. 'From a good family. And she has thrown it all away.'

'Did you know Terry?' asked Lena, trying to sound innocent.

'I know his sort,' said Vikram. 'Taking advantage of weak women.'

'You must be furious,' said Lena.

Vikram looked at her, his face suspicious. 'What did Rubilla tell you? She's a liar.'

'Nothing,' said Lena, wishing Rubilla had told her something. There was a secret here. 'When did you last see your wife?'

'She's no wife of mine,' said Vikram. 'Not after what she has done.'

'Have you seen her since what happened?'

174

'I do not have to talk to you,' said Vikram. 'Coming here, to my uncle's restaurant, and throwing around accusations. I am an educated man and I have suffered enough. Get out.'

Lena obeyed. This was a man who definitely deserved his place on her suspect board. She had no idea what accusations he was referring to, but she determined to find out.

That evening, Lena sucked her tummy in to avoid it spilling over the top of the faux leather trousers Sarika had given her. 'Are you sure we need to dress like this?' she asked as they approached the hotel. 'I feel ridiculous.'

'This is how rich Russians dress,' replied Sarika, her hands comfortably resting in the pockets of her imitation fur coat, which was longer than the tiny skirt she was sporting.

'I do not think all of them dress like this,' said Lena.

'Well, the ones on TV do,' confirmed Sarika.

'I do not see why we had to be Russian at all,' complained Lena.

'It is more convincing than rich Hungarians,' replied Sarika. 'People expect it. And he won't know the difference. Relax, you look great.'

'Where am I meant to hide my phone? I can barely fit a piece of paper in the pockets of these things.'

'I'll pop it under my fur coat,' said Sarika. 'Once I've secretly dialled in Mrs Kingston.'

'And I am not sure if I will be able to get these trousers off in time if I need the loo.'

'Stop fussing,' said Sarika, sounding like Lena for once. 'I wish you had let me do this on my own now. We're here. Don't slip on the marble floors in those heels.'

They entered The Anderson Hotel and Sarika scuttled forwards. 'We're meeting him in the Scottsdale bar,' she said. 'Follow me.'

It had seemed like a brilliant idea at the time. They were posing as wealthy potential investors for Jack Husky Capital. They'd secretly dial in Mrs Kingston so she could hear what he was saying, and perhaps then they could find out what he was up to. But now they were here, with Sarika overexcited and her own blood supply being cut off, Lena was not so sure. She couldn't work out how whatever he was up to could possibly tie to Terry's death.

'Come on,' said Sarika, sensing Lena's hesitation. 'We know Jack had a motive for murdering Terry. And we know he is up to something dodgy at work. Follow my lead.' She walked confidently up to Jack.

Lena wondered what the world had come to with her having to take the lead from Sarika. She put it down to the costumes they were wearing. Lena felt ridiculous, but Sarika seemed in her element. Lena tottered after her, marvelling that women who wore heels ever got anywhere.

'Ladies, welcome,' Jack stood up to greet them and gave each a kiss on the cheek. Lena sat down, feeling the leather bite right into her stomach. She leaned back awkwardly to stop her stomach piling over her waistband. She'd always been pretty lean – too thin if her mother was to be believed – but she was certainly not leather-trouser thin.

'I took the liberty of ordering a glass of champagne for us all,' said Jack. 'With the price of oil where it is, why not?'

Sarika's hand went under her coat and the girl winked, none too subtly, at Lena. 'We are the great fans of your show,' said Sarika, in what Lena could only assume was meant to be a Russian accent. 'You are very good businessman.' The girl crossed her legs, displaying a length of stockinged thigh. Jack glanced at it and then back to Sarika's smiling face.

'You flatter me,' he said. 'Sorry, I have to take this.' He grabbed his own phone, which Lena hadn't heard ring. 'Twenty thousand derivatives,' he said. 'Buy buy buy.' He turned back to the women. 'Sorry, when an opportunity comes you have to grab it,' he said. 'I'm always thinking of my clients.'

Sarika giggled. Lena struggled to retrieve Mrs Kingston's list of questions from the tight pocket of her trousers. She opened her mouth and thought about attempting to mimic Sarika's accent, then decided against it. This was hard enough already.

'I hope you do not mind, but I have some questions about your investment proposition,' she said, pronouncing the unfamiliar words carefully.

'Of course,' said Jack, shifting a little in his seat.

'Our money comes from our father,' explained Sarika, answering an unasked question. Lena shot her a glance, wondering why she was making up an unnecessary story. 'He is big in the caviar trade,' she continued. 'So we have lots of money. I have twenty-five pairs of Louboutins and thirty Jimmy Choos.' Lena rolled her eyes. Sarika was enjoying pretending to be rich a little too much. She felt a pang of guilt at Sarika's rapturous expression. Maybe she should pay her a little more.

'But he is very protective of us,' added Lena. 'So I need to make sure that the investment you provide is right.'

'I buy low and sell high,' said Jack. 'Equity bonds, government capital, venture derivatives.'

'What is your discrete year's performance,' asked Lena, reading from her paper. 'Over one, three and five years?'

'I always outperform,' he said.

'And your Sharpe ratio?' said Lena.

Jack looked down and then up again. 'It's very impressive,' he replied. 'Sharp as a knife.' He laughed. 'Little investment-manager joke,' he added. 'How much are you looking to invest?'

'Fifty thousand,' said Lena.

'Two hundred thousand,' said Sarika.

177

They looked at each other. 'Clearly my sister and I need to agree,' said Lena. 'We will discuss together and then meet again when we are ready to invest.'

'Of course,' said Jack. 'But remember, time out of the market is time wasted. I've got to get going. Helsinki is opening,' he said, standing up. 'Bonds to split.'

He left the bar. Lena quickly undid the top button of her trousers and breathed a sigh of relief. Sarika produced the phone from her coat. 'Could you hear okay, Mrs Kingston?' she said.

'Like I was there. But what he said made no sense. Gobble-degook,' declared Mrs Kingston, her voice excited but tinny through the phone.

'Is that an investment style?' asked Sarika.

Mrs Kingston laughed. 'Sorry, I mean that it is nonsense. He's just spouting buzzwords. I don't think he knows what he is talking about.'

'But he has clients,' said Lena. 'He was going to take our money.'

'I wouldn't trust him with a fiver,' said Mrs Kingston. 'He must be running some sort of scam.'

'Lena,' said Sarika, suddenly, grabbing her hands. 'What if Terry found out he was a fake? What if Jack killed him to keep his secret?'

'Do not overreact,' said Lena. 'But we need to flush him down. Out, I mean. Let's go, and decide what our next move is.' She redid the top button of her trousers, cursing Sarika as she did so. Thinking was much harder when your belly was squashed.

Lena stood at the bus stop. Sarika had decided to make use of the fact she was dressed up and had arranged to meet Lucia for drinks. Lena had declined. She just wanted to get home and put her tracksuit bottoms on. Perhaps even give the flat a quick clean to help her think about the implications of what they'd discovered.

It looked as if Jack was hiding in plain sight on *N1 Angels*. She couldn't help but wonder if Sarika was right. Terry could have stumbled upon his scheme, and Jack had to silence him for ever. Although Jack and Terry weren't friends, they would know each other fairly well. Jack must have realised that a drug overdose in a hotel room would be the perfect way to fool the police into believing it was accidental death. And if the police didn't believe that, he still had the cover of the woman he'd hired for the evening. Presumably at a hefty fee to make up for the risk she'd be taking. Lena knew there were plenty of women working in London desperate enough for money to take that on.

Her phone rang just as the bus approached. She expected it to be Sarika, urging her to join them. Glancing at the phone, she smiled. It was PC Cartwright. He wouldn't usually call her this late. Remembering Sarika's advice, she decided this was ideal. She hadn't exactly been on a date, but he didn't need to know that. And she was definitely not sitting at home pining for him. She picked up the phone and waved the bus on, keen to have a private conversation. The bus driver tutted at her as he closed the doors again and drove off.

'Hello,' she said. 'I am in town,' she told him. 'Out for the evening.'

'Oh Lena, it's all gone wrong,' declared Cartwright. 'Again.'

'What has gone wrong?' asked Lena. 'Where are you?'

'I couldn't bear it,' replied Cartwright. 'The way that Sutton is looking at me. So I've pretended to go to the loo but I'm calling you.'

Lena smiled. She was his support system. Excellent. 'Tell me,' she said. 'Perhaps I can help.'

'It's another operation, to catch Yasemin. The info is good this time and I'm convinced she has no idea we're after her.'

'Brilliant,' said Lena.

'But the informant hasn't shown up. He was meant to identify her. Without him, we've got no way of knowing if it's really her.'

'Arrest her anyway,' declared Lena. 'I can identify her after.'

'I can't get the wrong woman again,' said Cartwright. 'I'm already turning into a bit of a laughing stock. Gullins put on a black wig the other day and declared to me that he was Yasemin. In front of everyone.'

Lena bit her lip. 'Gullins is a pig,' she told him. 'You are a million times the policeman that he is.'

'Thank you, Lena,' said Cartwright. 'That's what I needed to hear.'

'It is tonight?' asked Lena.

'It is right now.'

'Give me the address,' commanded Lena. 'I will be there and I can identify her.' She thought a moment. What was the expression? 'In a jiffy bag,' she added proudly.

'What? Why? Oh, I see what you mean. No, I couldn't ask you to do that,' said Cartwright. 'It could be dangerous.'

'You did not ask,' said Lena, flagging down a black cab and trying not to think of the expense. 'I insist.'

CHAPTER 18

Lena found herself squeezed into the back of a police van between the cold hard door and the warm and beautiful PC Cartwright. For the first time that evening, she'd been rather pleased at what she was wearing. Cartwright had looked at her in surprise, and then she was sure a little admiration had crept into his features. Heroic and glamorous was what she was, she decided, and thought that maybe the trousers were not so uncomfortable after all.

There were two other officers in the van with them. She could have done without them leering at her. At her withering look, they'd all focused their attention back on to a small monitor. It reminder Lena of being in a cinema, except the tiny screen meant the proportions were all wrong. Despite the coldness of the evening, the inside of the van had an unpleasant odour, like the Danube flowing through Budapest in the heat of summer.

'We appreciate this so much, Lena,' said Cartwright. 'It is good of you to come.'

'This isn't protocol,' said the oldest of the policemen, introduced to her as DCI Sutton. He had the air of authority that comes with command. Lena wondered if he used to be in the army. 'But PC Cartwright vouched for you. It could be dangerous out there so you are to stay in the van at all times.'

'Of course,' said Lena.

'I'm not happy with this,' continued Sutton, somewhat rudely. 'But we've finally got Yasemin Avci where we want her. And Cartwright here tells me you are one of the few people to have met her in person.'

'That is correct,' said Lena, remembering when the diminutive Turkish gang leader had taken her hostage. She'd never forget her face.

'And it was you who told us we had the wrong person.'

'Yes,' said Lena. 'What do you need me to do?'

'Just stay in the van, watch the monitor and confirm it is her,' said Sutton. 'After last time, we can't risk arresting a decoy. It was not the force's finest moment.' He looked at Cartwright, who looked to the floor.

Lena remembered the flat she cleaned for Yasemin, before she realised who she was. No photos, no pictures, hardly any furniture. Just a room covered in dirty takeaway packets. And an underfed hairless cat that Cartwright had later adopted. 'Who was meant to be here to identify her?'

'We had her boyfriend lined up,' said Cartwright. 'He started informing on her after we caught him dealing drugs to a brothel. Charming chap, insisted on using the girls for free as part of the deal. According to him, Yasemin's got a massive drugs deal lined up with the Albanians and the exchange is happening here, in person. It's a new relationship and neither will trust it to their minions.'

'And where is he?' asked Lena.

'No idea,' said Cartwright. 'He hasn't turned up. I did not expect him to be late – he said that Yasemin would be here and gone quickly. He made a point of saying that she is not a woman to be kept waiting.'

'Cartwright, information is on a need-to-know basis,' said Sutton sternly. 'We appreciate what you are doing,' he said to Lena. 'But the less you know, the safer you'll be.'

'Yes,' said Cartwright. 'Sorry. Sometimes I forget that you're a civilian, Lena.' He smiled at her.

'The boyfriend did not show up?' said Lena, feeling uncomfortable. 'What happened to him?'

'Cold feet,' said the third policeman, introduced to her as Betty, although Lena was sure that couldn't be right. He was sweating, even though the car was cold. 'Wimped out.'

Lena nodded. Not all men were as brave as PC Cartwright.

'How long are we here for?' asked Lena.

'They should be here by now,' admitted Cartwright, looking at his watch. 'Perhaps they are running late.'

'Yasemin is never late,' said Lena. 'She left plates everywhere, but you remember her closet? Her clothes were neatly folded, in order of colour. She is precise. I think something must be wrong.'

'Calm down, Miss Marple,' said Sutton. 'Maybe she missed her bus.'

'Yasemin does not take buses,' said Lena.

'I was joking,' said Sutton. 'You foreigners don't get British humour.'

'To be fair to Lena, it wasn't very funny,' said Cartwright. 'Sir,' he added, awkwardly. He paused. 'How long shall we wait?'

Sutton looked at his watch and then back at the small screen. It still displayed the inside of the empty warehouse. Lena peered into the screen more closely. 'That is a funny box,' she said.

'Finally she finds something funny,' quipped Betty.

'No,' she said. 'Look at it. All the other boxes are crates, see, around the edge of the room.' Cartwright leaned in to look. 'They are clean and new. But that one, look, it is all grubby. There's some kind of liquid dripping off it.'

'Someone spilled their tea,' said Sutton. He looked at his watch again. 'Sorry, boys, I don't think we're going to get any joy tonight. Let's head off home. Overtime's up.'

'That is not tea,' continued Lena. 'Tea is thin and weak. That is thick, like kitchen cleaner. But dark, like . . .' Lena moved to stand up and banged her head on the roof of the van. She sat down again.

'We'll drop you back,' said Cartwright. 'I'm sorry we wasted your time.'

'I do not leave until I see what is in that box,' declared Lena. 'It is not right.'

'Betty, can you give that box of hers a poke before we leave?' sighed Sutton.

'Right you are, sir,' said the policeman. He jumped out of the van. Lena noticed the smell improved immediately.

'We call Betson Sweaty Betty,' said Sutton. 'For obvious reasons.' Lena ignored him, her eyes focused on the box. She saw Betson walk in, looking carefully around him. He walked up to the box and opened it, but his body was blocking their view. They all watched transfixed as Betson jumped back.

A man was in the box. His eyes were open in a stare, but he'd ceased to see. He was dead.

'God, Lena, I'm so sorry.' Lena and Cartwright were sitting on the sofa in her flat, both holding glasses of Sarika's Palinka. 'You shouldn't have had to see that.'

'I have seen worse,' said Lena, trying to sound brave, though really she hadn't. She'd seen some filthy places, even some drops of blood at houses she'd cleaned. But never a dead body. Timea's body was identified by DNA and then safely sealed inside a coffin for the funeral.

'I don't think I even need to say this,' said Cartwright, breaking her reverie. 'But you must keep everything that happened tonight to yourself. Not even Sarika can know. The investigation is still open, and now there's another murder to add to the tally.'

'The body was Yasemin's boyfriend?' asked Lena. 'It must be.'

'It's just been confirmed,' said Cartwright, looking at his handset. 'It was Deniz. She must have known he'd been working with the police. And she killed him because of it.' He paused. 'Because of me.' He took a sip of Palinka and coughed in surprise at the fierceness of the Hungarian spirit.

'It is not your fault,' said Lena, her voice gentle.

'He wasn't a decent fellow,' said Cartwright, holding the glass at a safe distance from his face. 'He was happy to make money from his girlfriend's drug deals, but just as happy to turn her in to save his own skin.' He paused again. 'But no one deserves to be murdered.'

Lena agreed. 'Life is too precious for anyone to take,' she said, thinking again of her friend Timea. Cartwright looked at her, and she could see in his eyes that he knew what she was thinking. He took her hand, but the contact made her want to cry. She took her hand away and gave herself a little pinch on the ear. She needed to pull herself together.

'That's pretty bold, leaving him right under our noses,' said Cartwright, pulling himself together too. Lena was grateful the conversation had turned back to practical matters. 'And we might not even have known. Imagine that, if the body was under police surveillance and the police missed it. Sutton was clearly impressed with you, even if he did think I'd told you too much.'

'The police cannot be expected to look inside every box,' said Lena, feeling generous now she'd regained control of her emotions.

'You were brilliant,' said Cartwright. He put his Palinka glass down and took her hand again. 'I'm sorry I've been rubbish,' he said. 'I've applied to join CID and I was so keen to impress Sutton that I got caught up in all this Yasemin stuff, with her boyfriend and all, and I thought catching her was more important than anything else.' He leaned forwards till Lena could smell the spirit on his breath. It smelled like home. 'Of course it wasn't.'

Lena leaned forwards too, feeling the stress of the evening melt away with the intoxication of this moment. She put her own glass down and reached up, running her fingers through his silky hair. It was as soft as Hungarian goose down.

'You have been rubbish,' she teased, gently tousling his hair.

'It would serve me right if you'd met someone else,' he said, gently caressing her hand.

This was her chance, thought Lena. Her chance to make him jealous, like Sarika had said.

'Actually, I was with another man when you called,' she whispered. 'A banker.' Cartwright leaned back again, removing his hand.

'Sorry,' he said. 'I had no idea. What an idiot I am.'

'No,' said Lena. 'It was not like that.' She was already regretting her words. 'It was an investigation.'

'No need to explain yourself, Lena,' said Cartwright. 'I know I've not been good enough. I couldn't expect someone like you to wait around for me. Not with you looking . . . like this.' Lena looked down at her trousers and cursed them again. 'I'll get out of your hair.' He jumped up and was gone before she had a chance to explain.

'*Szar*,' swore Lena. There was no one she wanted in her hair more.

Lena sat in the flat, alone. She was starting to wonder if she'd done the right thing keeping Sarika from fleeing the country. What she'd seen that evening reminded her what a dangerous place Islington could be.

Yasemin had murdered her boyfriend; sending a message that

she was not to be messed with. Lena wondered how long Yasemin had known he'd betrayed her.

And the boyfriend too. Deniz. He was hardly innocent: pretending to care for Yasemin while he was using her to secure his own freedom. They were as bad as each other.

Well, perhaps not quite as bad. Deniz was the one who was dead.

Lena wondered if the police would be able to prove that Yasemin was responsible for the murder. It seemed obvious, but the woman was a professional. She'd hardly leave a body for the police to find covered in her fingerprints. The police didn't even know what she looked like. But Lena did. And Yasemin knew it.

She tried not to worry. It was harder than she thought having Sarika staying in a hotel. The girl drove her crazy at times but Lena loved her. Despite the mess and silliness, she liked having companionship again. She'd been missing Timea so much.

When Timea was alive, everything had been better. Lena had a friend, a friend who was like a sister to her. She'd been more relaxed, even had a boyfriend, though she had to admit it was more for comfort than butterflies. She'd been happy, in her way.

Lena had been trying to find that companionship again with Sarika, but it was not the same. Lena needed to rebuild her own life. And she knew who she wanted to do it with.

CHAPTER 19

For once, Lena hoped that her client would be at home. She wanted to check that Mrs Ives was okay. And after what she had seen last night, she didn't feel like being in a house on her own.

Lena rang the doorbell. This time Mrs Ives appeared quickly at the door. Lena blinked. She wasn't wearing a nightie this time: she was smartly dressed, her hair was styled and she was made up to perfection. The wreck Lena had been expecting had gone. At least superficially.

'Lena, good to see you again,' said Mrs Ives, stepping aside to allow her to enter.

'Are you okay?'

'Couldn't be better,' she replied. 'Coffee?'

'Yes,' said Lena, coming in. 'What has happened?'

'Hang on a minute, I've some biscuits somewhere. Those nice ones with the block of milk chocolate on top. I think you'll like them. Have a seat.' Lena perched on the sofa and cast her eyes around for signs of Mr Ives. From Mrs Ives's disposition she assumed he must be back, but she hadn't seen his shoes by the door or his coat hanging up.

'Did you find Mr Ives?' asked Lena, taking a biscuit and trying to forget the memory of the leather trousers digging into her stomach.

'I was close,' said Mrs Ives. 'I should have been an internet spy.

Trolls, do they call them?' Lena shrugged. 'But in the end I didn't have to.' Mrs Ives smiled. 'He found me. I say found. He came crawling back, thoroughly ashamed of himself.'

'Where is he?' asked Lena, suddenly having a vision of him buried under the patio. Subtly, she glanced out of the back window. No signs of holes being dug.

'I sent him packing,' said Mrs Ives, her voice triumphant. 'Well, I say packing, but I didn't let him take any of his stuff. So I just sent him, I suppose.' Mrs Ives took a biscuit and then put it back down. 'I'm watching my figure,' she said. 'I'm going to have to find myself a new man.'

'Where had he been?' asked Lena.

'Just as I thought,' said Mrs Ives. 'With that girl from Bienvenue.com. They ran away together, then he claims he saw sense and came running back. But for all I know she ditched him when I cancelled his credit cards. There is no way I'm letting him back in our house.'

'Some men cannot be trusted,' agreed Lena, taking another biscuit.

'Who'd have thought such simple creatures as men could be capable of deceiving us women,' said Mrs Ives. 'On second thoughts,' she said, reaching for a biscuit, 'I think I'd rather have chocolate than a man any day.'

Lena pulled at her coat as she waited in line at the trendy coffee shop. She looked around for somewhere to sit, regretting her choice of venue. Every little table was a different style, but they were all taken. At the front of the queue she hesitated for a moment, wondering what Cartwright would like to drink. She ordered him an Earl Grey, assuming that some things never changed. Getting herself an Americano with an extra shot and resenting the cost, she carried both drinks awkwardly on a tray.

189

The only seats available were high stools, so she popped the tray down on a little ledge and hopped up with as much dignity as she could muster. When did people decide being seated at higher than bum height was such a good idea? It was called sitting *down* for a reason.

Cartwright appeared. He looked better than ever, wearing a padded jacket that made him look like a country gentleman and soft corduroy trousers that matched the sandy colour of his silky hair. Her resolve to tell him how she felt had already weakened at Mr Ives's betrayal, and now here he was, looking too good to be true. He waved to her and Lena hopped down from her stool again to greet him with a kiss on the cheek. She felt the soft warmth of his face under her lips and fought the urge to envelop him in a huge hug and never let go. Instead she gestured to the other stool and clambered back into her own with an awkward backwards scramble.

'This is a nice surprise,' said Cartwright, settling into his own stool with dignified grace. 'I thought you'd be busy with your banker.'

'No,' said Lena, wondering how to disentangle herself from her lie. She couldn't exactly admit that she'd been trying to make him jealous. 'What is happening with Yasemin?' she managed, eventually. 'You can charge her with murder?'

'It doesn't look like it. Unfortunately,' said Cartwright. 'Obviously she didn't kill him herself: she would not get her hands that dirty. There's no physical evidence to connect her to that body. With my informer dead, we're back to square one.'

'But she must have done it, or at least given the command,' said Lena, thinking how ridiculous the police could be. Yasemin's boyfriend's body in a warehouse where she was meant to be, and still no charges. 'She killed him, or as good as. She must have.'

'There's no proof. I'm sorry, I should never have got you involved.'

'I do not mind,' said Lena. 'There is much I would do for you.'

Cartwright didn't seem to hear her. 'No, Sutton was right. You're a civilian and I put you in harm's way. Yasemin is a very dangerous woman and she is always one step ahead of us. I know that Deniz had more to tell us about her new criminal enterprise, but he certainly can't spill the beans now.'

Lena took a deep breath. Then a sip of coffee. Then another deep breath. 'I want to tell you something,' she said.

'Of course,' said Cartwright. He put down his tea.

'It is about . . .' Lena paused. What was it about? Perhaps that was the wrong way to start. 'I feel that . . .' she stopped again and wiped at a few crumbs on the table. There was also a sticky coffee ring, and a bit of foam from someone's cappuccino. They should really wipe their surfaces more often here. With the price of the drinks, you wouldn't expect to stick your elbow in a splash of soy milk. She looked back up at Cartwright. He was fiddling with his phone.

'Sutton wants to see me,' he said, sounding worried.

'I thought it was your day off,' said Lena, feeling a mixture of regret that she'd not got her words out sooner, and relief that the moment had passed.

'I think this is it,' he said, looking at Lena with panic in his eyes. 'I think this is going to be when I am fired from the Met.' He put his head in his hands. Lena looked at his shiny hair, sticking out through his muscular fingers.

'You are perfect,' she told him.

'I don't know why I thought I could do this,' continued Cartwright. 'It devastated my parents when I told them I was joining the force. They wanted me to be a lawyer, like my dad. And when I studied maths and computing, they thought I'd do the second-best thing and work in the City. But I didn't want to. I wanted to do something real. Something that would help people. I didn't want to study any more. And I didn't even want to use my degrees to get ahead. I wanted to earn it, working my way through the ranks. But I haven't got anywhere.'

'You have helped me,' said Lena. 'You helped me bring the person who murdered my friend to justice.'

Cartwright lifted his head from his hands. 'Thank you, Lena,' he said. 'That means a lot.' He got up. 'I suppose I had better go and face the music.'

'Not on your own,' said Lena, getting up too. 'I'm coming with you.'

'You can't come in with me,' he said, with a half-laugh. 'DI Sutton already thinks I've told you too much.'

'Then I'll wait outside,' said Lena.

'Meet me later,' said Cartwright. 'Come to my flat at seven p.m.? I'll have pulled myself together by then. And I'd appreciate the company.'

'Of course,' said Lena.

'Thanks for the tea,' he said, weakly. 'And wish me luck.'

'No problem,' said Lena. She watched him leave. She hadn't told him what she wanted to, and for a moment she was pleased. What Cartwright needed now was a friend. And that's what she'd be.

Lena took a deep breath before she rang the doorbell to Kat's flat. She'd been putting off meeting with her, even though she was keen to know how Irina's sister was connected to Marsela. Kat was just so angry, all the time. She had a special hatred for Sarika that seemed to extend to Lena by association.

In a way, Lena couldn't blame her. Having your boyfriend stolen by your flatmate would be devastating. But then Kat had been angry before that too. She guessed it was the life she'd had to lead: working for an internet sex line to support her brothers and sisters back home, and having to lie about it too. Her father was a strict Russian Orthodox.

Kat opened the door and waved her in ungraciously. 'Come in then,' she said. 'What do you want?' She sank down on to the sofa and put her bare feet on the table, spread her toes and started painting her toenails a purple so dark it was almost black.

At least her feet were clean, thought Lena. 'I was talking to Irina . . .' she began. Kat's face softened.

'She is a good girl,' said Kat, with a smile. 'I think that she will make an excellent chef.'

Lena was surprised that Kat was so blissfully unaware of how little aptitude her sister had for cooking, let alone that she'd been fired. Perhaps it was hard to see the faults in those closest to you.

'Does she live here with you and Lucia?' asked Lena, looking around. She hadn't seen Irina since the dinner party they'd catered.

'Of course not,' said Kat. 'My sister does not know what I do for a living.' She looked at Lena. 'I am not ashamed,' she said. 'What I do, I do for my family. But my father, he would not understand.' Lena nodded. 'I paid the deposit for Irina to live in a nice flat in Crouch End,' she said. 'She is very happy there. Too happy to see much of her sister.'

'Actually, I am not here to talk about your sister,' said Lena. Kat looked surprised. 'But she told me something about you.' Lena watched as Kat's face hardened. 'Nothing bad,' she said, thinking Kat must worry that Irina knew her secret. 'Just that you are friends with Marsela Goga. From *N1 Angels*.'

'I used to be,' said Kat. 'What of it?'

'How do you know her?'

'Why do you want to know?'

Lena thought. Maybe a direct approach was best. 'You know her boyfriend Terry died? I think it could be murder and I think that she might be in danger too. Does she know anyone dangerous?'

'We used to work together for the same agency,' admitted Kat. 'A long time ago.'

'What kind of agency?' asked Lena.

'Do I need to spell it out for you?' said Kat. Lena looked back at her blankly. 'We were escorts,' she said. 'We slept with men for money.'

Thoughts raced through Lena's mind like greyhounds on a track. Marsela had been an escort. A prostitute. She found it hard to believe of this strong, independent woman who had put herself through law school.

But it was starting to make sense. Was that how she had paid for her education? Lena had heard stories of students turning to prostitution to meet their living expenses. Was this what Marsela had done?

The words of the receptionist came back to her. A prostitute had been with Terry. But Maria had been a fan of the show, she'd have recognised Marsela. If it was Marsela who Terry had been with, why not tell her?

And who else knew Marsela's secrets? Lena thought back to what Mrs Kingston had told her. Terry had placed Marsela on a pedestal. Then unceremoniously knocked her off. Had he discovered the truth about her past?

And what lengths would Marsela go to in order to keep her secret?

Lena found herself wondering if Marsela and Jack had plotted Terry's downfall together. They both had secrets to keep.

She had to find out what Jack was up to. But first, it was time to see Cartwright. Lena wondered what she should bring. When Sarika was heartbroken, she wanted alcohol. When Lena was at her lowest, she'd always go for chocolate. She realised she'd no idea what Cartwright would like when under stress. What did you give a policeman who'd been fired from the force?

Sympathy, Lena decided. And company.

It had been warm the last time Lena had stood outside this front door, back in June the previous year. It would be nice to see Kaplan again: he was the hairless cat that Cartwright had adopted when Yasemin fled the country. She'd promised Kaplan to visit more often, but she hadn't.

It wasn't her fault, she told herself. First Cartwright had been sent on assignment in Newcastle, then he'd been too busy to see her. It wasn't his fault either. He'd been devoting his time to taking a dangerous criminal off the streets. And now he was being penalised for taking those risks.

He shouldn't want any part of a police force that treated him like that, thought Lena, as she pressed the doorbell. And now he could do something else. Something else that would help people. And perhaps even something that would give him more time to spend with Lena.

He opened the door clutching Kaplan. 'At least I've managed to capture Yasemin's cat,' he said. Kaplan immediately started wriggling in his arms, clambered on to his shoulder, threw himself on to the floor and made a beeline for Lena's legs. 'For a moment at least,' said Cartwright. 'Some animals can't be tamed.'

'He loves you really,' said Lena. She leant down and allowed Kaplan to rub his bald head against her hand, emitting a healthy purr. 'I have missed you,' she told the animal.

Cartwright led her into the living room and offered her a glass of wine. Lena accepted, and looked at him expectantly when they both had glasses in their hands. 'You do not have to speak about it if you do not want to,' said Lena. 'But I have to ask you what happened with DCI Sutton.'

'I'm not in uniform any more,' said Cartwright.

'They do not deserve you,' she said. Kaplan ignored the anger in her voice and jumped on to her lap. 'The police are a waste of time in this country,' she continued. 'They are stupid, they are corrupt—'

'No,' said Cartwright. 'That's not what I meant.' He smiled at her. 'I've been accepted into CID.'

Lena looked at him. 'The Criminal Investigation Department,' explained Cartwright. 'You are looking at a fully fledged detective constable.'

'But that is brilliant,' said Lena, her happiness for Cartwright mingling with her sense that he would now have even less time to spend with her. 'You deserve it.' She raised her glass and chinked it awkwardly with his.

'Of course, I'm still constable level. But I'm on my way. It's finally happening.'

'And it should,' said Lena.

'Thank you Lena,' said Cartwright. 'I really think our work together helped. DCI Sutton went through my record with me. Solving Timea's murder. Bringing the art thief to justice last year. All the work to track Yasemin Avci after we identified her criminal activities. Finding Deniz's body. I couldn't have done it without you.'

Lena nodded. She agreed. 'And now I'm even more determined to catch Yasemin. That will really prove to the guys that I deserve my place in CID. There are new little pockets of crime everywhere, and I am sure that it is Yasemin pulling the strings. Whenever we catch someone, it's just some immigrant being forced into it and far too scared to implicate who is manipulating them.'

'Immigrants are not all manipulated criminals,' said Lena, with dignity. 'You should know that.'

'Of course,' said Cartwright, looking devastated. 'That's not what I meant; it's just that I know it's not always their fault . . .' His voice trailed off and they sat in silence.

'Congratulations,' said Lena, determined not to make this awkward. This was Cartwright's moment.

'Thank you,' he replied. Another slice of silence followed. 'So tell me,' he said, finally. 'I'm pretty sure you'll have found out more about Terry Tibbs since the last time we spoke.'

'I have my suspects,' said Lena. 'But I am going to get evidence before I share it with the important and fancy police constable.'

'Detective,' corrected Cartwright. He smiled again. 'Detective Constable Cartwright.'

CHAPTER 20

'Have you girls agreed?' asked Jack. They were in the same hotel bar in Mayfair, this time with an elaborately tiered afternoon tea platter in front of them. 'I can tell that you have good taste.'

Lena picked up a cucumber sandwich and took a bite. It was bland: she couldn't understand why the British didn't put paprika in their sandwiches. She'd been so busy worrying about Cartwright that she hadn't properly prepared for this meeting and wasn't sure how best to confront Jack with what they knew. Sarika's planning seemed limited to what they'd wear, and Lena shifted uncomfortably in her seat, trying to pull her skirt down to conceal more of her thighs. She wished she hadn't let Sarika dress her again.

'I should let you know that I do have a minimum investment threshold,' he said. 'But that shouldn't be a problem for ladies like yourselves.' Sarika just sat and stared at him. 'Of course, the more you invest, the more you'll get back. You have to speculate to accumulate.'

Lena took a scone and spread it with jam and cream. She took a bite. Even with the toppings, it was dry. There must be a subtle way to discover whether Terry knew about Jack's scheme. Maybe if she asked for a referral from another client, she could start to track who knew what—

'You're a conman and a murderer!' said Sarika, leaping to her

198

feet. Nearby people in the bar turned to look at them, the public's radar for drama kicking in.

Jack was staring at Sarika, open-mouthed. Lena shrugged. It would have to be the direct approach after all.

'I don't know what you're talking about,' he said. 'I'm a legitimate investment manager . . .' His voice trailed off.

'We all know that is not true,' said Lena. She put the scone back on the plate.

'Equity trades,' he said, feebly. 'Bond prices. Pork bellies.'

'You do not fool us,' said Lena.

'Who are you?' asked Jack.

'That is not relevant,' said Lena. 'Sarika, sit down. We might as well be comfortable while we wait for the police to get here.' She took her phone from her bag.

'Wait,' said Jack. 'There's no need for that. I can explain.'

'My Terry discovered your scam,' said Sarika. 'Because he is so clever. And you murdered him to keep it quiet.'

'What?' said Jack. 'Are you talking about Terry Tibbs? What does he have to do with anything?'

'Tell us everything,' said Lena, putting her phone on the table and leaning back a little in her chair in a futile attempt to get comfortable. 'Then I will decide if I need to tell the police. You are not a banker. Are you?'

'No,' confessed Jack. Sarika lunged at him but Lena pushed her back into her seat. 'I'm an actor.'

'And you impersonated an investment manager to steal money,' said Lena. 'Using the show as a means of generating publicity.'

'You've got it backwards.'

'Explain,' commanded Lena. Sarika sat and seethed.

'I'm an actor,' said Jack, miserably. 'And I was desperate for a part on *N1 Angels*. I knew I'd be brilliant on the show. It would be my big break. I just needed a chance to shine. But the producers didn't want actors, they wanted typical Islingtonites. Doctors, lawyers, entrepreneurs. And bankers.'

'So you pretended?'

'No, I acted. And I was good at it. They believed me, hook, line and sinker. I just shouted some words I'd heard on *The Wolf of Wall Street*. It wasn't doing anyone any harm. I got the role.'

'But you were doing people harm,' she said. 'You are taking money that you have no qualifications to manage.'

'I never wanted to,' said Jack. 'But one of the producers approached me and asked me to help him with some investments. I couldn't say no, he'd fire me if he knew I'd lied. So I took the money.'

'You stole it?' said Lena.

'No,' said Jack. 'I put it in a bank account. Then the FTSE fell, whatever that means, and he asked about the money and I said it was fine because I'd seen it coming and invested overseas. They wrote that into the show, with all the proper jargon, and after that loads of people started contacting me to invest. They thought I was some sort of investment genius. What was I meant to do?'

'Where is all the money?' asked Lena.

'I put it in a savings account,' said Jack. 'People assume I make a lot more on the show than I do, so no questions were asked. It's all still there. I can give it back to people anytime they want. I'm not even taking a fee.' He shrugged at Lena. 'No one is losing anything,' he said. 'Maybe we can just—'

'What about Terry?' said Sarika. 'What did you do to him?'

'Nothing,' said Jack. 'He had no idea that I'm not who I say I am. Even Marsela doesn't know. I wouldn't be surprised if she suspected though.'

'Why should we believe you?' said Lena.

'Terry's own uncle used to have money with me,' said Jack. 'I gave it back. Listen, I didn't like Terry all that much for how he treated Marsela, but I didn't do anything to him. I'm vegan, for god's sake. I wouldn't hurt a fly.'

'We will let the police decide that,' said Lena.

'But I'm innocent,' said Jack.

'Not really,' said Lena. 'You are a conman.' Jack looked at her for a moment, then jumped up, grabbed his coat and rushed from the bar. Lena watched him go, then rang Cartwright.

DI Damper had a pained look on his face while Lena told him what had happened. Like he was constipated, Lena decided. He could do with a cup of her mother's liquorice tea. She'd gone home from the hotel bar, peeled off her tight skirt and put on some stretchy leggings before coming to meet them at the police station. She knew it was urgent that she speak to the police, but some things were more urgent. Like the circulation to her pelvis.

DC Cartwright, on the other hand, was looking at Lena with the faraway look he got in his eyes when he was impressed. She remembered it from when she'd exposed Yasemin's gangster activities. And when she'd discovered Timea's murderer. And found that stolen painting. She smiled back at him, thinking that he was the most beautiful man she had ever seen.

'So you found out that Jack Husky is pretending to be an investment expert and is keeping people's money on false pretences,' said DI Damper.

'Exactly,' said Lena, grinning at Cartwright.

'And although you are not sure what the mechanics are, you think it might put Jack in the frame for Terry's murder.'

'I leave something for the police to do,' said Lena, feeling light-headed with victory.

'But instead of coming to the police with what you knew,' said DI Damper, looking as if his bowels were tightening further, 'you told him everything and he ran away.'

'It was an on-the-moment decision,' said Lena, feeling less sure of herself.

'You know it will take time for us to be able to freeze his assets,' said DI Damper. 'Even if what you have told us is correct, there are procedures that need to be followed. If he grabs the cash and flees the country, those people might never get their money back.'

'Steady on, Inspector,' said Cartwright. 'You can hardly blame Lena for that. Anyway, the financial services compensation scheme will kick in.'

'Great. Government money being wasted on that instead of keeping Bobbies on the beat. Result.'

'We don't even know if he will run away,' continued Cartwright. 'He might turn himself in.'

Damper laughed. 'Yes, that is what conmen do when they are exposed. Turn themselves in.'

'I don't think there is any need for you to take that tone,' said Cartwright. 'Inspector,' he added as an afterthought. 'Lena has found valuable information, off her own bat. She's a civilian and can't be expected to know police protocol.'

'Let's hope we don't need to add "wasting police time" to her list of indiscretions,' said Damper. 'You can explain to her what that entails. Seems to be her specialist subject, looking at her file.'

'You waste your own time,' said Lena, sick of this. '*Idióta.* Too stupid to see what is in front of you. I leave now.'

Lena walked out of the police station and was greeted by a blast of cold air. She was gratified to see that Cartwright had followed her out. 'Lena, I'm so sorry,' he said. 'I think Damper was just embarrassed that you found out something he didn't. Again.'

'Maybe I should have come to you before I saw Jack again,' said Lena, relenting a little.

'You have done brilliantly,' said Cartwright. 'Ignore Damper.'

He glanced at his watch. 'Maybe I can buy you a hot chocolate when my shift is over in half an hour.'

'I would love that,' said Lena. 'But I have someone else I need to talk to about Jack.'

'Is that nice policeman with you?' Marsela was standing in her doorway looking hopefully past Lena's head. 'He seemed such a gentleman.'

'No,' said Lena, trying not to sound cross. 'It is just me.'

'You seem rather obsessed with cleaning my house,' said Marsela. 'Business must be bad if you keep working here for free.'

'I am not here to clean,' said Lena. 'We need to talk.'

'What can we have to say to each other?'

Lena paused. 'I want to apologise,' she said. 'I know you did not write that note.'

'Apology accepted,' said Marsela, moving to close the door.

'There is more,' said Lena. 'Please, let me come in.'

Marsela gave her a puzzled look and stepped to the side to allow Lena to enter.

'I'm glad you know I didn't write the note to your friend,' said Marsela, as the women sat down in the living room. 'The police can verify that. My handwriting is not a match.'

'Okay,' said Lena, unsure whether she really believed Marsela. She took a deep breath, wishing she'd put together a better plan of what to say. Now she was inside, a hodgepodge of accusations were flowing through her mind like a *lecsó* stew. Marsela's dodgy alibi, her relationship with the fraudster Jack, her secret past as an escort. She fought her urge to go straight in with the punches and tried to start as tactfully as she could. 'I am sorry that I accused you,' said Lena, again. 'I was worried for my friend.'

'I understand,' replied Marsela, gracing Lena with a very beautiful smile. 'The first time you get a threat it can be frightening.

Terry and I have had so many that they don't worry us any more. Didn't worry us,' she added, looking to the ground.

'Maybe they should,' suggested Lena. 'He is dead, after all.'

'It was an accident,' said Marsela. 'A tragic accident.'

'You really believe that?' asked Lena. 'That he was on his own, in that collar, with those drugs?'

'Of course not,' said Marsela. She began to fiddle with her earlobe as she spoke. 'He was with some girl. Partying. He drank too much, took one too many pills. The girl will have been scared and ran away. Perhaps if she'd stayed and called an ambulance, Terry would still be alive.' She paused. 'But we can't blame her, even if we knew who she was. It's his own fault.' She took her hand away from her ear and looked at her fingertips, as if surprised by them.

Lena watched Marsela. It made so much sense when she said it like that. 'He took drugs often?'

'No,' admitted Marsela. 'Not that he told me.'

'He did not take them with you?' asked Lena.

'I wasn't into all that,' said Marsela. 'I think that's one of the reasons Terry liked me. I was different to the other girls he'd been with. "Square", the English call it.' Her hand reached back to her ear.

Lena shook her head, mystified. Marsela was curvy and beautiful, not shaped like a square at all.

'Sensible,' clarified Marsela, looking at Lena's face. 'I am always well behaved. Boring, maybe.'

'Boring?' queried Lena, thinking of Marsela's past.

'I had to be. Law school is not easy and I had no financial help. My parents are dead and my uncle . . . let's just say he was not supportive. But I was determined I was going to make something of myself and not end up drowning in a tonne of debts as a result. There was no way I wanted to end up in some menial job like . . .' she trailed off. Lena ignored the implication. Cleaning was no dead-end job for her. She was a business owner, albeit a tiny business. It would grow.

'So you worked while you studied,' said Lena. 'What did you do?'

'I worked in a bar,' said Marsela quickly.

Now was the time, thought Lena. 'No, you did not,' she said, speaking calmly and quietly. 'You were an escort.'

Marsela looked as though she'd been slapped. Then she swallowed, squared her shoulders and lifted her head. 'So the word is out,' she said. 'It was only a matter of time. Fine,' she added. 'Yes, I worked as an escort. I'm not proud of it but I'm not ashamed either.'

Lena looked at her in surprise.

'It's easy for rich people,' continued Marsela. 'Their parents pay for them to go to university, mess around for a few years and study just enough to scrape a degree. That degree gets them into a career, paid very little at first, but that doesn't matter because mummy and daddy put them up and supplement their income. I don't have parents; I had to do it on my own. And escorting was how I did it.'

'There are other ways,' said Lena. 'Plenty of people manage.'

'And I respect them for it,' replied Marsela. 'But I didn't want to be paying back loans for the rest of my life, and I was tired of being poor. That was my way.'

'Terry knew?' asked Lena.

'Not at first. But he found out, just before the second season started filming,' said Marsela. 'That was when he started treating me like crap, playing around. Because I wasn't the nice girl he thought I was. I fell out of love with him pretty quickly after that: I've had enough men treat me badly. I wasn't going to allow him to add to that list.'

'But you stayed together?'

'For the show. I let them give me all these ridiculous storylines where I'd take him back again and again. Apparently it helped the ratings. But in reality, we were over.'

'You were with Jack again?'

'That was always for the cameras,' said Marsela. 'He's a nice enough guy, but not my type. Plus he was getting himself into terrible trouble with that "investment company" of his.'

'You knew it was fake?'

'It doesn't take a genius to see he knows nothing about finance. Good for him: fools and their money.'

Lena thought. Marsela knew Jack's secret, but Terry knew Marsela's. Could she have killed him to protect it?

'I know what you're thinking,' said Marsela. 'I don't know who you really are, Lena, but you seem convinced that someone else was involved in Terry's death, and now here I am, his maltreated girlfriend, angry and with a secret to protect.' Lena felt cold air flood her mouth as it dropped open. She closed it again, quickly. 'Don't look so surprised,' continued Marsela. 'You've already accused me once, before you even knew that. But I was at Macaques all evening. There are dozens of witnesses.'

'No you were not,' replied Lena. 'You left early.' It was Marsela's turn to look surprised.

'I was working,' she said, quietly. 'Like I used to do.'

'As an escort?' asked Lena.

'Yes,' replied Marsela, her voice even quieter. 'I thought I was done with all that, but I had an offer I couldn't refuse. The client,' she leaned in and whispered, though they were alone in her house, 'he's a politician. Very influential. And married. It has to be conducted in the utmost secrecy. He paid me a great deal.'

Lena sat back. That was what the police were covering up.

'But . . . you're a lawyer . . . and a TV star. You don't need the money.'

'I always need the money,' replied Marsela. 'And I'm not a lawyer. Yet. Sometimes I wish I'd never got that part on *N1 Angels*.

I was so proud when I got my law degree. Do you know that – after everything I went through to get my damn degree – I've never even practised real law? I was just about to start my apprenticeship when my agent sent me the role.'

'Why did you even have an agent if you wanted to be a lawyer?' asked Lena, not feeling terribly sympathetic.

'He got me some modelling gigs,' said Marsela. 'And yes, they were topless. But I needed the money. Do you know how much they pay you for your first apprenticeship in a law firm? Probably a lot less than you earn cleaning. That's why only people whose parents can support them end up in decent jobs.'

Lena felt her sympathy levels increase. Marginally. When she was living in Debrecen she'd sold subscriptions to a magazine but had never been able to make ends meet. Wages were just too low. That's why she'd eventually moved to London.

'You have money now,' said Lena. 'You can still be a lawyer.'

Marsela laughed. 'I don't think any decent firm will take me seriously now,' she said. 'Not when I've aired my dirty laundry on reality TV.'

'You overestimate how many people watch your show,' said Lena. 'I had never heard of you.' She was surprised that Marsela looked more annoyed than comforted.

'I thought the ends justified the means,' continued Marsela, ignoring Lena. 'That once I qualified, I could stop. But now I'm famous the money is so much better than it ever was before. I get offered insane amounts of money to do . . . things. I know I won't be able to make money like this for ever, and if I can't practise law either . . . there's no way I'm going to be poor again. Not after the childhood I had.'

'I will not tell anyone about your past,' said Lena. 'And I do not think that the word is out.'

'It will be soon,' said Marsela. 'It's inevitable. And you're wrong about the motive too,' she added. 'Terry would never have told anyone my secret. He was ashamed and he begged me to keep it quiet. He couldn't have everyone knowing his perfect girlfriend's less than perfect past. I might as well go public with it now he's dead. I'll call my publicist, get the messaging right. Make sure it's my story that's heard. They'll probably make a storyline out of it if we get another season.'

Lena nodded. It seemed Marsela was a better actress than she thought.

'Those men were using me,' continued Marsela. 'But I was using them too. It's what we do to each other, all the time. It was different with Terry, at first. We were opposites, but we shared the same sadness. Deep down, we were both lonely. But in the end, everyone wants something. Money, sex, power: it's an exchange. Perhaps the world would be better if that wasn't the way it is. But I'm not here to change the world. I just played the hand I was dealt.'

CHAPTER 21

'This place is turning into a tip,' said Sarika. 'It isn't how Terry would have wanted it. Look at that barmaid! She isn't even wearing make-up.' Lena looked around N1 Demons. The sofa may once have had some structure, but it had been sat in for so long it was now just a soft bundle of comfort. There was music again but it was soft, relaxed and unobtrusive. The people looked happy, including Uncle Barry, chatting to punters at the bar while the new bartender Sarika had referred to efficiently pulled pints and smiled at customers.

But the atmosphere was not what Lena was here for. She wanted to find out more about Uncle Barry.

'Did you hear about Jack?' she asked him, once the people he was talking to took their drinks back to their seats.

'Marsela told me,' he replied. 'Luckily I'd already taken my money back from him after what happened with Anastasia. I needed it.'

'I like this place now,' said Lena. 'It looks busy too. Why did you let Terry have it the other way?'

'When he bailed me out of trouble he didn't do it out of familial love,' he said. 'He had me over a barrel and took half my share of this place.'

'You were lucky he was so generous,' snapped Sarika. 'To save you at all.'

'I was lucky he insisted on that insurance policy,' replied Barry. 'If one of us died, the other got his share of the business, a nice cash lump sum and the mortgage to this place paid off.' Lena looked at Sarika. She could see the girl's face filling up with suspicion. 'I'm pretty sure he thought I'd be the first to croak,' continued Barry. 'Seems a fair assumption. He was twenty-six and went to the gym twice a day. I'm fifty and haven't had a holiday since that girl from Bienvenue.com did her runner.'

'Bienvenue.com,' said Lena. She put her beer down, not wanting it to slow the whirrings of her brain. 'That is where you met the girl who stole from you.'

'I remember Terry telling you about her,' said Barry. 'He told everyone. So no point trying to hide what an old fool I've been. Imagining a girl like that would be interested in an old git like me.'

'So you got Terry's share of the business,' said Sarika. 'And a hefty pay-out.'

'That's right,' said Barry, looking at her. 'What are you trying to say?'

'You did not seem that sad when my darling Terry died,' said Sarika. Lena could tell she was a sentence away from accusing him of murder. It still didn't feel right to her, but she let the girl proceed. Her mind was busy.

Barry put down the tea towel he'd been using to wipe the bar. 'What are you saying, young lady? That I murdered my dead brother's only son to get my hands on his share of this bar?'

'Well, did you?' Even Sarika sounded unsure of herself.

'You knew Terry for what, a month? Two? I met him the day he was born. My April and I couldn't have kids, so it hurt her to hold him. But when he reached out and grabbed my finger with those tiny little hands of his, I swore I'd be there for him.'

'I didn't think you liked him much,' muttered Sarika, a little shamefacedly.

'Don't get me wrong,' said Barry. 'He grew into a little shit. I blame the Arsenal.'

Lena looked up at him, distracted from her thoughts for a moment.

Barry continued. 'He was a nice boy, football crazy like they all are. He loved a kick-about in Highbury Fields. We used to go every night after school. He got pretty good too. Very good. Had a try-out for the under-twelves and Arsenal took him on. You should have seen his dad's face. I was proud of him, but for his dad it was a dream come true. His son, who he'd raised on his own, on the path to becoming a Premier League footballer. He saw the glory, the fame, and – let's face it – the money. There was nothing my brother wouldn't do for that lad.'

'Terry told me he used to play,' said Sarika. 'But he didn't say why he stopped.'

'He was dropped, as quickly as he was picked. It's what happens to a lot of the boys they take. It's a numbers game. Terry was upset but his dad was devastated. And after that, Terry changed. He would never admit it, but I think he spent the rest of his life trying to get that same look of respect from his dad. He wanted to be rich and he wanted to be famous. He auditioned for *X Factor* but has a voice like a toad. He tried to get into acting, but could only play himself.'

'Then he got the job on *N1 Angels*,' said Lena.

'The irony is, he was so busy filming he didn't get to see his dad at the end. None of us realised how sick he was till it was too late. And then he was gone.'

Lena looked at Sarika. Tears were already forming in her eyes. 'Poor Terry,' she declared. She leaned over the bar and grabbed Barry as best she could in a bear hug. 'I am so sorry, Uncle Barry,' she said. 'I never should have suspected you.'

'No harm done,' said Barry, uncomfortably extricating himself from her hug. 'You weren't to know. Terry kept his cards close to his chest.'

'His beautiful, tattooed chest,' said Sarika. To Lena's horror, she grabbed the tea towel and used it to wipe the tears from her face.

'I'll get you a brandy,' said Barry. 'In fact, I need one too.'

'Okay,' said Sarika.

'And you?' he offered to Lena.

'No brandy,' said Lena. 'But a few questions.'

'Lena, leave Uncle Barry alone,' said Sarika.

'It is important,' said Lena, feeling excited about the idea that had started to brew in her brain. 'It is about the website. Bienvenue.com. You met the woman who stole from you there.'

'I should have known better. You won't meet a nice girl on a site like that.'

'Terry met me there,' interjected Sarika.

Lena ignored her. 'What was her name?'

'Anastasia,' said Barry, looking at her curiously. 'Do you know her?'

'You have a picture of this woman?'

'She'd never let me take a photo. She was really funny about that. In hindsight, I suppose it was a warning sign. She was always planning to con me.'

Lena nodded. A few punters were standing at the bar looking impatient.

'I need to help Hayley,' said Barry, gesturing to the barmaid. 'It's getting busy.'

'Thank you for your help,' said Lena. 'Come, Sarika, let us sit down.' She guided Sarika to a sofa.

'Mr Ives, he met a woman on that website, Bienvenue.com and ran away with her. She took money from him. Ten thousand pounds.'

'So?'

'And Mr Quincy,' she said, as soon as they sat down. 'You said you had seen him on that website too?'

'Dirty old man,' said Sarika.

'He is not yet forty,' corrected Lena, but her mind was elsewhere.

'Why are you so interested?' asked Sarika. 'I told you. Lots of men around here are on that site. And you must clean hundreds of houses. Of course you will know several men on there.'

'Uncle Barry too,' said Lena, ignoring her. 'He met a woman on the site who stole from him. Get your phone out,' she said. 'I want to look at this website.'

'Finally,' said Sarika, tapping away at her phone. She'd recovered from her earlier tears and cheered up at the prospect of helping Lena. 'It's about time you started dating again. For women, the profile picture is the most important thing. You have to upload a photo, but men get to choose whether they do or not. Some girls just put pictures of their bodies up there, but I don't think that's so classy. I wish I had taken a picture of you when we went to meet Jack. You looked hot.'

'I do not want to be on the site,' said Lena, feeling horrified at the thought. 'Just to look.'

'I'll log you in as me then,' said Sarika, looking disappointed. 'So you can pick the men you like.' She tapped at her phone again and passed it to Lena. 'Don't wink at anyone ugly,' she warned.

Lena took it and scrolled through. The men were a mixed bunch, but mainly had British-sounding names. Some had profile pictures, others didn't. The women were a cornucopia of nationalities. 'Why are the women foreign and the men local?' she asked Sarika.

'The site is designed to help women new to the country hook up with rich local men,' said Sarika.

'That seems sexist,' said Lena.

Sarika shrugged. 'That's why it's called Bienvenue.com. It is French for welcome.'

Lena tapped something into the search bar. 'I can't find Mr Quincy,' she said.

'He won't use his real name,' said Sarika. 'No one does. Give it here. I'll find him.' She messed around with the phone for a bit. 'He's not on the site any more,' she said. 'Maybe his wife caught him.'

'Maybe,' said Lena, thinking. Mr Quincy, Barry, Mr Ives.

Terry was on the site too. He'd met Sarika there. And now he was dead.

She took her phone back and scrolled through the pictures. Barry came over with their drinks. 'That's her,' he said, peering at the screen. 'Anastasia.' Lena looked. The name said Ekaterina. You couldn't see the girl's face in the picture – it was just a body shot of a voluptuous woman in sexy lingerie.

'How do you know?' said Lena.

'That body. My oh my,' said Barry, looking at the phone wistfully. Just a body, no face. It sounded familiar to Lena.

Mr Ives.

She was sure that when Mrs Ives found the photo of the woman he'd run away with, it had been a body shot only. No face. She bit her lip. Could it be the same woman?

'I've missed her,' Barry continued.

'She stole from you,' said Lena.

'She's a sight for sore eyes, though,' he said. 'Maybe Terry was right. She was worth the money.'

'Terry was attracted to her?' said Lena, her mind racing.

'He's a man, isn't he?' Barry said. 'Look at that body.'

'She probably had an ugly face,' said Sarika. 'Lots of women on this site just have sexy body pictures. I bet they all have massive noses.'

'Do you know where I can find this woman?' said Lena.

'She's not likely to come back to this bar,' said Barry. He looked at the picture again. 'More's the pity.'

The next day Lena sat on the bus staring out of the window. It was grimy; the dirty ghosts of dried-up raindrops taunted her. Outside, she watched a collection of new mothers struggle with their buggies over the uneven pavement, their babies' faces filled with stoicism at their bumpy ride.

'Why were you so interested in this website last night?' asked Sarika. She'd declared herself sick of the hotel breakfasts and the women had been to Louis Patisserie to indulge in Hungarian cakes instead.

Lena thought. 'Do you remember when Terry first went missing?' she said. 'We were catering that dinner party with Lucia and there was talk of another man disappearing too. Sebastian Brown?'

'Maybe there is a serial killer on the loose,' said Sarika, with a laugh. She looked at Lena's face and her own fell. 'Lena, you do not think I am right?'

'No,' said Lena, out of habit. 'But Mr Ives, he met a woman on that site too. She took money from him. The same thing happened to Barry. Something not right is happening with Mr Quincy, who you saw there too. I wonder if there is a woman, using the website to track down men who think with their *fasz*. We need to find out what happened with Mr Ives. I will visit his wife later today. Perhaps it is the same woman.'

'But Terry didn't meet that woman on the site,' objected Sarika. 'He met me there. And I have done nothing to him. Nothing but love him.'

Lena thought about what Marsela had said. Everyone was using everyone for something. Men were using this site to meet vulnerable women. What if there was a woman using it to turn the tables? Meeting wealthy men and stealing from them. She wasn't convinced that Sarika had been the only woman Terry had met on Bienvenue.com. She needed to find out more.

Lena was surprised that Mr Ives opened the door wearing an apron and a forlorn expression.

'Who is it?' called Mrs Ives, from the living room.

'The cleaner,' he called back. He gave Lena a smile of relief. 'I think this means I can take a break.'

'It means no such thing,' said Mrs Ives, coming to the front door. 'It's Saturday and she's popped in for a nice chat. Rupert is cleaning from now on. He'll still pay you, plus a tip of course,' she said, gesturing to her husband, who began rummaging through his pockets. 'Lena, put your feet up.'

'Don't you think this is getting ridiculous?' said Rupert, following the women back into the living room. 'You got me up this morning at five a.m. before the frost had melted to clean out the guttering and I've been working ever since. I'm shattered. If we're paying Lena to clean, why can't we let her do it?'

Mrs Ives turned on him. 'Lena was here for me these last three weeks while you were off gallivanting with that tramp. She's shown me more respect than you have. And I expect she has had a long day already too, haven't you Lena?'

'I have been busy today,' Lena confirmed.

'Well then, that's settled. Sit down and Rupert will make you a coffee. Do you like brownies?' Lena nodded. 'Excellent. Two brownies please, Rupert.'

'We don't have any brownies,' replied her husband.

'Then off you trot to Ottolenghi's,' said Mrs Ives. 'Try not to give any pretty damsels in distress ten thousand pounds of Alex's university money on your way back. I'd appreciate it. And don't forget the coffee first. Lena likes it strong, please.'

Mrs Ives turned to Lena and smiled as Mr Ives tramped back to the kitchen. 'In a funny way, things are better now,' she confided in a whisper. 'It's like having stomach flu. It's awful at the time, but then when you've recovered, you've lost half a stone and your jeans look great.'

'That is a good way to think about it,' said Lena, doubtfully. 'But I do not mind cleaning for you. Perhaps, if I can just do some dusting . . .' Lena went to get to her feet.

'Rupert!' called Mrs Ives. He scurried back in. 'Lena has noticed some dust in here. Get it sorted.' Rupert took a cloth from his back pocket. 'Make the coffee first, you idiot,' said Mrs Ives. 'Did your girlfriend take your manners as well as your money?'

Lena had never felt sorry for a man who cheated on his wife before. Not since her own father had run out on her and her mother, taking their savings and ruining their lives. But now even she was starting to feel sympathy creeping up on her like a spider on coving. 'Do you think you are being a bit hard on Mr Ives?' she said, quietly. 'I am sure that he is sorry for what he has done.'

'I didn't take you for a softy, Lena,' said Mrs Ives. 'But maybe he can have a little break. Rupert, you can bring us the chocolate biscuits from the tin and have a cup of tea with us,' she called to the kitchen. 'Then you can dust and vacuum. Then time to clean out the drains.' She turned back to Lena. 'More than the dirty sod deserves,' she said. 'But we are made of sugar and spice, after all.'

Lena looked at her, puzzled, and then decided to let it go. 'I wanted to talk to him,' said Lena. She leaned forwards. 'About what happened while he is away. I think there might be a connection to another man who disappeared.'

'Certainly,' said Mrs Ives. 'I've already heard more than I can bear to about the whole sorry business,' she said. 'So I'll leave you to it. Rupert, Lena wants to talk to you. I'm going for a bath with

217

the lavender you picked for me earlier. There had better not be any insects in with it.'

Mr Ives handed Lena her coffee and then sank into an arm-chair. 'I'm exhausted,' he said. 'It's like she is torturing me.' He looked at Lena in despair. 'I think she hates me.'

'She was very upset when you were gone,' said Lena. 'But you are lucky. I think she will forgive you, with time.'

'I hope so,' he said, taking a biscuit from the plate. 'Thank you for getting me a rest. I've been working so hard I feel like my arm will drop off.'

Lena took the duster from where he'd let it fall on the table. 'You have not dusted the skirting,' she told him. 'Do not worry, you can keep your arms on. I will do it, if you will answer my questions.'

'Anything for a break,' he said, leaning back on the sofa, putting his feet on the table and closing his eyes. Lena made a mental note to wipe the table off before Mrs Ives came back. This man had cheated, but for once she felt he was already being punished enough.

'The woman that you ran away with,' started Lena. Mr Ives's eyes popped open again. 'Do you still have her picture?'

'What? Do you think I'm crazy?' he said. 'My wife would castrate me.'

'On the internet maybe?' suggested Lena. 'Your wife showed me one before. I need to see it again, to compare it to something.'

'She tracks me online now, you know,' he said. 'I can't visit any of those sites, even just to look.'

Lena got out her phone. 'Find her on this,' she said. Mr Ives looked at her like it was a trap. 'Help me and I'll finish the cleaning and tell your wife it was you,' said Lena. 'I will even bring you another cup of tea.'

'Fine,' he said and took the phone from Lena's hand. 'There's only a body shot online, though. And she wouldn't let me take any photos of her face. Although I'd have deleted them now, anyway. Of course.' He tapped at the phone a few times and handed it back to her. Lena looked at the picture. Again it was just a torso in sexy lingerie. It might be the same girl who had swindled Barry, but without a face she wasn't sure.

'She took money from you, this woman?' confirmed Lena.

'Yes, but it's not what you think,' he replied. 'She wasn't a prostitute. We met on that site. I wasn't going to do anything on there. I was just looking. But then we got to chatting online and really got on. I thought maybe we could be friends.'

Lena raised her eyebrow. 'Your wife cannot hear us,' she said. 'The truth please.'

'Anyway,' he continued. 'We met and the connection was stronger than either of us expected. We couldn't keep our hands off each other, even though I tried. We ran away together. And then when she told me she needed money to help her son back in Russia, how could I refuse? She needed me. I haven't felt needed like that in years.'

'What went wrong?' asked Lena.

'I couldn't get enough money,' said Mr Ives, miserably. 'I gave her ten grand but that's the limit I could take from the joint account without my wife's signature. The next morning, Valentina left.'

'Valentina,' said Lena. Barry's girl had been Anastasia, but it was likely if she was out to swindle men on this website that she used a number of aliases.

'I realised what a fool I'd been and came home,' continued Mr Ives. 'I do love my wife. I always have.'

'You have been a fool,' agreed Lena. 'But I need to know more about this woman. Can you contact her?'

'It's like she's vanished,' said Mr Ives. 'She told me the money wasn't enough, left the hotel and never came back. Her phone hasn't worked since.'

Lena shivered a little. If the same woman had been in the hotel room with Terry, she'd left him dead. She wondered if Mr Ives had had a lucky escape. 'Have you spoken to the police?' she asked.

'Of course not,' said Mr Ives. 'We'd never get that money back, there's no point.'

'You did not report her missing?' said Lena. 'You were planning a future together and then she disappeared. How do you know that something did not happen to her?'

'She's got my ten grand,' replied Mr Ives. 'She'll be fine.'

Lena felt her sympathy for this man evaporating. 'Was Valentina seeing other men?' she asked him.

'If she was, she didn't talk about it with me,' he replied. 'In hindsight, I suppose she could have been.'

'I need you to remember a night: it is very important. Saturday the second of February, three weeks ago. Were you with Valentina then?'

Mr Ives looked to the ceiling in thought. 'No,' he replied. 'I was with her the night before,' he admitted. 'But my wife and I had ballet tickets on the second. Sadler's Wells. It was before I ran away with Valentina.'

'So she could have killed Terry,' said Lena to herself.

'What?'

'Nothing.'

Lena sat in front of her suspect board and looked at the pictures she'd printed from the website. The body of Valentina, and the body of Anastasia. Side by side, they looked very similar. It could be the same woman. She was definitely the nexus of activity. Lines went from her to Bienvenue.com and out to Barry and Mr Ives. Terry had met her as his uncle's girlfriend.

Lena had a bad feeling about that website. She opened up the page on her phone again. Next to a picture of a smiling, silver-haired man, it read: *Are you a powerful, successful gentleman? Why not give a warm Bienvenue welcome to an attractive woman, new to the country? She'll most definitely be grateful.*

Lena shuddered. Then there was a picture of a pouting woman, not much more than twenty, in a low-cut top. Lena read the caption: *New to the UK? Let one of our successful gentlemen look after you and treat you to the very best our country has to offer.*

Lena would never dream of using a site like that. But, distasteful as she found it, she could see why it might be successful. A woman coming to this country, alone, penniless and scared, could meet a man to take care of her in those early days. For a price.

And for the men, there were attractive and vulnerable women to date.

But Anastasia was not vulnerable. Lena hated deception of all kinds, but she couldn't help but respect how this woman had turned the tables on these men, taking advantage of their lust to line her own pockets. But had it gone too far? Terry was dead. He knew that Anastasia was up to no good – she had stolen from his uncle. Had he been lusting after her even then? Lena looked at the picture again. There was no doubting that she was sexy. Or was this some kind of trap – did Terry intend to meet with Anastasia to get his uncle's money back? Was that how it had gone wrong?

Lena knew how ruthless women could be. Had Anastasia silenced Terry for ever?

It was all guesswork, she knew. What she needed was proof. And she had a plan for how to get it.

CHAPTER 22

'Absolutely not!' Cartwright was looking at Lena as if she were a crazy person. They were sitting in the pub across the road from the police station on Cartwright's lunch break. 'That's entrap-ment,' he whispered, looking around as if to see if there were any of his colleagues nearby listening to their conversation.

'Yes,' said Lena. 'A trap.'

'No,' replied Cartwright. 'En-trap-ment. The police should not incite someone to commit a crime. I can't do it. Especially now I'm CID. It's not the right thing to do.'

Lena usually loved how moral Cartwright was. Right now it was frustrating. 'But it is the only way,' she said. 'The only way to prove what she has done.'

'We don't know that she's done anything,' said Cartwright, taking a sip of the sparkling elderflower drink he'd ordered. 'Explain to me again why you even think she is involved.'

Lena found herself starting to get annoyed. Usually Cartwright could quickly follow her thoughts, but it was as though he was being purposefully obstreperous now. Maybe becoming a detective had gone to his head.

Lena took out the photo she'd taken on her phone of her sus-pect board. She zoomed in and pointed to the lines running to Valentina like veins to a heart. 'I think that Valentina and Anastasia are the same woman,' she explained. 'She uses Bienvenue. com to meet men and then cheat them. She ran away with Mr Ives and convinced him to give her money. Ten grand, but she tried for more. She dated Barry Tibbs and then stole fifteen thousand pounds from the safe in his pub. I do not yet have evidence, but I think that perhaps she blackmailed Mr Quincy. Terry used the same dating site. I think that she met him there and was going to blackmail him too. Something went wrong and it looks like she might have killed him.'

'Lena, that's quite a theory, but extremely tenuous. You need proof.'

'I know that,' snapped Lena. 'That is why you must go on the site, pretending to be a wealthy businessman. She will contact you and try to seduce you. But we will be ready and catch her in the act. Perhaps stealing from you. Perhaps blackmail. But then we will know.'

'It's unethical,' replied Cartwright. 'And it's hare-brained. I'm sorry, Lena, but there's no way I'd ever get involved in something like this.'

'You will not help me,' said Lena.

'I am helping you. You need to stop this. I never thought I'd say this to you, Lena,' he said. 'But I think you need to leave this to the police. There's a team working to find out what happened to Terry. Let them do their job.'

'They do not even believe it is murder,' she scoffed. 'I do not believe anyone is working on this. Anyone but me. And I need to keep Sarika safe.'

'Why would this woman be threatening Sarika?' asked Cartwright, voicing a question Lena had been asking herself. 'Sarika is not a wealthy man.'

'I do not know,' said Lena. 'Maybe it is her connection to Terry. But that is something that we need to find out.'

She looked at Cartwright. He looked away. 'The police have

nothing,' she surmised. She shrugged. 'Fine. I leave it with you.' She slurped her Coke. 'We are finished here,' she said. 'You can go.'

'My lunch break isn't over yet,' said Cartwright. 'I thought we might have a sandwich together.'

'You eat,' said Lena. 'I have things to do.' She stood up and walked out.

Cartwright wasn't the only man around. If he wouldn't help her she needed someone who would. Someone without his ethics. She smiled to herself. She knew just the person.

'So let me get this right,' said Raz. He was leaning against the wall round the back of the Boots by Angel, on his break. He took a swig from the plastic bottle of green sludge he was clutching. Lena scrunched up her nose in disgust. 'You want me to sleep with a beautiful woman?'

'I said "date",' corrected Lena. She took a sip from her paper coffee cup and despaired at Raz's slowness. All his blood must have rushed to his stomach to deal with an assault from the kale, spinach and spirulina smoothie he was glugging.

'Exactly,' replied Raz, replacing the cap on the bottle and giving the dregs of the liquid a shake. 'Show me the picture again.' Lena showed him her phone. 'Smoking body,' he said, nodding approval. 'But what if she's got an ugly face?'

'That is not relevant,' said Lena. 'It is one date.' She saw Raz frowning and changed tack. 'She is pretty,' she said. 'I have been told that by two men. Terry said it himself, do you remember?'

Raz nodded again. 'And you will be very grateful to me if I do this?'

'Of course,' said Lena, wiping off the small drop of green liquid that had escaped to her coat. He grinned at her.

'Count me in,' he said. 'There's no downside.'

'Do not take extra risk. You go on a date and act normally. Do not ask too many questions,' warned Lena. 'You must not make her suspicious.' She took another sip of coffee and tried to make him understand. 'This woman, she might try to get you into a compromising position.'

'Compromising positions are my favourite,' he replied with a wink.

'She might try to steal from you.'

'Nothing to take,' said Raz. 'I'm broke.' He grinned at her.

'Do not tell her that,' said Lena. 'She must think you are wealthy.'

'Everyone does,' he replied. 'I've been on telly.'

'You must not do something you are not comfortable with,' continued Lena. 'She might threaten to sell pictures to people who should not see it.'

'I'm a single lad,' said Raz. 'And even my gran's seen it all. I gave her the *N1 Naked Angels* calendar for Christmas.' He gulped the remainder of his drink and flashed Lena another smile, his white teeth flecked with green. 'She loved it,' he said, proudly. 'I can get you a copy half price,' he added. 'Since it's almost the end of February.'

Lena ignored his offer. 'It could be dangerous,' she said, her voice serious. 'If I am right, this woman killed Terry Tibbs.'

'And we'll catch her,' said Raz, sounding grave for once. 'Terry was my friend and I want justice.' He flashed Lena another smile and was back to normal. 'And I can handle myself,' he said, flexing his muscles. 'Two hours in the gym before work every day, coconut quinoa porridge for breakfast and a green goddess smoothie twice a day. Don't you worry about me.'

Lena attempted to return his smile, but couldn't get over the feeling of dread that was mingling with coffee in her stomach. 'Sarika will put up your profile on Bienvenue.com,' she said. 'You are a celebrity like Terry, so I think you will appeal to her. But you must text me as soon as the date is over.'

'So after breakfast then.' Raz winked at her and laughed. 'Only joking,' he added. Lena ignored him. She was wondering if this was such a good idea after all.

'That board is sick.' Raz was sitting in Lena's living room with a cup of tea and a look of admiration on his face. 'Super-cool. It's like *CSI*.'

'It helps me to organise my thoughts,' said Lena.

'You're really clever, aren't you?' said Raz. 'I could tell there was something about you. You're different.' Lena shrugged. 'You should put a picture of the investigation team there too,' said Raz. 'I can give you my photo. I'd be great on *Heroes of Law*.'

'The board is for the victim and the suspects only,' said Lena. 'I do not want to confuse things.'

Raz grinned at her. 'I'm like your Dr Watson. The Jude Law to your Robert Downey Junior.' He reached out and brushed her arm with his hand. 'Except you're not a man.'

Lena moved her arm out of his reach. 'Sarika,' she called. 'How is Raz's profile coming along?'

'Almost done,' replied Sarika. 'But I could do with more glamorous pictures.'

'Are you kidding?' asked Raz. 'There's tonnes of me with my top off.'

'That's not what I mean,' said Sarika, looking up from the laptop. 'I want pictures of you enjoying the high life. In a Porsche. Travelling by private jet. On a yacht.'

'Oh,' said Raz. He paused. 'Those must be on my other phone.'

Lena smiled. 'It does not matter,' she said. 'Sarika, just say in the profile description that he is a wealthy TV star. That should be enough bait.'

'No one reads the descriptions,' muttered Sarika. 'But I'm doing it.'

'So tell me the plan again,' said Raz.

Lena looked at him. They'd been over this several times already that afternoon. 'We will put your profile live now,' she said. 'I hope that it will be enough to attract this girl they call Anastasia, or Valentina, very soon.'

'It will be,' said Raz, confidently. 'It's got my picture.'

'Anyway, you must arrange a date with her as soon as you can. Try to take a photo of her face without her seeing. Whatever you do, you must not drink anything she gives you in case it is drugged. She might not try anything the first date: with Barry and Mr Ives she lured them in first and then tried to rob them. But with Terry . . .'

'Don't worry, I can handle myself,' said Raz.

'And you must call us as soon as the date is over. I want to know everything. There might be something we can use straight away, without this having to go any further.'

'It's live,' said Sarika. They all sat and looked at the screen. 'What if no one wants to date him?' asked Sarika.

'We only want that woman,' said Lena. 'And we know she is on the hunt for people like Raz.'

A pink love heart flashed up on screen. 'Yess!' said Raz, pumping his fist. 'Got a bite. Come on the Raz-ster.'

'Sarika?' said Lena. The girl clicked on the heart. A body shot came up. A lacy black bra barely concealing a voluptuous chest. A toned stomach that made Lena regret the two Krispy Kremes she'd had with her coffee earlier.

'That's her,' said Sarika. 'She's calling herself Ivanna now, but it's Anastasia/Valentina. And she wants to meet Raz. Tomorrow night.'

The next evening, Lena checked her phone again on her way home from work. It was only eight p.m. – an hour into his date – but Lena wished Raz would get in touch. She'd hardly been able to concentrate at her cleaning jobs all day; she was too worried. Maybe it hadn't been such a good idea to set Raz up on this date.

He'd called before he left; too confident for Lena's liking. She wasn't convinced he really understood how dangerous this woman might be. And it made her feel guilty: like sending a tiny lamb to battle a thousand goblins.

She went into the entrance to her apartment block and gathered a few bills from her mailbox. Realistically, ten or eleven p.m. was the earliest she could hope to hear from him. Probably much later. She paused and looked up the staircase, then pushed the button for the lift. Life was hard enough without climbing unnecessary stairs.

'Lena!' The voice was a hissed whisper, redolent with fear. She looked around. She was on her own. 'It's me.' Lena looked again, wondering if she were losing her mind. The door to the communal laundry room stood slightly ajar. A pair of frightened eyes stared out at her. 'Get in.'

'What are you doing?' asked Lena.

'Just get in,' said Sarika. 'I don't know when she is coming back.'

Lena obeyed, going into the small room. Sarika shut the door and then turned the light on. The room was just big enough for a washing machine, a tumble dryer and one person. Lena pulled herself on top of the washing machine so she didn't have to stand with her face right against Sarika's. There was a basket in the corner full of unclaimed orphan socks and a stray pair of grey Y-fronts. Sarika sat too, perched on the dryer. She pulled her feet up into her and hugged her knees.

'What are you doing in here?' asked Lena. 'Why are you not at the hotel?'

'There is someone in our flat,' said Sarika. 'I came over to get some clean clothes, but then I thought some wine would be nice while I packed and I popped out to buy a bottle and when I came back I could hear someone moving around in there.'

'Have you called the police?' asked Lena, feeling dread rise inside her.

'I left my phone in the flat,' said Sarika. 'I was only gone a few minutes.'

Lena's mind whizzed. There had been no notes for a week, but that didn't mean the threat to Sarika had gone. Or had the date with Valentina gone wrong already and the woman was coming for them?

'Lena, I'm scared,' said Sarika. Lena took a deep breath. 'Who do you think it is?'

'Maybe a burglar,' said Lena, trying to sound collected. 'I will call the police,' she said, fishing her phone out of her bag.

'I might have left the door open,' said Sarika. 'I was only out five minutes and my key is stiff. What with my shaking hands after Terry died and all those awful notes I don't always . . .'

Lena began to dial.

'Lena, no,' said Sarika. 'What if it is the woman who sent that note?'

'Even more reason to call the police,' said Lena, raising the phone to her ear.

'What if she is planting evidence?' said Sarika. 'Evidence that I killed Terry. What if that is what she is doing right now?'

Lena looked at her cousin. 'That is the least likely explanation for what is happening,' she said.

'Don't do it!' said Sarika. She snatched the phone away. Lena leaned forwards to grab it but Sarika scrambled to her feet and stood on top of the dryer with the phone held above her head. 'I will smash it,' she threatened.

Lena looked to the concrete floor. That would be easy to accomplish. And if she attempted to tackle her, Sarika might fall too. She looked wobbly on her feet already.

'Sit down,' said Lena. 'Just for a moment. I will not call the police. Tell me what you heard.'

'Shush,' said Sarika, slowly crouching back down. 'Did you hear that?'

The women sat in silence, listening. Lena couldn't hear a thing. 'This is silly,' said Lena. 'We cannot stay in the laundry room all night. How about I call Cartwright?'

Sarika considered.

'Off the record,' said Lena. 'If it is not too serious, he can help us. And if it is serious, he can call for back-up.'

'Okay,' said Sarika. Lena dialled. His phone went to voicemail. She left as coherent a message as she could.

'I do not know when he will get that,' said Lena. She took a deep breath. 'I am going up there.'

'Lena, it could be dangerous.'

Lena was determined. 'It is probably a squirrel in the flat,' she said, to calm Sarika down. 'I saw a programme about them scrabbling into apartments and causing chaos.'

'We are on the fourth floor!' said Sarika.

'Squirrels can climb,' said Lena, hoping she sounded more nonchalant than she felt. She looked around for a weapon. A mop sat next to the sock bucket. That would have to do. 'Come on,' she said. 'I will go first. We do not want to be robbed.'

'I thought you said it was squirrels.'

'Let's find out,' said Lena. Sarika squeezed her knees more tightly into her chest. 'I will tell you what,' said Lena, relenting. 'I will go and see what is happening. You wait. Here is my phone: if I do not come back after five minutes then call the police.'

'Okay,' said Sarika, a little too quickly for Lena's liking. 'That is a good idea. If something happens I will raise the alarm.'

Lena stood up. 'Right,' she said. 'I am off.' She went to leave the laundry room, clutching her mop. Sarika grabbed her and enclosed her in a tense hug.

'Be careful,' she said. 'And thank you.'

Lena left the room and made her way softly up the stairs. She wanted to be able to listen to what was happening in the flat. From a distance.

Lena hoped Sarika had imagined the intruder. The thought of someone rummaging around in her stuff with their dirty hands filled Lena with horror, whether or not it was Valentina come with malevolent intentions. Once she'd received a tearful phone call from her client Mrs Hills after she'd been burgled. Lena had come to clean up as soon as the police had finished. It had been awful: clothes scattered everywhere, furniture upturned, not to mention the treasured belongings that were gone for good. Lena had felt a strong sense of satisfaction when she found a selection of fat fingerprints and pointed them out to the police. These burglars would be punished for the mess they left behind.

Lena stood outside the door and listened. The banging had stopped and she could hear what sounded like a gentle whimpering. Squirrels don't whimper, she thought to herself. But then again, she didn't think most burglars would either. Carefully, her mop clutched in one hand, she turned her key in the lock with the other and pushed the door open. She stepped inside.

It was worse than she'd feared. Nothing was in its place. Clothes were strewn all over the apartment, shoes were flung all over the open-plan kitchen and even Lena's precious bottles of homemade cleaning products were lying on their sides on the floor. The television was still in place and, opening one of the cupboards, she found the biscuit tin where she kept a small stash of cash. The money hadn't been touched.

Lena tried to keep her head and looked around for the perpetrator. She could see no one. She stood in silence for a moment, listening. A timid whimper, this time coming from her room.

Dreading what she'd find inside, Lena crept through the hallway and into the bedroom.

Crumpled in a heap on the floor was a shaking girl, clutching a pillow to her chest and sobbing. Lena felt her anger at the state of the flat evaporate as she looked at the wretched creature. She took a step closer and the girl looked up. Even with her make-up smudged all over her face, she recognised her as Rubilla Patel.

'Has it been washed?' the girl said. 'Please tell me it hasn't.'

Lena looked at her, completely baffled. The girl pulled a face at her. 'You are not Sarika,' she said. She chucked the pillow away as if she'd just realised it was covered in venomous spiders. 'Has he slept in this bed?'

'Who?' said Lena. No one but her had ever slept in that bed, she thought regretfully. Certainly no men. She kept a firm hold on the mop and reached in her pocket for her phone, before she realised she'd given it to Sarika.

'You know who,' she replied. 'Has he slept with you too?'

'What are you doing in my flat?'

'He's not yours. He's mine,' the girl suddenly shouted. 'He's not Marsela's and he's not Sarika's. He's mine. I will punish you for what you've done.' Lena recognised the familiar words. They were from the notes Sarika had received.

'I've seen your family,' said Lena, realising Rubilla wasn't in her right mind. 'They want you to come home.'

The girl sprang up, suddenly as nimble as if she were a squirrel. She rushed to the window and thrust it open. It was almost as tall as she was and cold air flooded the flat. 'I need something of his,' she shouted at Lena. 'I need something that hasn't been washed. Something with his smell.'

Lena watched her, puzzled by her need to be by the window. Was she going to light up a cigarette?

232

'There is nothing that belongs to Terry in this flat,' she told her. 'And everything here has been washed,' she added, with a touch of pride. 'He has never even stayed here. Sarika and he used to go to a hotel. And please close the window,' she added. 'You have to go outside if you want to smoke.'

The girl let out a cry and stepped out on to the window ledge. 'No, I did not mean there,' said Lena, aghast. 'Come back in. It is not safe.'

'I couldn't have him and now no one can,' said Rubilla. Lena looked at the girl. Was that a confession?

'You made sure of that?' asked Lena.

'He told me he loved me. I have never done something like that before, but I believed him. I did not know that there were photographers. I didn't know those people on social media would call me a slut. I have brought shame on my family. And I will not let him leave me after what we did together. I will not let him go. Never.'

Lena thought for a moment, choosing her words. 'You were with him, that night at the hotel? When he died?'

'I'm always with him,' declared Rubilla. 'Even when Vikram was beating me, I was with him. Here,' she added, putting her hand to her heart.

'Vikram beat you?' asked Lena, her horror at the violence making her lose focus for a moment.

'A little, at first,' said Rubilla. 'When I did not want to quit my job. But then when he found out about Terry . . . I thought I was going to die. But when I came around, I had the strength to run. And now I wish he had killed me. Because then Terry and I would be together again.'

'And what happened?' asked Lena, slowly moving closer to her like a cat stalking a sparrow. 'What happened that night?'

'He's gone,' replied Rubilla. 'He's gone for ever. I've already been to the hotel. And to Marsela's house.' She looked back at

Lena. 'There's nothing left,' she said. 'Nothing that's been next to his skin. Nothing to remember him by.' She turned and looked back to the road below. 'So I need to join him.'

'Wait,' shouted Lena, horrified. 'Do not jump.' She tried to think quickly, watching Rubilla swaying by the window. 'We do have something of Terry's,' she said, edging towards her. 'I have remembered. It is in Sarika's room. Come with me.' She held out her hand.

'You said there was nothing,' said Rubilla, her voice suspicious. 'What is it?'

'Come with me and I will show you,' said Lena. Her mind raced through things she could pass off as Terry's. There must be something that could vaguely be passed off as belonging to a man in Sarika's room. Lena grimaced as she thought. She'd have been better off pretending it was in her room. She had a few manly shirts that might do. But Sarika wouldn't be seen dead in anything like that. Still, with Sarika's room in the mess it was, she could pretend to look for a good long while, keeping Rubilla away from windows in the meantime. Perhaps Cartwright would finally arrive and help her.

Lena watched as Rubilla hesitated. She decided that was all the signal she needed, and reached out to grab the girl's hand. It was cold in her grasp. Lena held it tightly, pulling her back into the room. Rubilla stumbled, then clung to Lena's arm.

'Let's get you a hot drink too,' she said, gently. 'We have some of the hot chocolate that Terry used to drink,' she lied, never having seen Terry drink anything non-alcoholic. But Rubilla was definitely in need of heat and sugar and, in fact, Lena would say anything to distract her from splattering herself on the pavement outside her flat.

To Lena's relief, it seemed the adrenalin had drained out of Rubilla, leaving her quiet and malleable. She silently nodded and allowed Lena to lead her out of the room and sit her on the sofa.

Lena packed a blanket around her and went to put some milk on the stove to boil, keeping an eye on her to make sure she didn't make a run for it.

When Lena bought the drink over, Rubilla was crying again. Lena handed her a tissue and then the hot chocolate. 'This will make you feel better,' she told her.

'Nothing will do that,' said Rubilla. 'The love of my life is dead and it is my fault.'

'Your fault?' confirmed Lena.

'Yes. It is my fault that he is dead. I wanted to hurt him and I did.'

It was a confession.

Despite the fear she and Sarika had been living in these past two weeks, Lena felt sorry for Rubilla. She was clearly unstable and needed help. Thank goodness she'd called Cartwright. He'd make sure Rubilla was taken somewhere where she couldn't hurt herself. Or anyone else.

Lena was exhausted. She let Sarika go straight to bed after Cartwright had led Rubilla away: her cousin was exhausted by fear and deflated by relief. At least she didn't have to stay in a hotel any longer. Lena took some time to put her flat back together before she'd allow herself to sleep.

It was a good result: Rubilla would get the treatment she needed. Sarika was safe. Terry had justice.

And Cartwright had looked at Lena the way he used to. She'd seen admiration in his eyes again as she presented him with the murderer.

So Rubilla was the murderer. Lena thought about the girl she'd found in her apartment, the girl who had confessed. The motive was clear: jealousy, obsession, and despair. Terry had slept with her and then cast her aside. Lena expected he had done that with

235

many girls, and maybe would have done the same with Sarika, eventually. But with Rubilla he had chosen the wrong woman. She was already on the edge, driven by misery at her arranged marriage that had turned violent. She had threatened Terry, threatened Sarika and Marsela, the women he had chosen over her, and eventually followed through and killed him. If she couldn't have him, no one could.

Lena wondered how she'd done it. She must have lured him to that hotel room for a final night of passion. Once she had him there, she'd given him the fatal cocktail of Rohypnol and Ecstasy. Perhaps he'd died in the throes of passion, making him forever Rubilla's, in some twisted way. Could forensics find that out, she wondered? It was probably too late.

Not that she minded. She didn't need to know the sordid details of Terry's last moments. So long as Sarika was safe.

But what about Raz? It was past midnight, and still no news. She checked her phone again. Nothing. She dialled him. No answer. Maybe she was being paranoid, she decided. Midnight was probably still early for him.

Lena found her eyelids were heavy and the strain of keeping them open seemed unnecessary. Sarika was finally safe, that was something. She'd find Raz in the morning.

CHAPTER 23

'I can't believe that crazy woman murdered my darling Terry,' said Sarika. Lena blinked her eyes awake. 'And threatened me too.'

'What time is it?' asked Lena. It felt like the middle of the night, though light was streaming in through the windows.

'It's ten a.m. I let you sleep. You've been looking awful recently. And I'm the one who has been living out of a suitcase.'

Lena struggled to her feet. She must stop sleeping on the sofa. It wasn't doing her back any favours. 'Has Raz called?' She looked at her phone. Nothing. 'I am worried about him. We have not seen or heard from him since his date last night.'

'On it,' said Sarika, tapping her phone. She called him, but there was no reply. 'I'll go through his Instagram account and see if he's posted anything. He normally has by now. Then we'll track him down. But first you need a shower.'

Lena had to agree. She'd been wearing the same clothes since yesterday. She padded to the bathroom and brushed her teeth while she ran the shower to allow the water to heat. When the mirror was covered in mist she knew it was hot enough and stepped in. She couldn't help but think about the Patels. Their daughter had murdered Terry, and was now suicidal herself. They were not a family that deserved something like that to happen.

Lena couldn't afford to luxuriate in the shower today. As she dried off, she tried to figure it out. Rubilla wasn't the woman on

Bienvenue.com. She must have been wrong about the connection to that site: it was just coincidence. Perhaps karma, she thought to herself. Men who cheated getting what they deserved.

But then where was Raz?

She dressed quickly and went back to the living room. 'Nothing on Instagram,' said Sarika. 'Not on Twitter or Snapchat either, and no check-ins on Facebook. Not since yesterday afternoon, when he posted a picture of himself with a matcha latte outside Boots.'

'I will go there,' said Lena. 'Perhaps he is at work.'

'I'll get my stuff and check out of the hotel,' said Sarika. 'Then I'll do some Instagram digging and make a list of where Raz usually spends his time. We can try those places next.'

'Sorry love, he didn't come in today.' Lena looked at the Boots employee. His name badge said *Gareth*. 'Can I help you?'

'I need to find him,' said Lena, feeling her panic mounting. It had been bad enough when Sarika told her he hadn't posted a picture on Instagram since before the date. Now he was missing from work.

'Nothing I can help you with?' asked Gareth, breaking her reverie.

'It is . . . personal,' said Lena.

'The lady's sanitary products are at the back of the store,' he told her. 'And painkillers are right here. You do look a little peaky.'

Lena put her hand to her forehead and realised it was covered in sweat, despite the freezing temperatures outside. 'That is not what I mean,' she said. 'I know Raz. I need to find him.'

Gareth laughed. 'That man is a legend,' he said. 'Where he finds the energy, I don't know. Just last night he had a hot date lined up with some Russian chick, now you're here desperate for him. Russian too, are you? Got any hot friends for me?'

Lena pulled a tissue from her pocket to wipe her damp brow.

Gareth misinterpreted. 'Don't cry, love,' he said. 'Did you think you were the only one? Don't worry. I'm sure he's got plenty to go round.'

Sarika was waiting for her outside Boots. 'According to his Instagram, Raz spends most of his time in Body Fanatics near the Arsenal. It's the gym he and Terry used to go to together. But he still hasn't posted anything online since before he went on that date. Not even a "story". Normally he posts at least five times a day.'

'We will go to the Body Fanatics,' said Lena. 'And see what we can find out.'

They headed to the bus stop. 'I think Raz will be okay,' said Sarika. 'Rubilla is the murderer and they don't even know each other.'

Lena thought. 'Are you sure they did not? You did not know Rubilla had been with Terry.'

'He didn't have to tell me everyone he had ever slept with before we met,' said Sarika, defensively. 'He needed to keep some mystery.'

The bus pulled up and both women climbed on. 'Do you know what I think?' said Sarika, swinging on one of the bus poles while Lena took a seat in front of her. 'I think that Raz and that woman hit it off and they've been together ever since.'

'I hope so,' replied Lena. They got off the bus.

Lena pushed open the door to the gym and heard screaming. She blinked in the darkness while her eyes adjusted to the strobe lights. 'Can I help you?' said a voice, apparently unperturbed by the screams. Lena focused. There were punch bags hanging from the ceiling, weights in the corner and the air conditioning was on full blast. A row of red-faced women stared at her as they did squats. In the corner was a mat covered in toys. And babies. One of them was screaming as if the world was about to end.

'I do not think I am in the right place,' said Lena, trying to make a swift exit.

'It's our mother-and-baby class,' said the woman. 'Did you leave your little one at home?'

'There is no little one,' said Lena. She looked at the screaming baby. Its mother had picked it up and was trying to put it in a sling. Once in, the baby grinned at Lena. The mother valiantly resumed her squats.

'Do you know Raz?' she asked, realising she had no idea what his surname was. A muscular man appeared from behind the counter. 'He's our best customer,' he said. 'Eliza, you carry on with your class. I'll take over the enquiry.'

Lena watched as the mothers switched to walking lunges. 'Impressive, isn't it?' he said. 'I wouldn't fancy doing that with a twenty-pound baby strapped to my chest.'

Lena nodded. Sarika had gone to the mat with the babies and was cooing at them. Lena turned her attention back to the man. 'When is the last time you saw Raz?' she asked.

'It's awful what happened to Terry,' said the man. 'Those two were great workout buddies. They used to pummel those punch bags together then spot each other on the weights.'

'Has Raz been in today?'

'Nope. And he never usually misses a session.'

Lena looked at Sarika. She was tickling one of the babies, who giggled back at her with glee. The mothers continued their workout, clearly thinking baby-loving Sarika was a perk of the class.

So Raz hadn't been here either.

Lena thought. It was too early to be worried, she told herself. She'd do her cleaning jobs for the day, but if there was still no news by the evening, she'd have to report Raz missing. Even if it meant confessing to Cartwright what she'd done.

★ ★ ★

'You're back,' said Cartwright, his words waking Lena with a jolt. She realised that she'd dribbled on to her collar and wiped hurriedly at her chin. Her breath tasted disgusting and must smell even worse. After searching for Raz all morning, she'd had to work late cleaning to catch up and had drifted off in the warm police waiting room. She had no idea how long she'd been asleep for.

'You'd probably have been more comfortable in a cell,' said Cartwright. 'At least they have beds.'

'I need to tell you something,' said Lena. 'I am very worried.'

'I need to tell you something too,' said Cartwright. 'It's about Rubilla.'

'What has happened?' she asked. 'Do you have her confession?'

'Yes,' said Cartwright. 'But listen, you don't look too well. Why don't you go home and get some sleep. You must be exhausted after everything that happened last night. And knowing you, you'll have been tidying up that mess in your flat all night, and working all day.'

'I am fine,' said Lena. She pulled herself to her feet. 'I am pleased it is over with Terry's murder,' she began.

Cartwright looked away. 'What is it?' asked Lena. She could tell something was wrong. 'What are you not telling me?'

'We'll talk tomorrow,' said Cartwright.

'We will talk now,' replied Lena. She sat back down and ran her tongue over her teeth. They felt furry, as if they were coated in velvet.

'Rubilla did not murder Terry,' said Cartwright. 'She has an alibi.'

'An alibi like Marsela?' questioned Lena, wondering what conspiracy this was.

'She was in hospital,' answered Cartwright. 'She'd taken an overdose of pills. Not enough to kill her, but enough to cry pretty loudly for help. A dozen staff at the hospital can vouch for her being there when Terry died.'

'But she confessed,' countered Lena. 'She confessed to me. And you just said that you have her confession too.'

'She's very confused,' answered Cartwright. 'And extremely unstable. We're getting her into a psychiatric ward, where they can take care of her. And we'll make sure she's protected from that husband of hers. He'll not be getting anywhere near her ever again.'

'But she did write the notes,' said Lena. 'She must have done. Did you test her handwriting?'

'She's in no state,' replied Cartwright.

'She quoted almost directly from them,' said Lena. 'I am sure the handwriting will match. All the notes must have been from Rubilla.' She thought a moment. Were the text messages from her too?

'Then Sarika is safe,' said Cartwright. 'You can stop your investigations.' He smiled at Lena. 'It is time to let this one go,' he said. 'You have done a good thing, bringing Rubilla to us. She'll get the help she needs.'

Lena took a deep breath. 'There is someone else missing,' she said. 'A man called Raz. He was on the show with Terry.'

'Surname?' Lena had asked Sarika to look it up.

'Gosper. He has not been to work or the gym.'

'You've tried his home?'

'I do not know where he lives,' confessed Lena.

'What's his relationship to you?' Cartwright sounded as though he was trying to be casual.

'He is a friend.' Lena paused, wondering how much she needed to tell him to get his help.

'I will look into it myself,' said Cartwright. 'I owe you a favour after all the assistance you have given us.'

'Thank you,' said Lena. She got up and turned hastily to leave, lest Cartwright try to give her a kiss on the cheek and get a whiff of her breath.

'If it was not Rubilla, it must have been Anastasia Valentina,' said Sarika, using the names like first names and surnames. 'Maybe you are right and Raz is not okay after all. Do you think Anastasia Valentina has murdered him too?' said Sarika, hurrying along behind Lena. Lena had got home late and collapsed into bed, but she couldn't sleep for long, not with the ghost of Raz already haunting her dreams. She had dragged Sarika up early that morning and hit the road. 'She is a serial killer,' continued Sarika. 'A black widow. Killing the best-looking men in Islington.'

'I am sure that Raz is fine,' replied Lena, not believing it herself. Cartwright had reported no answer at his house and was checking whether he'd used his phone or credit card in the last twenty-four hours.

'He's dead,' declared Sarika, with a hint of triumph. 'Just like Terry.'

'That is not helpful,' replied Lena. The icy air was hurting her lungs. She slowed her pace a little. 'We need to find him.'

'Where are we going?' asked Sarika.

Lena stopped in her tracks and allowed her breathing to calm. Nice clean cold air, that's what her brain needed. Her brain told her that it would quite like a coffee too, and her cold hands agreed. No time.

'You don't know where we are going,' said Sarika. 'It is not helping, us standing here in the cold. Maybe if we stop for breakfast, get a drink . . .'

'No drinks,' said Lena, to herself as much as to Sarika. 'We must think.' She paused. 'If it is Anastasia, how do we find her?'

Sarika shrugged back at her, and Lena wished Cartwright was here. She rubbed her hands together then breathed some warmth into them. She should tell Cartwright the whole truth of what she'd put Raz up to: if she'd been thinking straight last night she would have told him then.

'Barry doesn't know where Anastasia is,' said Sarika. Lena frowned at the unhelpfulness of that statement. 'And Mr Ives doesn't know either,' she added.

Lena thought for a moment. 'Mr Quincy!' she said.

'That creep?' replied Sarika. 'Why would he know?'

'Come on,' said Lena, starting to walk again. 'He was on that site, you said?'

'Yes,' said Sarika.

'And he was suddenly short of cash – he tried to cancel me, pretending to go to South Africa. But he never did.'

'So?' said Sarika.

'It is a long shot,' admitted Lena. 'But I wonder if he was targeted by Anastasia too. It would make sense.'

'I suppose,' said Sarika.

'Come on,' said Lena. 'We must go to his house. It is possible that he can tell us something that will help.'

Lena fished the keys out of her bag, opened the door and charged in.

'Lena!' exclaimed Mr Quincy. He was standing in the kitchen stirring a wooden spoon around a mixing bowl. Lena could smell sweet vanilla and it made her stomach rumble.

'You are back from your trip,' she said, well aware he hadn't been anywhere.

'What? Oh, yes. My father-in-law is much better.'

'I thought it was your mother-in-law who was sick?' said Lena.

'That's what I said.' Mr Quincy turned back to his baking. 'What are you doing here?'

'Are the children home?' asked Lena.

'One's at nursery and the other is with her grandparents,' he replied.

'Good,' said Lena. She grabbed the spoon and the bowl from a surprised-looking Mr Quincy. 'Sit,' she commanded. 'Did you have an affair with a woman from Bienvenue.com?'

'This is an outrage . . . I have never even heard of that site.'

'No time for lies,' said Lena. 'You need to answer my questions truthfully. Right now.' She gave Mr Quincy a small push until he was seated. She towered over him. Mr Quincy looked at Lena and then glanced over at Sarika, who had taken up a position near the kitchen knives.

'Did my wife send you?' he asked.

'You do not need to know who sent me,' said Lena, starting to enjoy herself a little. It was like being a gang leader, she decided. Like Yasemin. Except no one was going to get hurt. But he didn't know that. 'We need facts. We know that you were having an affair with this woman,' she said. She nodded to Sarika, who got her phone out of her bag and showed him the body shot.

'I don't know what you're talking about.'

'Sarika, pass me that rolling pin.' She held it in what she hoped was a vaguely threatening manner, like her mother would if she saw a mouse in the kitchen.

It worked.

'Okay, okay. Yes.' He nodded.

'Where is she?'

'I don't know,' he replied. 'In hell, I hope.'

'She was blackmailing you,' said Lena, a little more softly.

'Yes,' he replied. He looked around. 'Listen, my wife hasn't been interested in me for years. A man has needs.'

'Do you have an address for her?' said Lena again.

'I only met her the one time,' he insisted. 'But it was here.'

'You slept with another woman in your wife's bed?' exclaimed Sarika.

'It's my bed too,' said Mr Quincy, miserably. 'My wife was away on business and my parents had the kids. But that girl set up some sort of camera and videoed the whole thing. I've been paying her ever since or she'll show the video to my wife.'

'How do you get the money to her?' asked Lena.

'A man comes to the house and collects it,' Mr Quincy said.

'What does he look like?'

'Big and scary,' he said, with a shrug. 'I used my savings to pay him, at first, back from when I used to work,' he said. 'Then I had to economise on the housekeeping budget so I could still make payments. I'm cleaned out now. There's no more money but they keep coming. What am I going to tell my wife?'

'You must have a way of contacting this woman?' said Lena. 'It is important. We need to find her.'

'No. They always call me.' He paused. 'It wasn't worth it,' continued Mr Quincy, miserably. 'She promised to cook me breakfast, she said she was a chef. But it turned out she couldn't even fry an egg.' He put his head in his hands. 'Don't tell my wife what I've done,' he implored. 'She'll throw me out.'

Lena looked at Sarika, who looked back blankly. 'How tall was this woman?' she asked.

Mr Quincy sniffed, looking a little bit calmer. 'You won't tell my wife?'

'Tell me how tall she was,' Lena repeated.

'She was little. Maybe five two, in heels,' he replied. 'Why do you want to know?'

'Come on, Sarika,' said Lena. 'We need to go.'

'Don't tell my wife. Please,' begged Mr Quincy. Lena shut the door without replying.

'Call Lucia,' commanded Lena, once they were on the street.

'Why?' asked Sarika. 'And why all the interest in Anastasia Valentina's height?'

'Don't you remember?' said Lena. 'She could not fry an egg.'

'So?' said Sarika. 'Do you want Lucia to give her a cookery class? We don't even know where the woman is. That does not seem like the priority.'

If Lena had not been so worried she would have laughed. 'Who else do we know who is short and cannot fry eggs?' she said. 'Who could pass for that picture of Anastasia?'

Sarika looked at her blankly.

'Irina,' said Lena. 'Lucia's trainee chef.'

'Kat's sister?' said Sarika.

'I saw her,' said Lena. 'Ice skating. With an older man. The type of man she would meet on Bienvenue.com.'

'But she is not called Anastasia. Or Valentina.'

'You told me everyone uses fake names,' said Lena. 'Call Lucia. Perhaps I am wrong. Perhaps it is not her. But we need to make sure.'

CHAPTER 24

Lucia said she had not heard from Irina since Terry's funeral. Lena went straight to the kitchen where she worked anyway, dragging Sarika with her. She found her pounding a slab of meat that could have come from any large animal.

'I tried to keep her on for Kat's sake,' said Lucia, punctuating her sentences with a pound of the pummel. 'I ignored how terrible a cook she was. So careless. Salt where sugar was called for, tablespoons not teaspoons. Fluttering her eyelashes instead of stirring the pot. But I told you, in the end she quit, the day of the funeral. I was not sorry.'

'And no news since?'

'I did her a favour, giving her that job. Not one word of thanks. Not even a text message since she left me in the lurch.'

'What does Kat say?'

'I'm not a monster,' said Lucia, picking up the raw meat and flipping it before pummelling the other side. 'I didn't tell Kat. You know how terrifying she can be.'

Lena and Sarika both nodded. 'Do you have a phone number for Irina?' asked Lena. 'And an address?'

'Of course,' Lucia replied. 'I needed it for my employee records. Everything by the book.' She put down the pummel and delicately sprinkled the meat with oregano. 'Why are you so interested?'

'No time to explain,' said Lena. 'We need to find Irina.'

Irina's phone rang out. There was no answer at her building. A neighbour told them he hadn't seen her for days. Lena decided she'd have to talk to Kat. She sent Sarika home – the girl had stolen Kat's boyfriend after all – and although Lena was not her favourite person, she was less hated than Sarika.

Lena knocked and waited at the door to Kat's apartment. Kat opened the door in a dressing gown, rolled her eyes at seeing Lena and gestured her in. 'I'm working,' she said. 'Wait in the living room.'

Lena took a seat on a faded sofa, noticing how much tidier the flat was without Sarika and Dragg living there. She tried not to listen to the sound of Kat's seductive work voice, purring from the other room. Lena wasn't sure what she was expecting to find out. She thought about Irina, the chef who couldn't fry an egg. Could she really be involved in all this? But why would she want to do harm to Terry? And more importantly, where had she taken Raz?

Finally Kat emerged, now dressed in jogging bottoms and a loose T-shirt. She went to the kitchen and made herself a coffee without offering one to Lena. She came back to the living room and took a seat, cross-legged on the sofa. She took a sip of her drink and lit up a cigarette. 'So what do you want?' she said, finally. 'Your cousin has been arrested again and somehow you think I am to blame? I have done nothing to that boyfriend-stealing bitch.'

'No,' said Lena, trying not to cough as Kat blew smoke her way. 'It is not about Sarika. It is about Irina.'

Kat leaned forwards. 'What do you want with my sister?' she asked.

'I want to find her,' said Lena. She thought a moment. She didn't want to give anything away, not until she was sure. 'Lucia has a pay-cheque for her that I need to deliver.'

'Then send it to her flat,' said Kat.

'You are not expecting her here? A visit soon, maybe?'

Kat laughed. 'Not where I work,' she said. 'Try her flat.'

'The flat in Crouch End?' said Lena. 'That is where you think she is?'

'Yes,' replied Kat, stubbing out her cigarette. 'Why?'

'Lucia . . .' began Lena.

'Lucia can speak to her at work,' said Kat, starting to look worried. 'Why would she send you here when they see each other so often?'

Lena battled with her conscience. Maybe she was overreacting and Irina had nothing to do with all this. She didn't want to get her in trouble with her sister. But what if she was at the centre of it all? She had to find Raz.

'Irina quit her job with Lucia,' said Lena. Kat slammed down her coffee mug, the hot liquid slurping over the edges. 'She said that she was too pretty to have to slave in a kitchen. I am worried that she is involved in something she shouldn't be. And I think she might have something to do with my missing friend.'

Kat laughed. 'You are crazy,' she said. 'My sister is a good girl.'

'I think that she might have got into trouble.'

'You have evidence?' asked Kat. 'Evidence that she is. in trouble?'

'None,' admitted Lena, aware that the egg would be unlikely to sway Kat. 'Not yet. And I hope I am wrong.'

'I know you are,' replied Kat, standing up. 'Now get out of my flat.'

★ ★ ★

It had gone on long enough, decided Lena, as she walked into the cold February air. A light smattering of snow began to fall, each flake floating down gently. It was much more leisurely than rain, in no hurry to reach the ground and turn to sludge.

But Lena was in a hurry. She dialled Cartwright: she had to tell him everything. The wind howled around her, chilling her fingers as she gripped the phone. Cartwright answered. 'I'm glad you called,' she made out, the rest of his words being swept away by the wind.

'I cannot hear you,' she said, looking for somewhere to shelter from the wind. She chose a lamppost, which proved itself not at all up to the task.

More hissing down the line. 'A body,' she heard. 'We've found a body.'

'Who?' she shouted. The line crackled and hissed and was taken by the snow. 'I meet you at the station,' she said to the phone, although the call was over.

Raz, she thought. He was the second man to lose his life at the hands of Anastasia Valentina. And this time it was her fault.

Lena sat in the waiting room of the morgue. She'd stormed into the police station, only to be driven by a chatty young police-woman straight to the morgue. The woman had drivelled for the whole journey about the increase in crime that Islington had experienced in the last months, but knew nothing about the body Lena was coming to identify. 'Not a close friend, I hope?' was all she'd managed.

'No,' replied Lena. 'But a good person.'

'They said it wasn't a relative,' the woman replied, cheerily. 'That's something.'

Cartwright came out and sat down next to her in the waiting area. 'I'm sorry I doubted you, Lena,' he said. He took her hand

and Lena felt shivers run right up her arm. 'I should have known better, after everything you've done before.'

'I've got a theory about who this body is,' he continued. 'But I'm hoping that you will be able to confirm it. Once we have a name, we can contact the family for a positive identification.'

'What was cause of death?' asked Lena.

'A single bullet wound,' said Cartwright. 'The body wasn't long dead when we found it. And in the cold it is perfectly preserved. It almost looks like sleep.'

Lena stood up. 'I am ready,' she said.

Cartwright led her into the room and kept hold of her hand until he released it to draw back the sheet.

Lena gasped. 'This is a woman,' she said.

'Yes,' replied Cartwright, looking surprised. 'Is it Anastasia, or Valentina, the woman you suspect from that website? She matches what little description you gave.' Lena realised she'd never told Cartwright she hadn't seen Anastasia's face. But it didn't matter.

She recognised this girl.

'That is Irina. Irina Ivanov.'

Cartwright looked at her, his face a question mark. 'She is Kat Ivanov's little sister,' explained Lena, still staring at the dead girl. 'She worked for Lucia, until recently. I thought that maybe she was involved in Terry's death.'

'But she is not Anastasia?' said Cartwright. 'Not Valentina? I thought she was your suspect.'

'Maybe,' said Lena. 'We have much to discuss.'

Lena cradled a brandy and stared into the log fire. The pub sofa was old and comforting, and for a moment she felt as if she could forget about it all and just enjoy the crackle of the wood burning and the smell of the smoking embers.

Cartwright came back from the loo and sat down next to her.

His weight on the soft cushions sucked her towards him with a gravitational pull. She let it, enjoying the warmth of his leg next to hers. It was better even than the heat of the real fire.

'We've sent an officer to tell Kat the news,' he said. 'I remember her from our last case. How do you think she'll take it?'

'She'll be devastated,' said Lena. 'It is her little sister.'

'Of course,' said Cartwright. They both sat in silence for a moment. Lena took another sip of her brandy. 'So what do you think she was involved in?' asked Cartwright. 'Why was she murdered?'

Lena thought a moment. 'I do not know,' she said honestly. 'But I think it was to do with Terry's death. So many men were on this site and then ended up being stolen from, or blackmailed.'

'And you think this Irina girl could be behind it all?'

'I do not know,' she said again. 'I did not think she was so smart.'

'I'm sorry, Lena,' said Cartwright. 'I should have helped you when you asked. I couldn't do what you suggested, of course, but I could have done something.'

Lena took a deep breath. The scent of brandy mixed with the soft smokiness of the fire, a double dose of warmth and comfort. 'When you called I was not expecting it to be Anastasia that you had found,' she said. 'I was expecting someone else.'

'It was someone else,' said Cartwright, looking confused.

'I was expecting a man,' said Lena. 'And I am glad that it was not him.'

'Who would it have been?' asked Cartwright.

'Raz, the man I asked you to check on. I did not tell you why.'

'Go on,' said Cartwright.

'When you would not help me, I did not give up,' confessed Lena. 'I thought that one date, just for research, might be all we needed to get some proof.'

'What did you do?' asked Cartwright. He moved his leg away from hers. It felt cold where he was not, despite the heat of the fire.

'You are not the only man I know,' she said. 'I knew that Raz would not share your scruples. He was a friend of Terry.'

'And now he is missing?'

'Yes,' said Lena. 'It went wrong. I have not seen him since Monday, when he went on the date.'

'The date with Anastasia?' asked Cartwright.

'I thought so,' said Lena. 'But it might have been Irina that he met.'

Cartwright stood up and reached for his police radio. 'And now Irina is dead,' he said. 'Murdered.'

'Do not think that,' said Lena, reading his mind. 'Raz would not do that. I am worried about him.'

'You should be,' replied Cartwright. 'I'll issue a report to see if we can track him down. You should have come to me with this information sooner.'

'I know,' replied Lena.

Cartwright left the pub without saying goodbye. The door let in a gust of wind as he left and Lena shivered.

Lena fumbled with her key, her icy hands uncooperative. She clapped them together for warmth, then tried again. She could hear voices from inside her flat. She listened for a moment. Both female, and angry by the sound of things. She didn't know if she could face it, and thought about turning round and going back into the cold night. Her trainers had once again proved themselves permeable to water, her socks were sodden and she'd lost all sensation in her feet. She visualised her cosy slippers waiting for her just inside and pushed the door open. She trod on a small envelope on the mat with her name scrawled on it in handwriting she didn't recognise. She bent down to pick it up, frowning at the dirty print of her trainer patterned upon it.

Then she was set upon.

'Oh, thank God you're back,' said Sarika, in Hungarian. 'Kat is here. I almost didn't let her in but then she started crying in the hall so I opened the door and I wish I hadn't because she's been a right bitch to me ever since.'

'Her sister has just been murdered,' said Lena.

'Speak English,' said Kat.

'I am sorry,' said Lena. 'Maybe you would like a drink?'

'No,' said Kat. 'You were asking questions about my sister, and a day later she is dead. What do you know?'

'Nothing for certain,' said Lena. She thought a moment. She might as well share all she knew with Kat. 'But there was something I was looking into. A number of bad things have happened to men who were using a dating website. Bienvenue.com. Do you know it?'

Kat nodded. 'A hook-up site for immigrants and wealthy men,' she said.

'Yes. Well, two men had substantial sums of money taken from them by girls they met there. Another was being blackmailed. Terry Tibbs was using the site too. And he was found dead.'

'What does this have to do with my sister?' Kat's face had turned white. 'I will have that drink,' she said. Sarika disappeared to the kitchen.

'The man who was blackmailed gave me a description of the girl he had been with. She sounded very much like your sister.' Sarika returned and gave a glass of Palinka to Kat. She took a sip of the liquor and coughed, then downed the rest, gesturing to Sarika to refill her glass. 'But I do not know,' Lena confessed. 'It might not have been her. I might be wrong.'

They sat in silence. 'I was approached,' Kat said eventually, looking at her glass all the time, 'by someone who used to work on the same internet sex line as me. She told me about a new business venture using some website.'

'Bienvenue.com?' asked Lena.

'I don't know which site,' said Kat. 'They wanted people who would sleep with the men.'

'Prostitution?' asked Lena.

'Yes,' replied Kat. 'With a difference. They were not just sleeping with the men for money. The women would also be looking for ways to get more out of them. Blackmail if they were married. Stealing if they were careless. It was organised by a woman. Apparently she'd been cheated on and instead of just getting revenge on her boyfriend, she turned her anger into a business. And it was a good deal for the girls too. They said I could keep thirty per cent of whatever I took. The boss would protect us if anything went wrong.'

'Who was behind it?'

'I don't know. I am not a prostitute,' said Kat. 'Not any more. The internet is safer. No one touches me. I said no.'

'Could Irina . . . ?' began Lena.

'I would say no,' said Kat. 'But I remember now. She was in the flat when the woman came. She was in her bedroom, I thought she was asleep. After that I made her move out. I didn't want that sort of person around my little sister. It was bad enough her being around me.' Kat put her head in her hands and sobbed. 'But I couldn't keep her safe,' she said. 'It's my fault she's dead.'

'No it is not,' said Lena, putting her hand tentatively on Kat's shoulder. 'When my friend Timea was murdered, I felt I was to blame,' she said. 'But I was not. It was the person who killed her. The murderers are the ones to blame. The same with you. And I will find that person. I will bring them to justice.'

'Don't bring them to justice; bring them to me,' said Kat, her eyes fierce. She downed the rest of her drink and stood up.

'One more thing,' said Lena. 'I need a picture of your sister.' If she had a picture, she could show it to Barry, and to Mr Ives to find out if Irina really was Anastasia and Valentina.

'I will text it to you.'

Lena showed Kat out and then stood by the door and closed her eyes. Timea's death came flooding back to her. She'd been like a sister to Lena, and now she was gone, for ever. Lena fetched a glass of Palinka for herself and sank heavily on to the sofa.

But she didn't have time to wallow. Raz had been missing for two days. She had to take action.

Lena looked around her. She was surprised that she'd been able to arrange this for that same evening. She supposed there was a benefit to these men being absolutely terrified. When she'd demanded they meet her, all had meekly obeyed.

Barry Tibbs, James Quincy, Rupert Ives, all sitting around a table at the back of Barry's bar. All men who had met women on Bienvenue.com and suffered as a result. All the ones who were still alive, that is. She'd printed out all the shots Sarika could find of the lingerie'd bodies on Bienvenue.com and now lined them up. There were six photographs, all with different names, but it was impossible for Lena to tell if they were all of the same woman.

'You have all been victims,' she said. The men looked down, miserable. 'You, Barry, you were robbed. You are the odd one out because you are not married.'

'Not any more,' agreed Barry. 'Not since my Maeve passed away fifteen years ago. I still wear my ring though.'

'Rupert Ives,' she continued. 'You had an affair with a woman who persuaded you to leave your wife, only for her to dump you when the money ran out.'

'Ten grand gone and my wife hates me,' said Mr Ives, miserably. 'Valentina told me her son was sick and needed treatment back home in Russia.'

'And you, James Quincy,' continued Lena. 'You had a one-night liaison with a girl from Bienvenue.com. She took a video and blackmailed you.'

'I'll always regret it,' said James.

'The reason I've brought you all here,' said Lena. 'Is that Terry Tibbs also used Bienvenue.com. He checked into a hotel room with a woman we believe to be a prostitute. And he did not come out alive. I want to establish if there is a connection.'

The men were silent for a moment. Perhaps their own misfortunes suddenly seemed trivial in comparison.

'Mine was called Anastasia,' started Barry. 'We dated for three weeks before she robbed the safe. Terry knew her, so he'd have recognised her that night. He did always have the hots for her, though.'

'Do you think that your nephew would knowingly meet a woman, for sex, who had stolen from his uncle?' asked Lena.

'Maybe,' said Barry. 'Randy bugger. Or maybe he didn't know it would be her.'

'Valentina was beautiful,' said Rupert Ives. 'Don't tell my wife I said that. She seemed really genuine, till she disappeared.'

'Beautiful how?' said Lena. She reached into her bag and pulled out the final picture. 'Like this?' she said, a printout of the photo Kat had sent of Irina on the table.

'No,' said Rupert. But James Quincy gasped.

'That's her,' he said. 'Natalia, she told me her name was.'

Lena prised the photo from his hands and showed it to Barry. 'Not my Anastasia,' he said.

So it wasn't just one woman. But Irina was one of them. 'This was Irina Ivanov,' said Lena. 'She has been shot. I identified her body.'

'She's dead?' said James. Lena could tell from looking at his relieved face that he thought that meant he was off the hook for blackmail. She liked him even less.

'Yes,' said Lena. 'But I do not think she was working alone. Barry, I know Anastasia would not let you take photos of her. Describe her. Especially things she couldn't change, like her height. Rupert, listen carefully. I want to know how many women we are dealing with.'

'Well, you can see her body there so there's no point telling you she was smoking hot,' began Barry. 'She had a gorgeous face too, but a long thin nose.'

'Valentina had a stubby little turned-up nose,' said Rupert. 'I thought it was cute.'

'She was tall,' said Barry. 'Maybe five nine or ten.'

'That clinches it,' said Rupert. 'I'm only five eight and Valentina was shorter than me.'

Three woman, thought Lena. That she knew of. All with a similar way of working – and one that sounded like the business Kat had described. It wasn't a definite connection, but it was the best she had.

'Do any of you have any way of tracing these women?' she asked. 'A man's life could depend on it.'

All three shook their heads. Lena dismissed them and they shuffled out. She put her head in her hands. She wasn't any closer to finding Raz.

Barry came back. 'There was one thing,' he said. She looked up. 'Marsela knew Anastasia.'

'They met when you dated?'

'No, it seemed like she knew her from before. They never said how, but they were pretty pally. But then Marsela claimed to have no idea what she was planning, and said she couldn't help me track her down afterwards.'

CHAPTER 25

Marsela.

It all made sense. The wronged woman who turned revenge into a business.

Marsela had been a suspect since the beginning. She was the one with the motive to murder Terry. He'd cheated on her, publicly, over and over. And after what she used to do for a living, she would have contacts in the sex industry. She had plenty of reasons to hate men. She'd been used by them for years.

Lena cursed herself for not thinking of it earlier. But then, she'd only just seen the connection between the women. Marsela was smart: she'd dragged herself through law school. But would she really have murdered Irina? Why? The girl had done as she was told and, if Lena was right, had killed Terry in cold blood. Perhaps Marsela was covering her tracks. It seemed ruthless, more ruthless than Lena could believe Marsela to be. But she'd seen the evidence. Irina's body, in a cold slumber from which she'd never wake.

Lena sat down on her sofa. She heard a crinkle of paper. The note. She'd forgotten all about it.

Lena fished it from her back pocket and looked at the envelope. Her footprint stared back. A lot of trouble had been caused by notes, she thought, and hoped this one would be nothing. A reminder from the building managers to put the bins out. An apology from the people next door for the noisy party they had thrown a few weeks back. She opened it.

I can help you. I know where your friend is. Meet me under the Caledonian Road railway arches at midnight tonight. Come alone and tell no one or I can't do anything for him.

Lena looked at her watch. It was already 11.30 p.m.

She had no time to spare, no time to think even. Was this a trap? Or could someone help her find Raz? She looked at the note again and memorised its content. Without thinking, she scrunched it up and threw it in the already full kitchen bin. It could have been from one of the women Marsela employed — maybe they had found out what happened to Irina and were scared. Maybe they wanted to help Raz. She had no way of knowing.

She knew the note said not to tell anyone, but Lena couldn't take that chance. She rang Cartwright. No answer. She paused, wondering how to leave a coherent message about her theory and what she was about to do. Voicemail really wasn't the medium for that. She'd try him again on the way.

Lena looked around, and grabbed a kitchen knife, wrapped it in a tea towel and put it in her bag. She didn't know what her plan was, and she didn't have time to work one out. She'd have to take her chances if she wanted to rescue Raz.

Lena shivered. The night air was even colder under the railway bridge than it had been elsewhere — the bricks acted as a shadow, preventing the sun from ever warming this air. It reminded Lena of a cave she'd passed in the Transylvanian hills: even the air around it was chilled, as if a ghost was spreading its icy fingers.

And it was dark. The streetlight on one side of the bridge was broken, so she just had the pink glow of a single light to see by. The moon was blocked out by the brickwork.

She'd run most of the way here, not trusting a taxi or bus to deliver her in time. Her sweat had soaked into her jumper, making her even colder. She shivered again. She'd have felt much better if she could have spoken to Cartwright, but he'd still not picked up his phone. In the end she'd left a garbled voicemail, realising halfway through that if he showed up, the meeting would be ruined. She'd ended the call without telling him where she would be. And she certainly didn't want to phone Sarika. The last thing she needed was the girl stumbling into more danger.

Lena took a deep breath of cold air. She was here to get information about Raz. Information that she could then relay to Cartwright and together they could rescue him. Raz had been there for her when she needed him. And now, because of that, he was in trouble.

She heard footsteps; the uneven clatter of heels on cobbles. Lena turned to look. The figure was approaching from the darker end of the tunnel. Lena felt like an actor on stage: she could see nothing, but in comparison it was like a spotlight was shining on her.

'Lena,' said a voice. It had a foreign lilt that was familiar to Lena. 'We meet again.'

The shadow stepped forwards. Lena saw a five-foot-two woman who filled her with horror. 'Yasemin,' she said. 'Yasemin Avci.'

'I thought you'd remember me, Lena Szarka,' replied Yasemin. 'I certainly haven't forgotten you.'

'What are you doing here?' asked Lena. 'What have you got to do with Raz?'

'He's my guest,' replied Yasemin. 'He was asking rather a lot of questions, so one of my girls thought I should look after him after their date.'

'Your girls,' repeated Lena.

'Yes. Mine. Surprised? I know you are aware of my interest in drugs, but these days I've branched out. I was inspired by a nice bit of treachery.'

'Your boyfriend,' said Lena, remembering the body she'd seen. Yasemin's boyfriend had cheated on her and betrayed her – and ended up dead.

Yasemin looked surprised for a moment. 'It seems everyone knows what that cheating little snitch did to me,' said Yasemin. 'Still, I suppose that is for the best. No one will ever do it again.'

'He only died a few days ago,' said Lena. 'Your scheme has been going for months.'

'Keep your enemies close,' said Yasemin. 'The scumbag thought he could cheat on me with prostitutes and get away with it. That's where my business idea came from. I let him linger while he was still useful. But then when he tried to turn me in to the police? That was the time to make an example of him.'

'So you set up the site?'

'No. That site is degrading to women.' Lena looked at her in surprise. 'I just used it to my advantage. My girls target wealthy men they find there. Cheating men with a lot to lose.'

Lena looked around. Yasemin was the last person she wanted to be with, at midnight, in a dark spot. She couldn't see a world where she'd provide Lena with useful information that would help Raz. She needed to make a run for it.

As the thought crossed her mind, two heavyset men appeared from the shadows. 'I know you're a fast runner, Lena,' said Yasemin. 'So I brought some friends along.' Lena turned around. Three more men were behind her. She didn't stand a chance.

'My friend at the Goswell Hotel told me you'd been sniffing around his staff,' she added. 'So I gave you a little warning. A nice little fire in your flat. But you carried on sticking your nose into my affairs, Lena,' said Yasemin. 'You haven't been through my bins this time, but you have been rummaging around my dirty laundry. I've been watching you.'

'I was just trying to keep my cousin safe,' said Lena. 'After what happened to Terry.'

'Ahh, Terry,' said Yasemin. 'That was unfortunate.'

'Why did you want him dead?' asked Lena. 'Were you together? Did he cheat on you too?'

Yasemin laughed. 'Of course not. He was just another client. Another man who couldn't keep his dick in his trousers. He deserved to pay. And that was all we were going to do. Make him pay. A few compromising pictures, the type that would lose you your sponsors if it got out, and a little blackmail.'

'What went wrong?' asked Lena.

'The cheating fool wouldn't play along. He thought he was hiring Anastasia for the night – his uncle's girl. But we wouldn't send her, not back to the same family twice. It was too dangerous. So I sent Irina. He got difficult when she showed up.'

'So you murdered him?'

'Of course not. Irina slipped him a few drugs to loosen him up. Except the stupid girl got the dosage wrong and killed him.'

Lena listened. That did sound like Irina.

'So you see,' said Yasemin, 'in a way, the police were right for once. It was an accident.'

'And now Irina is dead.'

'You know me, Lena. I don't mind the odd body; it's the cost of doing business. But Irina was nervous. First she sent you those text messages, and then she started talking about turning herself in. I couldn't have that. She was a loose end. Like you. And I do hate loose ends.'

Lena shivered again, this time with fear. She found her fists were clenched tightly around something. The strap of her backpack, slung over one shoulder. 'Where is Raz?' asked Lena. She needed a distraction. She stepped forwards, trying to find herself a darker space.

'None of your business.'

'The note said you'd help me find him.' Lena quietly reached into her bag. She felt the tea towel and unravelled it as best she could.

Yasemin laughed again. 'You must stop believing everything you read, Lena,' she said. 'It will be the death of you.' She gave a nod and the men approached. Lena saw a gun glinting in the streetlight.

Soon it would be too late. Lena knew it was desperate, but it was her only move. She jumped and grabbed Yasemin, pressing the knife to her throat. The woman cried out in surprise. 'Drop your guns,' Lena shouted at the men. 'Or I will kill her.'

CHAPTER 26

Lena realised that Yasemin was quivering, like Timea's son Laszlo used to do when he was afraid of the dark. Lena was holding her in a twisted hug: one arm across her chest, but the other gripping the knife to her throat. A drip of sweat fell from Yasemin's face on to the knife. Yasemin wriggled and then yelped like a puppy and Lena looked down. She'd sharpened her knives last week, and there were already a few drops of blood running down Yasemin's neck, staining her coat. Lena stared at the blood, transfixed.

This had already gone too far. She had no idea what she was going to do next.

All five men were staring at her. They didn't know what to do either. Everyone seemed to expect Yasemin to take charge, but she was shaking in Lena's arms, speech eluding her.

'Drop the guns,' repeated Lena. They looked to their boss, who gave nothing back. The first man dropped his gun to the ground and it clattered on the cobbles. Then the others followed suit.

'Get back,' shouted Lena. She needed space and she wanted to be able to see all the men at once. 'All of you, against that wall.' They obeyed. Lena looked down to Yasemin again. Panic was flooding her eyes. 'Where is Raz?' she asked, her voice quiet. This might be her only chance to find him.

'We have him,' stuttered Yasemin. 'In the old builder's warehouse on Caledonian Road. It's nearby.' Now she'd found her voice, Yasemin seemed to grow calmer. She stopped shaking. Lena felt some of the power ebb away from her and be absorbed into Yasemin. 'Let me go,' she said. 'And we'll bring you Raz.'

Lena had no intention of releasing Yasemin. Not while there were five strong men and guns littering the ground like deadly confetti. 'No way,' she said. 'Not until Raz is safe.'

'That is fine,' said Yasemin. 'I will send one of the men to fetch him.'

Lena thought. She didn't know how many people Yasemin had working for her, but she was pretty sure it extended beyond these five. If one man went, he could fetch others to overpower Lena. And she wasn't sure how long she could hold on to Yasemin. Already she could feel the woman straining against her, testing her strength. Lena squeezed tighter and heard a catch in Yasemin's throat. She'd inadvertently dug her knife deeper.

Lena resisted the urge to apologise, trying to figure a way out of this. She could see the men getting fidgety. Someone was going to come up with a plan soon. There were six of them including Yasemin, all ruthless gangsters. Against one Hungarian cleaner.

'Mehmet can go,' said Yasemin. 'He will bring Raz. We will exchange. Me for him.'

'No,' said Lena, before the man had taken a step. 'No one leaves.'

'We can't stay here all night,' said Yasemin.

'We can do whatever I say,' said Lena, clutching the knife more tightly.

'What are you going to do, Lena?' asked Yasemin. 'If you kill me, my men will kill you.'

'If I let you go,' replied Lena, 'your men will kill me.'

'No,' said Yasemin. 'We will let you go. You have my word.' Lena didn't believe that for a second, but she could feel herself tiring. Her arm was starting to cramp and she adjusted her grip on the knife.

Suddenly she was filled with pain. The knife was on the ground. Yasemin was free, her mouth bloodied. Lena realised too late what had happened. Yasemin had bitten her hand. The men rushed forwards. One charged at her, the others were going for the guns. This was it.

Lena was blinded by a flash of white light. One of the men must have reached a gun. She felt the cold stones scrape her hands then her knees hit the cobbles with a painful jolt. It was as if she'd been running in the playground and taken a tumble.

Except this time she might not get up.

Lena could hear shouting. She opened her eyes. The men were running towards her. Then past her. Running away. They were running away. Yasemin was trailing them. Shouting. Her short legs and high heels were not designed for speed. Suddenly Lena saw her tumble, metres from her. Lena forgot her own injuries and jumped to her feet. She threw herself on top of Yasemin, pinning her to the floor.

Only then did Lena wonder what was going on. Why were the men running? What was she going to do with the diminutive Turkish crime boss prone beneath her body? The men would come back for her. Then what?

But they didn't. The lights grew brighter. She realised there were more lights. Flashing blue. And sirens. Police sirens.

The body underneath her squirmed. But Lena didn't care. The police were here. She looked up. Not just any police. DC Cartwright was running towards her. She was safe.

'You got my message,' said Lena, wrapping the silver foil blanket around her more tightly. It rustled and she felt like a sandwich. A warm, cosy, rescued sandwich. Yasemin had been bundled into a police car and the other officers had given chase to her hench-men. She'd told Cartwright about the warehouse on Caledonian Road and he'd sent more police there to look for Raz. So, for the moment, it was just her and Cartwright, sitting on the cobbles. Waiting.

'The one that said you were in danger but didn't say where you were going? Lena, I've never been so worried in my life,' said Cartwright. He stared at the cobbles, then looked back at Lena. 'Thank God Sarika showed up when she did. She stormed into the police station and told me you'd be here and that I needed to help.'

'How did she know?' asked Lena. She hadn't told Sarika any-thing about where she was going.

'She found a note, apparently. In your bin. Lena, you shouldn't have come. It wasn't safe.'

'I know that now,' replied Lena.

'It looks like you gave Yasemin quite a fright though,' said Cartwright. 'And her five henchmen. Was that blood on her neck?'

'A little,' admitted Lena. She shuffled, and her silver foil rustled again. 'She confessed,' she said. 'She was responsible for Terry's death. It was Irina who killed him, but accidentally. But Yasemin ran the prostitution ring that was using Bienvenue.com. The women were under orders to drug the men, steal, blackmail, whatever they could.'

'I still can't get my head around it,' said Cartwright. 'We knew she was up to something, but this . . .'

'Can you charge her?'

'I hope so,' said Cartwright. 'Now we know what she's been up to we should be able to pull together the evidence. The hard thing about Yasemin is catching her in the first place. You've managed that with aplomb.'

Lena smiled. 'I hope Raz is okay,' she said. 'I never should have got him involved.'

269

'Why did he get involved?' asked Cartwright. 'Are you two . . .'

'No,' replied Lena, quickly. She thought about the events of the past weeks. The notes from Rubilla. The texts from Irina. The fake relationships, the lies, the lengths to which men and women would go to manipulate each other. She wanted no part in dirty games or messy affairs. She wanted something clean. Something simple. Something real. 'There is only one man I want,' she said.

Cartwright glanced behind him, as if expecting her to be talking to someone else.

'It is you,' she said. And she leaned in and kissed him.

CHAPTER 27

'So really, I saved both of your lives.' Sarika smiled and raised her glass of prosecco. They were comfortably settled on the sofas in N1 Demons. 'I think a toast to me is in order.'

Lena and Raz both lifted their glasses and the three chinked amiably. 'Although, I have to say, the real hero here is Lena,' said Raz. 'She discovered the prostitution gang, confronted the leader, and held her at knife point until she revealed where I was being held prisoner.' He reached out and put a hand on Lena's leg, gazing at her adoringly. Then he looked back at Sarika. 'All you did was empty a bin, find a note and tell the police.'

'I am very pleased that Sarika emptied the bin,' said Lena, removing Raz's hand and placing it gently back on his own leg. 'It is what saved me.'

'I knew you would be pleased,' said Sarika. 'You are always telling me to do my chores. So when I saw stuff poking out of the bin, I decided to take the rubbish out. And I rescued you both in the process.'

'Raz, I am so sorry for what happened to you,' said Lena. 'It must have been terrifying.'

'It was awful being a prisoner,' said Raz, with a shudder. 'One minute I was on a date with this gorgeous woman; then we got chatting about Terry, I asked a few questions, and the next thing I know I'm tied up in a cold warehouse.'

271

'It is my fault,' said Lena. 'I should never have sent you.'

'I didn't know what they were going to do with me,' added Raz. 'I thought perhaps I would have been sold as a sex slave. What with my body looking like this, and all.'

'I know,' said Lena. 'Sarika showed me the interview.'

'The one in *Heat*?' asked Raz, smiling. 'Or *Hello*? Or *Chat*? I've been interviewed everywhere. Never has anything been so awesome for my profile. And you'll never guess what. I've been offered a leading role in the next series of *N1 Angels*. My storyline is massive.'

'More cause to celebrate,' said Sarika, topping up everyone's glasses. 'That is brilliant news.'

'Well done,' said Lena.

'There is something else,' said Raz. His hand had found its way on to Lena's leg again. She went to move it, but found his hand was suddenly clasping her own. 'They need a co-star for me. A girlfriend.' He looked into Lena's eyes.

Sarika shrieked with excitement. 'Lena, you could be on TV!'

Lena extracted her hand from Raz's grasp. 'I am grateful for your help, Raz,' she said. 'You have been most brave and I think you are a very impressive man. But I have had enough of reality television and its relationships for show. I have found something real. And I want it to be private.'

'Fair enough,' said Raz, taking a gulp of his prosecco. He forced a smile. 'I'm not sure you would have got through the auditions anyway. They want someone who will do a steamy shower scene with me topless.'

Sarika burst out laughing. 'Lena would make the worst reality TV star in the world,' she said. 'When she is not cleaning she just eats biscuits and naps on the sofa.'

'And solves crimes to protect her cousin,' said Barry. He'd come out from behind the bar to deliver a large bowl of freshly fried chips.

Sarika nodded, conceding the point. 'Maybe she is not all boring,' she said, grabbing a chip. 'Anyway, well done on the role, Raz. I am sure that Terry would be happy for you.' Sarika took another swig of her prosecco. 'I still cannot believe that he cheated on me,' she said. 'Or tried to, at least, with Barry's ex.' Barry stopped and listened.

'I have been thinking about that,' said Lena. 'Perhaps that was not what he was doing. Perhaps he tracked Anastasia down on Bienvenue.com, like we did, and booked to go to the hotel room to confront her about what she did with his uncle. Maybe even try to get some of the money back. When it was not her, he did not want to go ahead.'

'I suppose we'll never know his motives for sure,' said Barry.

'We already do,' said Sarika, a grin filling her face. 'Of course that is it. My lovely Terry was a hero.'

Lena smiled back at her, feeling generous. She doubted that was the explanation, but didn't see any harm if that was what Sarika chose to believe. People needed their memories.

'Chips are on the house,' said Barry. 'Prosecco too. Just this once, mind.'

'What's going to happen to Yasemin?' asked Sarika. But Lena wasn't listening. Her heart felt as though it was scrambling up her windpipe into her mouth. She'd seen Cartwright come through the door and walk towards them. He stood awkwardly by the table for a moment. Raz spotted him and jumped up.

'Cheers mate,' he said, taking Cartwright's hand and shaking it enthusiastically. 'You saved my life.' He let go of his hand and enclosed a surprised Cartwright in a giant bear hug instead.

'It was Lena, really,' said Cartwright, his voice muffled through Raz's shirt.

'And me,' chipped in Sarika.

'I was just doing my job,' said Cartwright, disentangling himself and giving Raz an affectionate pat on the back. 'Can I join you?'

273

'Here,' instructed Lena, moving over on the small sofa to make room for Cartwright. 'You sit by me.' He obeyed, hesitated for a moment, then leaned in and gave Lena a quick kiss. On the lips.

Lena took his hand and they sat and smiled at each other for a while. Sarika shrieked again. 'About time,' she said.

'Congrats guys,' said Raz, a little sternly. 'I suppose you will be happy.'

'I expect Lena will mess it up,' said Sarika, with a laugh. 'But I hope she does not.'

'Thank you Sarika,' said Lena. 'I hope not too.'

'So what is happening with Yasemin?' asked Sarika.

'Since she's been in custody we've had much more luck getting people to come forward,' said Cartwright. 'I think she seems vulnerable, so all the people that were too scared before have found a bit of courage. I can't name names, of course, but I'm hopeful we'll have enough to convict her for a number of crimes, including ordering the murder of her boyfriend and Irina.' Cartwright paused. 'But that's not what I'm here for. Lena, I have booked a table for dinner. I hope you will accompany me?'

'I will,' said Lena. She stood up and took Cartwright's hand. Together, they walked out of the bar and into the Islington evening.

ACKNOWLEDGEMENTS

Many thank-yous to my editor Krystyna Green: I'm thrilled that this is her favourite of my Lena series to date! She's got a talented editorial team working with her at Little, Brown and I'd like to thank Amanda Keats and Hannah Wann for all their hard work. Penny Isaac has done a terrific job as always at copy-editing; Jo Wickham impressed me again with her achievements generating press for the books; designer Hannah Wood and illustrator Sara Mulvanny have created a beautiful cover yet again. Thanks too to my agent Euan Thorneycroft at A. M. Heath and Jo Thompson for all their advice and assistance.

Philippa Pride has continued to be a fantastic mentor to me and I feel lucky to have her support and wisdom. She, together with the fabulous Next Chapter writing group, provide me with great feedback and a lot of fun. Special thanks to Kelly, Tanya, Jenny, Debbie, Elvie (sorely missed) and new addition Otter.

My talented mother Susan is my constant consultant and once again gave me many creative suggestions that have made this book much stronger. I can't thank her enough for all that she does. My husband Sui deserves special mention: not for his messiness this time, but for being such a brilliant father to our toddler Teddy and whisking him away for a couple of hours at the weekends so I could finish writing this book.

My two children, Teddy and Violet, were my writing companions. Newborn Teddy snuggled up and napped on me when I started this book, and Violet hiccupped and kicked inside my belly as I finished my edits. I couldn't wish for better company.

AUTHOR'S NOTE

The inspiration for the Lena Szarka mysteries struck the first time I visited the flat of my, until then, rather promising new boyfriend. He was lovely: funny, successful and very smart. Then I saw his flat . . .

There were half-eaten, mouldy pieces of toast under his bed and cups of cold tea, used as ashtrays, littering the living room. I don't think he'd ever done a load of laundry. Unwashed boxers and dirty socks were piled high on the bathroom floor – I had to clamber over them to find the toilet.

He was embarrassed at my horror and hired a cleaner the next day. It struck me that this employee, whom he'd hardly ever met, would know more about his private life than any of his colleagues. That's when I decided a cleaner would be a great, if unconventional, detective: they have such intimate access to their clients' dirty secrets.

I doubt if many cleaners are interested in the state of their clients' sheets or the contents of their bins. But what if a cleaner were to suspect their client of a crime? What if it were a crime against a fellow cleaner, her closest friend? What if that friend were to go missing, leaving only a list of clients, the keys to their houses and a mop? That's what happens in Lena's first mystery, *In Strangers' Houses*.

At the same time, cleaners are vulnerable to accusations. If an object goes missing, the finger often points to them. This is an area I wanted to explore. Lena's force of character makes her far from vulnerable, but in the second novel in the series, *A Clean Canvas*, suspicion turns to her agency when a valuable painting is stolen from a gallery she cleans. Seeking to clear her agency's name, she sweeps her way through the art world and its pretentions to identify the real thief.

But there is another reason why I felt a cleaner would make an excellent sleuth. Many cleaners are immigrants to this country; outsiders looking in. My detective, Lena Szarka, works in London, but I chose to make her Hungarian; my own great-grandmother Magdaléna emigrated from Hungary to America just before the First World War. Magdaléna was an early economic migrant: she'd been told that in the States the streets were paved with gold. She ended up in rural Indiana, raising her six children in a house with a dirt floor.

Magdaléna inspired Lena: her heritage, her recipes (one of which you'll find overleaf), but also her willingness to uproot everything in the hope of discovering a better life. As part of my research for my series, I interviewed several lovely cleaners, all of whom had more prestigious jobs back home: nurses, teachers, insurance brokers. But in their native countries it was hard to make ends meet, let alone ever hope to buy a house. Leaving everything they knew to come to the UK meant that they had a chance for a better future.

I feel sorry for the cleaner who landed the job with that messy boyfriend of mine. I'm sure it's not what she had in mind when she came to the UK, full of hopes of a fresh start. But she's done us both a favour: she not only inspired my crime series, but she also meant that I eventually made that boyfriend my husband.

That's how the series came into being, but inspiration for *A Messy Affair* came, I have to admit, while watching television. I feel a bit like Mrs Kingston about reality shows. I don't want to like them, but I find myself getting sucked in. I wrote this book while on maternity leave with my first baby, and an addiction to *Made in Chelsea*. I'd recline on the sofa, with the newborn on my chest and the laptop balanced on a cushion in front of me. And when I was too tired to write, I'd reach for the remote.

I'd never watched the show before and started right from season one on catch-up. Like most people, I assumed much of it was made up: I knew it was semi-scripted and I knew the scenes were contrived – they had to be, of course. The cameras were there.

But something very real happened. One of the stars fell pregnant with her onscreen boyfriend's baby. The borders were confused: fiction fed reality, and reality fed fiction. It was this dynamic that gave me the idea to set my book in this world. Did every character have the same view of where the show ended and reality began? If they didn't, that could lead to emotions so damaging that perhaps they'd take revenge into their own hands.

That's only part of the story: the inspiration for Terry's death itself came years earlier. I had been having drinks with a friend who'd been seeing a new man. He seemed perfect: keen, handsome and they'd had some amazing dates – she felt that elusive 'connection' and was beginning to imagine a future together. Then he just disappeared. He didn't answer her calls, didn't reply to her messages: it was as if he'd been wiped from the face of the earth.

Now of course the most rational explanation was that he'd lost interest. Men do – and women do too. Perhaps he'd met someone else. Perhaps he was married. Perhaps he'd decided he didn't like the way she laughed or the shape of her little fingernail.

But none of that was comforting. It was only when we speculated that maybe he'd been hit by a bus that my friend started to feel less rejected. So in *A Messy Affair*, when Terry starts 'ghosting' Sarika, I decided it would be because he was really dead. Whether their relationship would have lasted otherwise is unclear, but his untimely demise allowed Sarika to continue to believe that it would.

Writing these notes, I've just had my second baby: she entered the world four days before my second book, *A Clean Canvas*, was published. I'm looking forward to seeing what ideas come to me writing with a newborn cuddled on my chest again. And I won't feel guilty if I reach for the remote.

Did you enjoy A Messy Affair? Please do leave a review and get in touch: you can connect with me on Facebook, Instagram and Twitter @ElizabethEMundy or visit www.elizabethmundy.com to find out more about the Lena Szarka mysteries.

Recipe for Lena's Hungarian *kiflis*

These *kiflis* are nut-filled pastries named after their crescent shape. My Hungarian grandmother made them every year at Christmas, and Lena's mother Greta would have done the same. There are many variations of the recipe but here is our favourite: it is from my Aunt Nancy and the one that my mother uses.

Lena makes *kiflis* for Cartwright in the second book in the series, *A Clean Canvas,* but she is a terrible baker and they turn out hard and dry – I expect she had them in the oven for too long. Follow this recipe and you'll have moist, tasty *kiflis* that are perfect with a strong cup of coffee.

For the dough
300 g flour
225 g cream cheese (cold)
225 g softened butter
2 large egg yolks
2 tablespoons sour cream
1 teaspoon vanilla

Mix the cream cheese and butter together. Add the eggs, sour cream and vanilla. Cream together. Add the flour. Mix together.

Make small balls, about 3 cm in diameter. Refrigerate overnight.

For the filling
240 g finely chopped walnuts

225 g sugar
1 teaspoon vanilla
Milk (add as needed)

Icing sugar

Mix the walnuts, sugar and vanilla together. Add milk very gradually until the filling holds together and is slightly sticky, but don't make it soupy.

To finish
Roll out the dough balls and place on a greased baking sheet, about 2 cm apart.

Put a small piece of filling in the centre of each ball. Don't overfill, or the filling will leak out. Turn the side edges in slightly, then make a roll from top to bottom. Put the seam underneath. Bring the ends in to make a crescent shape.

Bake at 350°F/180°C for 15 minutes. If not a little brown, bake 3–4 minutes longer. Remove from the baking sheet immediately and place on a rack to cool.

Once cool, sprinkle liberally with icing sugar and serve.